imPERFECT BONES

C.N. ROWAN

By C.N. Rowan

The imPerfect Cathar

Vinci Books

vinci-books.com

Published by Vinci Books Ltd in 2026

1

A CIP catalogue record for this book is available from the British Library.

Paperback ISBN: 9781036710774

The EU GPSR authorised representative is Logos Europe, 9 rue Nicolas Poussion, 17000 La Rochelle, France contact@logoseurope.eu

Foreword

Hello and welcome to this, adventure the fourth in the imPerfect Cathar series.

If you haven't read the first three I'd say STOP!

Then COLLABORATE!

And finally LISTEN!

While this is a story in and of itself – and I do try and fill in the backstory as you go – you'll be missing out on all the fun of the fair that came before. Plus, if you do decide to go back you'll – THE HORROR – have read spoilers. And that might lessen your enjoyment. I want to embiggen your enjoyment instead.

If you are determined to proceed then know you're in for dark humour, strong language and graphic violence. Also, I am for my sins – numerous and immeasurable as they are – a Brit, and the writing will be in British English. You may expect an excess of extra S to make the X cess (which is French for cease – do you like how I managed to slip in a little bilingual joke there?) Also all of the U's too. This is for U, and U, and U, and U at the back as well.

Foreword

Now let us return to where Paul was last. In the place no human would ever want to be. The Wilds of Faerie.

Luckily, he's not alone…

Chapter One

Sometimes escaping from the dark doesn't mean you leave it
behind. Sometimes, you just carry it with you.

I don't know why all my ancient ghosts keep getting dressed
up in suits stitched from skin.

There was a time when phantoms knew their place.
One simple job — hang around in musty old mansions,
bewailing their miserable existence, in desperate need of a
psychotherapist to help them learn to just let it all go.
Worst-case scenario was one chucking a tin of beans at you
if they felt particularly pissed off.

Now they all seem to be eager to try their long-
discarded flesh on for size again, like a wedding dress pulled
out from the back of the cupboard by a widow at a nursing
home. It seems like everyone I've ever cared for and had to
watch die has come back for a visit. After sipping several
pints of evil juice first.

My best friend and student from my life as a Cathar

Perfect tried to punch a hole in reality in order to jump off the reincarnation Ferris wheel and take me with him at the same time. Then Susane, my dead wife, turned up just in time to stab me in the back. Why? Apparently for our son, who had been ripped from her belly, supposedly killed, when she'd been murdered the first time.

Except the ghost pretending to be my son, wasn't him at all. Couldn't be, in fact, because I became infertile the first time *I* died. And our believed miracle baby was never mine — something I didn't find out until Simon De Montfort — yet another ghost— revealed he, too, had jumped onto this flesh-again fad. But where I can reincarnate into the nearest dead body regardless of its relation to me, Simon's spirit can only reincarnate in the bodies of blood relatives.

I avoid thinking too much about how he made that happen without Susane's knowledge, else I'm likely to go mad and start killing everyone in sight until I wrap my hands round his wretched neck and watch the light dim in his eyes one last, final time. Well, *more* likely. And more mad.

Plus, I don't yet feel like I've been reunited with the whole wretched gang of ghosts. When Ben first pulled his "fuck the world; I wanna get off" manoeuvre, I intended to look into whether Arnaud Almeric, the psychotic priest known as the Butcher of Beziers, might also still be kicking around in another body. My reincarnation and Ben's and, it turns out, Simon De Montfort's, were all caused by being splashed with the essence of stolen Cathar souls when I broke the Holy Grail during a magical tug of war with the treacherous Bogomil Cathar Papa Nicetas back in the twelfth century. Nicetas got blown up along with the Grail, but Almeric caught a bit of the ectoplasmic backsplash along with the three of us, so it seems highly likely he might still be around.

I lie huddled up inside my blanket, thinking about all this inside the lean-to shelter Aicha and I hammered together in the Wilds of Faerie. It's less warm and dry and honestly, probably less safe than the cave we left, but there's no way I'd ever have managed to get a good night's sleep in there. Even with water now dripping through the roof of woven wide-leaved indigenous ferns directly onto my nose, I sleep better. Too many of my own ghosts, fragments of myself I left lingering, hang around that cave full of vacuum-packed corpses, where Simon left me to go insane, starving and dying of thirst over and over again.

I'm still inside my blanket when Aicha comes back. For most people, Aicha Kandicha's a closed book. Not just closed but bound in five-inch-thick chains, then locked with an industrial-sized padlock. Then put in an uncrackable safe that would make George Clooney think twice. Then covered in concrete and buried at sea. Unreadable is the point I'm making. I, though, can gather more than most; her micro-expressions, tiny movements, and creases in her otherwise immobile face tell me box sets of stories missed by everyone else.

For example, at this moment, having come in and dumped down the miscellaneous weird vegetation she's identified as edible, she seems completely emotionless. Her short dark hair clings to her forehead, slicked by the soaking she chose to take rather than burn her *talent* to keep the rain off her. Features that are sharp enough to cut yourself on —or for her to do so with a swiftly delivered headbutt— are hard to see in the half-light, but the siyala tattoo on her chin stands out still, the curling fronds around the black dots a story of personal growth worn for all to see. Her coal-black eyes would be unreadable to most, buried behind the shadows of a nose Cleopatra would have killed for. But I can read the concern, the worry she carries for me — the relief that we've patched things up marred by whether I'll ever be quite the person I was before my imprisonment. I can see her heartache where no one else can.

She turns and sees me looking, obviously reading her thoughts. 'Are you over that whole bullshit yet, or are you still being a massive pussy, dickhead?'

See? Totally torn up inside by angst over my wellbeing.

'What are you staring at?' She waves her hand up and down. 'Woohoo, Earth to Major Knob?'

I snap out of my reverie. 'Sorry, *laguna*, miles away for a minute there.'

She grunts an acknowledgement and turns back to preparing a salad gathered from her foraging. Again. Bless her, she must be utterly fed up with the whole thing. Aicha isn't vegetarian, but she's been keeping our diet strictly herbal for two reasons. First, because I am vegetarian unless necessity really leaves me no choice. Second, just because something is four legged and furred or feathered doesn't mean it isn't sentient in Faerie. Hell, you have to double-check half the mushrooms aren't going to burst into song. And then try to eat your ankles.

I scoot over. While it might not be entirely watertight, we've made a reasonable and camouflaged space about ten metres squared. The failed waterproofing isn't surprising. The weather in all its forms in the Wilds (the unclaimed part of Faerie between Summer and Winter we're currently in) lives up to the area's name. The heat is baking; the cold is biting; the wind is tempestuous. And the rain? The rain is incessant.

It comes down in sheets. It drizzles like a fine mist. It hits with droplets that feel as large as my thumb. No matter what we do, it always finds a way in, and we've learned to live with constant damp as a companion. Aicha's affinity with the elements means it's bearable; she operates as a portable radiator, cranking heat out of her pores to dry the place and keep us warm. It stops us having to use a fire that might give away our position. Of course, it means she glows in the magical spectrum instead. Still, we're on a plane made of magic. Practically everything is luminescent with *talent* here. Apart from me, of course.

I got my magic back for a while. Well, not mine, as such. Reincarnating inside a fae body gave me access to their wild form of natural power, and it was a giddy feeling to be *talented* once again. Of course, Simon De Montfort made sure all the bodies he stored in the cave were normal, unTalented human ones. He didn't want me using fae magic to get out of his trap.

Now I'm fucking useless again. That's the official diagnosis. An acute case of *fuckingus uselessosis*. The worst I've ever seen. If I were a dog, they'd put me down. Sadly, because of my reincarnation magic, I'd just pop up again like a bad penny in another body. A fucking useless bad penny. Not even a bad penny. A mediocre penny.

Aicha can see I'm tormenting myself again. It's like a knife in her gut to see me so reduced, so full of self-doubt. She rubs at the corners of her eyes.

'Oh, boo hoo,' she says. 'I'm Paul Bonhomme, and I'm so very, very sad. I can't do much magic, and I had a rubbish couple of weeks, so I'm just going to sit here and whine and cry rather than doing anything about it. Weaaaaaahhhh.'

Okay, that one was just mean. Still, she saved me from that hellhole trap of De Montfort's making. 'You've made your point. I've not been coming up with much in the way of a plan. Have you?'

'Yep.' She carries on tearing the vegetation up, shredding it with one of the innumerable blades she keeps concealed around various points on her body.

I wait for a minute. A very annoying minute. 'Do go on?' I eventually prompt.

'Go to Winter. Find Simon. Kill the queen if she doesn't give up Simon. Go home.' She chops up something that doesn't look a million miles away from pak choi...if someone dipped some in neon paint and then injected it with gadolinium.

'Hold on, what?' I can't believe my ears. 'That's not an "Aicha" plan. That's a "Paul" plan. That's a "the plan I present and then you tell me it doesn't even count as a plan and that I need to sit in the naughty corner and think about what I've done until I come up with something that is actually a plan" plan. You can't put *that* forward as a plan! That's my job.'

Aicha is entirely unfazed by my outburst. 'Tell you what, dickhead. If you don't like that plan, come up with a better one.'

'All right, I will!' I feel righteously indignant. I'm the act-now-regret-it-later actor in this partnership. She holds the plan-rigorously-and-save-Paul's-bacon-with-it role. Not content with making me stop sitting around and moping, she's going to make me think as well. It's outrageous. Outrageous!

I sit furiously (which is quite a skill — taking a simple action and imbuing it with a ten-megaton emotional charge). Aicha pays me precisely zero attention and just gets on with preparing our food.

After a while, the intensity of my anger reduces, and the thinking starts properly. 'The problem is,' I say as she plonks down what looks like a bunch of leaves shredded into smaller leaves and served on one huge leaf, 'that we don't really know what we're up against.'

Aicha widens her mouth into a shocked O shape. 'You don't say?' she deadpans. 'Please, Mister Obvious, please tell me more of these reality-shaking revelations.'

'Queen Maeve rules Winter,' I continue, choosing not to dignify her sarcasm with an answer. 'We can only assume that if we go into her territory, she's going to know about it. Instantly. So we're going to be targets the moment we arrive, with no idea where Simon is or where the portal to get out of Faerie and back to Earth is. If we don't come up with a proper plan, we're fucked.'

'Paul,' she says, rolling her dark eyes, 'that's not a plan; that's a precis.'

'Yes, I'm aware of that. I'm hoping if I lay it out clearly, maybe it'll jumpstart my brain into actually coming up with a solution.'

'Is it working?'

I shake my head. 'Nah.'

'I can slap you really, really hard. Maybe that'll get your grey matter going again?' She bats her eyelashes at me hopefully.

'It'll get my grey matter going, Aich. It'll get it going straight out of my nose and splatter it across the nearest wall.'

'Right, which might —and hear me out— actually make you smarter.' I look at her in disbelief. 'Well, it can't make you any stupider, can it?'

'Okay, tell you what, let's take that idea, okay, and put it over here, on the conveyor belt into the incinerator.' I mime the required action and then watch it until it passes out of sight. 'Now, let's never talk about that ever again.'

'Still haven't got us any closer to an actual solution though, have you, *saabi*?'

'It'll come! Just give me some time.'

She finishes up her hardcore leaf-on-leaf food action, then sighs. 'You've had time, Paul. Plenty of it. We need to do something.'

I understand her frustration. For all the jokes, we are both creatures of action. Part of being extremely *talented* and virtually indestructible is it makes you more ready to get up in the mix, more quick to throw down when the moment demands it. Problem is, we're a long way from Kansas. We're on the Winter Queen's home turf, and I just can't see any way this is going to end well.

We sit in a companionable silence, and I bash my head against the problem from every angle. It seems impossible to crack. Luckily, my head is exceptionally hard. An idea suddenly comes to me.

'How did you get here again?' I ask Aicha, the first hint of excitement creeping into my voice.

She shakes her head at me. 'A deal with the White Lady. I already told you I can't tell you the details, and it was a one-way trip. She can't help us here.'

'Okay, no, I get that, but hear me out. How did you find the White Lady the first time?'

'I can't tell you that either. That was when I was off hunting down the Nazi bastards.'

Interesting. She mentioned having met the White Lady before, but I didn't realise it was so relatively recent. It's beside the point though.

'Okay, the second time — or the second-to-last time — or, fuck, I don't know how many times you've actually met the White Lady. Right, the time you got through Melusine's barrier with her help, how did you find her?'

Aicha rubs her chin slowly. 'I called in the favour the Red Nain owed us, settling his debts.' A sudden grin splits her face. 'I guess you could call it Red Nain Redemption.'

I groan. 'Dreadful, Aich. Still, it didn't settle *our* debts. It settled yours.'

I reach into my etheric storage, which is still accessible with some difficulty despite my depleted power level thanks to years of practise. Rummaging around, I pull out a shiny red finger, the knuckle-bone protruding at the bottom.

I grin. 'I can think of a winter fae who still owes me a favour.'

Chapter Two

I guess it's time to knuckle down and really put a finger on the problem.

Aicha looks carefully left and right, then raises a hand. I point the dismembered Nain finger at her. 'Yes, you, the annoying one at the back with the Takeshi 6x9 tribute facial tattoo?'

Aicha blinks disbelievingly. 'Okay, well, first, I'm going to skin you alive and then make you tattoo, "I must not mock ancient and wiser cultures like an ignorant fool" on your flayed hide five hundred times using your sharpened little finger as the needle for that comment. But after that, last time I looked, we aren't in the Pyrenees.'

'Look, I get it. You're right…'

She interrupts. 'Say it again.'

I pause. 'Err, you're right?' I'm not sure which bit she means.

'And again.'

I sigh. 'You're right.'

'And one more time'

'You're right.'

I can see she's deep in thought. 'Nope,' she says at last. 'I'll never tire of hearing it. Sorry, go on.'

'Right, thanks, The Incredible Id-Woman. Look, this is my thought process. What the Nain Rouge gave us is summoning magic, okay?'

She nods. 'Yep, totally.'

'So why did he say that we had to be in the Pyrenees to use it?'

She shrugs. 'Because he lives there.'

'What, in the whole of the Pyrenees? That's a massive bit of land to claim as property. I'd think some other monsters and magical beings might dispute that slightly.' I'm a lot tougher than him — or was before my magic got eaten by Melusine, and I only own the city of Toulouse, France. Not that I'm in a measuring contest with him, but he isn't exactly a "capable of keeping strong Talented out of an entire mountain range" kind of guy. He's a "use sly magic to trap a more powerful Talented inside a dumbass escape room and then shriek like a little bitch when said Talented gets out" kind of guy. 'Plus, we know he lives in a collection of shipping containers in a pocket dimension. So why the Pyrenees?'

I can see her chewing it over. She's not looking to take the piss out of me anymore. Playtime's finished. She's got her serious thinking hat on. 'Because he feels an affinity or a connection with the mountains?'

It's my turn to nod now. 'Right. That's his focal point on Earth. Now, again, pocket dimension. Do you think he's powerful enough to have just carved that out of the ether?'

I can see her joining the dots together as I say it. 'No,

not at all; else, he'd have made a better show at resisting when I kicked his arse and burned his house down.'

'Right! He's a trickster — sneaky, clever even but not a magical powerhouse. So where is his pocket dimension likely to actually be?'

'Inside of Faerie!' She grins suddenly, just for a moment. 'Bloody hell, *saabi*, every now and then you're not a complete idiot.'

'Thanks?' I'm not entirely sure how to take that.

'So what's the plan? Burn his finger?' That's how we can summon him. A flame flickers up on her fingertip.

I shake my head. 'Not straight away and not here. We already said he's got an affinity with the mountains. I say, let's look for any serious hilly area in the Wilds and do it there. What do you reckon?'

'That is actually very sensible and extremely well-reasoned out.' She puts her hand on my forehead. 'Are you sure you're not running a fever?'

I push her away and get to my feet. 'That's just the radiant heat of my genius. Come on. I've spent enough time waiting for you to get your shit together. Let's rock on.'

I manage to half-duck the cuff she aims at the back of my head as I waltz past, so it only makes half my brain bounce off the front of my cranium like a crash-test dummy. I try not to let her see me wince as I carry on towards the exit of the shelter that has been a safe haven for the past few weeks and into the unknown weirdness of the fae Wilds.

It's harder than I expect, walking out from that shelter. And I'd known it'd be difficult. I've witnessed the effects of trauma firsthand a hundred times over, probably more. Still, it's something else to feel it. That sensation like a physical barrier; an unpassable air-wall that squeezes you tight as you try, all the way inside to your very heart. My lungs must be compressed. I can't get my breath.

Aicha doesn't help. Not physically. She doesn't grab my arm and yank me out, however much a part of me might wish she would. She stands. And waits. And that in itself — having her just calmly standing, as if she has all the time in the world — is enough to get me moving. With a last shaking push I force myself through that self-imposed limit to my world and sail off the edge of my traumatic map.

Those first few steps are infant-like, a trembling toddle out into the unknown. Every step is an opportunity for terror; my heart is palpitating, leaping each time a leaf crinkles. The wind whispers threats that fill my bones with lead. I was once attuned to the Wilds. Not now. Not when my head is full of prey-thought.

Luckily there's an apex predator by my side to keep me safe. And more than that, her presence lends me the strength to still move forwards.

We walk for about half an hour, tromping through feathered bracken that crackles like brushfire under our feet, stamping past curled, thorned vines that seem to snatch at our ankles, winding themselves into the perfect position to obstruct our way before Aicha asks me the most important and pertinent question possible.

'So where exactly are we going?'

I stop suddenly. 'Ummm.' I was so taken with the whole "get off my arse, stop moping, and actually do something", that I didn't give any thought to *where* I should go once I did it.

Aicha sighs, a long-suffering sigh. 'And Bonhomme is back with a vengeance. I suppose it was too much to ask that thinking things through became a habit rather than just a once-in-a-blue-moon occurrence. So I take it that means you've no idea where the high terrain is then?'

'Err, not precisely,' I say, trying to work out how to save the situation. 'I mean, I know I'm keeping equidistant from Summer and Winter, so I thought…'

'You thought you'd just keep walking until you stumbled over a mountain range? Because obviously it would *have* to be in the middle between the two courts? Because the fae are so well organised and logical and love everything to be neat and tidy?'

'Hobs do!'

'Hobs are just brownies with OCD; doesn't count.'

'Do you have a better plan?'

'Absolutely.'

There's silence for a moment. Fucksake. 'Can I hear said plan?'

'Yep.' She nods. 'It's very simple. You ask me if I know where there are any mountains.'

'Aicha Kandicha, Druze Queen, good friend, and massive pedant, do you know where there are any mountains?'

'Of course I do! I thought you'd never ask. Follow me, dickhead.'

She brushes past me. I guess that one was payback for my comment as we left the lean-to. I can't really argue with her. Plus, after my time trapped underground and then huddled up under dripping fronds, trying to hide from my sense of failure, getting out and just going for a walk is doing me the world of good. I suspect that's why she left it so long before mentioning it to me. She's just glad to see me doing something, *anything*, again.

Once Aicha corrects our trajectory (or 'turns around

and goes the actual right way instead of just wandering about like a dickhead,' as she puts it), I lapse into silence, my earlier high from a sense of positive action dissipating. Instead, I find it harder and harder to catch my breath, my lungs feeling too small for anything but tiny, shallow ones. I can hear my heartbeat in my eardrums, which is weird as I'm fairly sure it's supposed to be in my chest, and my palms become slick with sweat despite it being tenaciously cool in the forest. Then we break through the foliage, and the mountain Aicha has been leading us to comes into view.

This enormous wave of relief hits me, and the weird symptoms reduce down to manageable levels even if they don't disappear entirely. I realise suddenly that I was terrified Aicha was taking us back to the hill I'd been imprisoned under, that maybe that place was the high terrain she was thinking of. It's only now that I see it isn't, that I realise how terrified I was of going back there.

Aicha seems not to notice, but considering she can spot a leaf falling unexpectedly half a mile away in sheeting rain, I think that's pretty unlikely. I appreciate the effort of her pretence.

The forest breaks against the slope of the mountain like a green wave, sparse hardy trees clinging to rocky outcrops. It looks almost vertical, and I feel dizzy just considering trying to clamber up it.

'How far up do you think we need to go to get it to work?' I ask doubtfully. I'm having second thoughts about the entire plan.

Aicha already did me the favour of ignoring one moment of weakness from me. She's not about to make a habit of it. 'How far do you think?'

I point at where the first of the tenacious few boughs poke out at what looks like almost ninety degrees. 'There?'

The tremor to my voice is just to underline the question…
Though the trunks do look threateningly high. At least two,
maybe three metres off the ground.

Aicha points at them, then lets her finger trace the path
of the ascent all the way to the top. It's only when she
swivels her hand around to point at me after that I realise
it's her middle finger.

'The top, you twat,' she says, kissing the tip of her digit,
then pretending to blow smoke off it. 'All the way to the
tippy-top.'

Of course. Looks like I need to get my climb on. Fuck
my life.

I might be from the lowlands of the Haute-Garonne,
but I've spent literal lifetimes in and around the Pyrenees. I
would normally be moving up this path like a sprightly
mountain goat. Instead, someone seems to have surreptitiously operated on my kneecaps and swapped them out for
jellyfish when I wasn't looking, which is a bitch move, in my
opinion. I heave myself up one wobbling step after the
other, from trunk to trunk, trying not to lose my trembling
footing or face-plant when my sweaty mitts fumble as I
crawl up a particularly steep bit. It's, well. It's frankly
humiliating.

Even Aicha can't ignore it or just continue to take the
piss out of me. 'Are you all right, *saabi*?' she asks eventually,
after she comes to a grinding halt to allow me to catch up
for what feels like the zillionth time.

I sink down against the tree I used to heave myself level,
keeping my back to the slope, using the gritty irregularities
of the wood to anchor myself into it, to feel safe. I don't
mind if it scratches my skin. It makes me feel more
connected to the mountain, less likely to slide back down all
the way I climbed up.

'No, I'm really not, Aich.' I can't deny it. 'It fucking sucks. I lost my *talent* — or as near to all of it as matters, and now the slightest difficulty has me shaking like a leaf. In my head, I feel fine, but nobody seems to have passed that information to the body I'm borrowing because it's on the verge of having a heart attack every time I see my own shadow. And I'm sick of it, Aich. I want to get out there and kick De Montfort square in the nuts, and at the same time, I want to go hide in the nearest dark hole.' I shudder. That's not true. 'Actually, not a dark hole. The opposite of a dark hole. Yes, to the hiding. No, to the dark hole. '

I never expected this. I don't know what I had expected, but it wasn't this. I was so blasé for so many years about the idea of being trapped. Sure, someone might torture me, I might suffer and die, but then I'd just dust myself off in a new body and get on with my life. The cave was the first time I really felt imprisoned, totally ensnared. The situation seemed helpless, the trap inescapable, and I really thought I was going to spend the next sixteen years, roughly three days for each corpse De Montfort had left down there for me, living it over and over. The first sixteen days alone reduced me to a shadow of who I once was.

I'm furious with myself for being so affected by it, but it doesn't change the truth. I'm terrified of dying now. Terrified I'll end up back there. That somehow Aicha didn't destroy all the bodies with her fire and didn't leave the hole open. That I'll wake up back in that cave again and never make it out. Each time my foot slides on the loose gravel, my heart feels like it's ten sizes too big for my chest, like someone hooked it up to one of those air compressors used to blow up a bouncy castle and threw the switch to maximum pressure. Just moving at all is taking every inch of my willpower, and I'm sick of it.

'It doesn't get better, you know,' Aicha says quietly.

I blink. 'What?' If this is her idea of a pep talk, she needs to do some serious work on her people skills.

'It doesn't get better. That sort of trauma. It just gets… usual.'

'Usual?' Apparently, although it's starting to look like my career as a wise-cracking, ass-kicking magician might draw to a close, at least I'll have the job of "annoying parrot" to fall back onto.

Aicha scratches the nape of her neck, knocking away whatever little flying beastie is trying to feed on her. Because we are in Faerie, I think I hear it vaguely cursing her out in a Scottish burr as it flies away. The drunken weave to its movement certainly looks Hebridean.

'You don't get over these things, Paul; you know that. Did you ever forget watching Ben bleed to death at your feet when you couldn't move? Can you honestly say that if you closed your eyes right now, you can't see Susane lying in a pool of blood on your wedding bed?'

I don't trust myself to speak, so I just shake my head. There's no way I can say that.

'So why weren't you still weeping into your pint for Ben's loss when we first met? How come you aren't still elbow deep in an opium den, blotting out your existence right now over Susane?'

I think about it for a minute. Even though I did fall back into the pint after I lost my magic, and Isaac, my father-figure and mentor, had to pull me out, he only managed to pull me out because *I* was ready. 'Because it won't help.'

That gets me the gun fingers. 'Bingo. It won't. When shit goes catastrophically tits up, we all catch a grace period where everything is allowed to fall to pieces. Might not be straight away. Might have too many other pressures. Too many responsibilities. Others who need us to hold it together. But the collapse, when it comes, is understandable. Maybe it's a week, maybe it's a year. Maybe it's just ten minutes of screaming and punching the wall. Not my place to tell anyone else how to handle things. Eventually, though, you've got a choice. Do you stay there? Or do you live again? If you choose the latter, it doesn't mean suddenly it all just goes away, does it? Just pack it all up neatly. Then carry it with you forever. Get so used to carrying it, sometimes you forget you even are, but when you think about it, it's always there. Over time, it just becomes usual.'

I ponder this. 'Have you ever thought, *laguna*, that we might be in desperate need of some serious therapy?'

She rolls her eyes. 'Well, duh. Let me know when you find a therapist who won't yeet themselves out of the nearest window if we start telling them our story.'

It's a valid point. Looks like there's a market opening for a Talented therapist. Maybe that could be my fall-back career if I never get my powers back. I'd be rubbish at the whole "caring, listening ear" thing, but at least when I add to their trauma instead of helping them heal it, they can Cathartically murder me at the end of the session. It could be the equivalent of one of those rage rooms where you pay to smash the place up. Don't like my advice? Stab me in the face. I'll make a killing. Well, they'll make a killing, but you get what I mean.

The changing light shakes me from my reverie. The shadows are elongating, dancing across the carpet of fallen leaves to intermingle, grouping together to solidify darkness' hold on the land itself. Night doesn't so much fall as hurtle downwards at terminal velocity in Faerie, and if we want to make it to the top before it becomes pitch-black, we need to get going. I'd rather defend the high ground if any of the

Wilds' hungrier denizens come sniffing about in the nighttime.

I push myself off the supportive bough, feeling like I have a second wind. I guess I just need to get used to my new normal. Funnily enough, I do feel better. It doesn't make sense; I've just been told I'll be carrying this forever. But maybe it's because I've now accepted that as the case instead of fighting myself every step of the way. Okay, I'll be more afraid, more nervous and cautious. To be honest, my overconfidence and reckless behaviour didn't really stand me in good stead. I can do with being a bit more careful in my everyday actions.

When I think back to my first life, I was terrified plenty of times. Hell, I was a named heretic with the considerable combined weight of the Catholic Church and feudal society chasing after me with a tinderbox and a bunch of kindling. Maybe I need to get back to my roots. Not in the religious sense — that's never going to happen, but in terms of finding a bit of courage even when I'm scared stiff. There's no bravery in genuine fearlessness. Just idiocy.

I use the gnawing worry about falling as a tool to choose my next branch to grip more carefully, to think out my path more precisely. I look farther ahead, working out where I'm going. If I don't want to plunge off the side of the mountain —and I don't want to plunge off the side of the mountain — then I better do something about it.

I feel Aicha prowling behind me, far more graceful and confident in her movements than I am. I mean, she's far more graceful and confident in everything than me, but it's the moving part that stands out right now.

'Appreciate it, *laguna*,' I say softly. 'Appreciate you.'

'Yeah, yeah, soppy bollocks. Less talking, more climbing.' Her words might be disparaging, but I notice she stays behind me, positioning herself in just such a way between this tree *here* or next to that boulder *there*, that if I slip, she can catch and brace me. She's back again in her role as my safety net. Only literally this time.

It's good to have friends who love you. Even if they'd rather swallow their own tongue than tell you that.

Chapter Three

TOULOUSE, 20 FEBRUARY 1973

There's about half a second as Aicha hisses for quiet when I walk in, where I consider playing with her. Perhaps slamming the door or bellowing questions at her about what she wants for breakfast and why do I need to be quiet, fixing my decibels at just-below-eardrum-popping levels. Then I see her face and realise precisely what effect that will have on my life expectancy for this body and probably several other bodies as well.

Aicha isn't the most outwardly expressive person, excluding her artistic use of violence that she can use to express anything from slight annoyance to utter contempt. If there is a message to be given, it won't come couched in a grimace or a frown. It'll be visible in her eyes. Right now, they burn like coals dropped in the snow, the smoke rising off them almost visible. She is, as the kids these days would say (and even thinking that makes me feel every single one of my eight hundred years at once), "buggin' out".

A moment or so after deciding not to commit seppuku

via Aicha, I clock what has her attention — the wireless radio chattering away in the background.

'*...since the evening. Both the gendarmes and the military police are blocking all access points from the Ile d'Yeu but believe that the thieves may already have absconded off the island with the coffin prior to the forces' mobilisation. Authorities are appealing for any witnesses in the case of this egregious crime to contact them immediately. The telephone number to do so is...*'

Aicha leans forward and switches off the radio, tension radiating from the swift precision of her movement, as though it took all her concentration to stop at turning the knob to off rather than tearing it from its Bakelite frame. I suspect, had she done so, it wouldn't be the first time she tore a knob off.

'What's going on?' Part of me, the selfish part that values my own well-being, wants to just back out of the room slowly. This is my friend though, and if she needs to vent her spleen, I'm here for her. Even if venting her spleen means stabbing me in mine.

Aicha turns to me, swivelling on her heels before brushing past as she marches out the door. 'Tell you on the way to the Ile d'Yeu,' she shouts, stomping upstairs.

I sigh. Apparently, we're going on a road trip.

It's a long drive up to the island situated just off the west coast near Nantes. Work has started on a major motorway between Toulouse and Bordeaux that will knock a fair chunk of time off the route, but for now, we're stuck bumbling down single-lane roads, limited more often by haulage traffic or the occasional tractor than we are by the speed limit of a hundred kilometres per hour. It's frustrating. I've only just picked up my Citroen DS23, its burgundy spaceship curves as fabulously aerodynamic as they are impossibly futuristic, and I'm desperate to open it up and see what it can do. The other road users make that an annoying impossibility.

I let Aicha stew in her fury for an hour or so. Once she simmers down, letting a little of that righteous anger evaporate into a condensed but more controllable amount, I risk trying to extract some information out of her.

'Know what I love?' I inject a breezy tone into my voice to match the whipping air currents sliding in through the cracked window. Despite the winter month, the sun's strong enough to heat the cabin up sufficiently as to want some fresh air. Also, the pressure of Aicha's fury is stifling.

'Being a twat?' Good. She's still got her sense of humour. Because of course she's joking. Of course.

'Besides that. I love going for nine-hour drives to the other end of the country without knowing the reason why.'

'Not the other end of the country. Toulouse: southwest. Ile d'Yeu: northwest. West even, arguably. Hardly fucking Calais.'

I wonder if it might be advisable to look into a future career in dentistry because this is like pulling fucking teeth. 'Yeah, I think you might have focused on the wrong part of that sentence. It wasn't so much the geographical precision I was concerned by.'

I catch the faintest flash in her eyes. We've been friends for closing in on thirty years now, but she went off hunting Nazis for a good portion of that and was an almost entirely closed book prior. Even after her return, she's hardly thrown it open, pages out on display like some form of hussy literature, parading its verbs and adjectives for all the world to see. No, just occasionally, she'll crack open the tiniest sliver.

So now, twenty-eight years since I got her out of that hell-hole at La Rochelle, I'm still only just learning to read her. Most people wouldn't have noticed that micro-expression. The few who did would probably have interpreted it to be tamped down rage considering the rest of her body language and demeanour. I'm pretty confident it is amusement. We're developing a way of talking to each other, a back-and-forth banter that I hope will help her relax and open up further. Generally, I say something, and she insults me. It seems to work well. So I'm confident what I saw was amusement. Either that or tamped down rage, and I'm about to get murderised. One or the other.

She huffs slightly, the tiniest expulsion loaded with all the wearying weight of having to be in my company on a daily basis. See — told you I'm getting through to her. 'Not hear the news?'

'Not really.' I shrug. Normally it would be a wasted gesture, what with her eyes being fixed on the road, but I know perfectly well that Aicha sees more with her peripheral vision than most people see when they're looking straight at something. 'I was too busy hunting for the particularly gigantic snake hissing at me like it was about to strike when I came to offer you breakfast.'

She ignores me. 'Actually been listening, might have realised why. Took Petain's coffin.'

I sit upright. Ah. 'Who?'

I see her shake her head, doubtless in disbelief at my stupidity. 'Who? Fucking Nazis.'

I slink back in my chair, abashed. Right. Who else? Petain was a French hero in the First World War, a respected general at the start of the Second…and then a reviled traitor by the end. He set up the Vichy regime, the collaborative government that surrendered to the Nazis and was responsible for loading up Jews, travelling folk, homosexuals, and basically anyone Hitler didn't like onto train carriages, heading off towards Auschwitz and the like, never to be seen again. After the war, he landed a death sentence, but that got commuted to life imprisonment.

Post war, Germany grappled hard with what they did; there was soul searching aplenty. They acknowledged how much they'd fucked up — the evils done either by them or in their name.

But France never really went through that same self-analysis. Everyone miraculously became a former member of the Resistance, statistical evidence be damned, and there's a significant element of the hard- and far-right wingers that try exceedingly hard to gloss over the truths of the Vichy Regime. They want to present collaboration as having been a good thing — saving lives rather than the cowardly craven surrender it actually was.

Part of that whole "reframe our evil deeds" drive has been to present Petain as some sort of military hero who bravely defended France by licking Hitler's boot. I've not paid too much attention to it. I try to avoid listening to fascists' demands as it makes me want to kill large swathes of humanity, ironically. I know they want Petain buried in one of the main national cemeteries with full presidential honours. I have no idea which. Doubtless Aicha knows. Stick him in a plague pit or a pauper's grave, far as I'm concerned. None of his previous actions repudiate what he did when the Nazis came knocking.

A thought occurs to me, and I narrow my eyes. 'Did you kill Petain?' I can't remember the details.

Aicha scoffs. 'Yep. Made him be ninety-five years old. Super-secret Druze magic called "time".' She sobers. 'No.

Thought about it. But he was found guilty. Imprisoned. Enough. Just.'

Of course, that makes sense. Aicha had only "gone hunting", as the note she left me said, after news of some Nazis having slipped away, often getting quietly scooped up and pardoned by countries like the USA, came to light. Most of us who are Talented aren't big on killing ordinary mortals, though for particularly execrable scumbags like Nazis, we might make exceptions. That's obviously the line in the sand Aicha has drawn for herself. If they are caught and tried and found guilty by the authorities, she'll leave them be. If they escape the law, well. Then they're fair game.

I consider the information I've got now. 'Do you think it could be magic? Is that why we're getting involved?'

I see her start to shake her head, but instead, she cocks it, obviously intently listening to her own internal dialogue, considering my question. 'Possible. Not considered it. More likely not. Still, it'll become a rallying point for the Nazis. Breathe life back into their ideology here. Not having that.'

Again, it makes sense. Considering her own suffering at the hands of the far-right regime, she'll not want to see it coming back into prominence ever again. End of the day, this is fascists doing fucked-up fascist things. Enough of a reason for her to get involved. And if becoming their worst nightmare helps to keep her own nightmares under control, I'm happy to come along for the ride.

We pass most of the rest of the journey in silence. I occasionally re-tune the radio as we pass out of range of one antenna, chasing a new station that started up a couple of years back called FIP. Their music selection's eclectic, covering a plethora of modern wonders from around the world, particularly some of the more obscure funk and

Motown you aren't likely to catch on the other French stations. Even better, they don't allow adverts, and most of the interruptions between songs are semi-snarky traffic advisories, as useful as they are amusing. I pore over the Michelin road map, guiding us away from any hot spots. I don't want Aicha to end up taking a traffic jam personally. In her current mood, she's likely to explode the other cars to clear them out of our way. After getting the occupants out, of course. Probably.

By the time we arrive on the island, night hasn't just fallen, it's tripped over its own feet and then face-planted spectacularly, so that seeing anything outside of the halogen glows of the streetlamps is difficult. The carpark on this side of the ferry dock is much like the other side was — a mixture of official vehicles, TV and radio branded minivans, and the rest undoubtedly ghoulish sightseers. Aicha pays them no mind but heads the short distance to the Pont Joinville Cemetery. It's a quick drive, less than five minutes, and all we have to do is follow the general traffic and buzz. Parking is more of an issue, but we find a spot on a side road where traffic can pass without side-swiping my gorgeous motorcar, then get out.

The front of the cemetery is a mass of bodies pressed up against the official cordon, where several police officers wearing harangued expressions more crumpled than their uniforms push people back. Occasionally they force an opening to allow senior ranking detectives, their jobs as clearly displayed on their faces as the stripes on the beat bobbies' shoulders, access in and out. It's a media circus, full of noise, a hubbub of hullabaloo. I need to check my copy of *Dante's Inferno*, but I'm fairly confident this is one of the circles of hell he described with such great accuracy. There are certainly enough politicians around for it to be the Underworld.

I turn towards Aicha to suggest coming back at a quieter time, like in about three years, only to find she's already marching with great purpose and determination towards the throng.

Looks like we're going to be fighting our way through the lion's den of press and police after all, exactly the sort of mundane humans I desperately try to avoid whenever possible. This is just what I want to be doing on a Monday night.

Chapter Four

When Diana Ross wrote, 'Ain't No Mountain High Enough', she clearly wasn't on a walking holiday in Faerie.

We make it to the top of the mountain before it plunges into absolute darkness. That's a win. Faerie is full of wild, insanely dangerous creatures, the Wilds even more so. Luckily, I'm human — the most dangerous animal of all. Except for honey badgers. Those little bastards are vicious as fuck. Also — Aicha. I have Aicha. She's even more vicious than a badger. High praise indeed.

It's mainly a level surface at the top, the scrubby grass broken by rocks that push up and out like undead trolls digging themselves out of their graves. If that doesn't sound like a particularly cheery mental image, this is not a particularly cheery place. It's freezing cold, the wind whipping up the slopes behind us and accelerating over the top before launching into free fall down the other side, trying to carry us with it. The rain is holding off for once, though, so I'm thankful for small mercies.

Aicha does her award-winning impression of a portable radiator, and the whole place becomes more bearable. I'd love to start a fire as well, but that would be akin to shooting fireworks off that explode into a beautiful arrow pointing straight at us with the words 'COME GET YOUR WALKING BUFFET' picked out in twinkly curly script. I've enough *talent* left I can augment my night vision a small amount, meaning I can keep watch on a part of the perimeter, at least. I huddle over my sword, the cold returning as Aicha walks the rest of the boundary of the open space, securing our six. Attacks can and probably will come from any direction. Knowing how and where they are likely to come from is essential.

I beckon her over when she makes her way back. Simply improving my night vision fractionally has taken it out of me, so I hand the severed Nain Rouge finger over to Aicha.

'Burn that for me, will you?' She plucks it from my outstretched hand. Without her even blinking, it ignites, a momentary miniature beacon that I know she effortlessly wraps a protection around to keep it from keen predatory eyes. In a matter of seconds, the finger turns to ash, disintegrating into dust as the wind whips it away.

'Now we wait.' I crouch down next to Aicha, resisting the urge to warm my hands against her like a fire as that would be a good way to get them snapped off at the wrist.

'Yep. Thanks for stating the obvious, Hermione.'

I notice that although she's turned her back, she's angled herself to be closer to me. The temperature warms accordingly, and it's a massive relief. My teeth stop chattering, and I bask in not feeling like my bone marrow has been hollowed out and replaced with Mr Freeze ice popsicles (which would be as painful as it would make your skeleton delicious).

We don't have to wait long. There is a puff of red smoke because the Nain's a showy bastard, and the little red-devil-wannabe steps forward, out of the last few plumes before they disappear.

He's an ugly bugger. That's only by my, admittedly human, standards. Maybe for other vertically-challenged fae, he's a prime specimen, but shiny bright red leathery skin has never been my cup of tea. The stubby little bumps on his forehead, too tiny to even really be considered horns, don't help. As for his personality…he's the sort who thinks sticking your leg out and tripping someone over is peak hilarity. If they face-plant onto a bed of spikes, all the better. The Nain Rouge is a vindictive little trickster and an all-round shithead.

He capers forward, probably thinking he looks mysterious and otherworldly instead of how he actually appears, which is like a proper twat. 'Hello, hello Cathar…' he starts, then blinks. He looks around, whipping his head back and forth, his brow furrowing like a field ready for sowing. 'Where are… Where are we?' He backs up a couple of steps, his head still swinging around wildly. 'You're in Faerie — we're in *Faerie*!' The first trickle of sweat forms on his temple. 'What are you doing in *Faerie*? *In the Wilds*? Are you fucking suicidal, Good Man? Why, why would you call me *here*?'

His screeching gets higher and higher in pitch. He starts to make sudden tense movements. Each step carries a juddering readiness that speaks of the fight-or-flight mechanism, and if I'm any judge, he's about to make a run for it.

'Wait!' I hold up my hand. 'You owe me a favour.'

'A favour? A *favour*?' I can see his little hoofed feet

scraping at the floor, gouging a hole in the soil. 'I'm here now with you, aren't I? I'd say that's the favour done. Good day, Cathar. I need to get somewhere less deadifying.'

He tries to bolt, but Aicha was waiting and seizes him by the scruff of his neck so that his momentum just makes him do a pretty good impression of a fairground Pirate Ship ride, his skin folds operating as the pivot point. Once he swings back from the horizontal, he dangles from her grasp above the ground.

'Not how this works, Nain. You know that.' There's a tone to Aicha's voice that promises a detailed explanation of why can easily be forthcoming. It can involve diagrams and everything. Carved directly into the retina with a red-hot knife blade. 'You owe us a favour, and it has to be agreed to by both parties.'

The Nain continues to flail his stubby legs as if he thinks he might suddenly get purchase with the ground half a metre below them and disappear in a cloud of dust. 'This isn't fair! Isn't fair!' he wails. 'I stated to call me in the Pyrenees, and I'd come. I said nothing about Faerie.'

'Well, true,' I say. 'But that's because you never expected us to be in Faerie. And the fact you've turned up suggests the magic you made doesn't see the difference. As long as it's somewhere you're attuned to. And last I looked, you're still fae.'

'Very wriggly fae, actually,' Aicha pipes up, watching in intense fascination the Nain's entirely unsuccessful attempts to work himself free and head off.

'Still not the agreement, not the agreement, was it?' The creature looks like he's about to burst into fits of tears any moment. 'Do you even know where you are right now?'

I roll my eyes. 'Well, duh. You just said it at least once. We're in the Wilds of Faerie.'

'No, no, you dunderhead. Do you know where in the Wilds you are?'

I resist the urge to poke holes in him with my sword for the insult. Just. 'No, my geographical knowledge of "Lands where humans never willingly go" is somewhat limited. Lack of serious cartographers and all that.'

'This is Coin Mountain. Coin Mountain!'

I scratch my head. '*Con* Mountain? Like, there's a lot of *connards*, dickheads, that congregate up here?'

'No, no!' the creature shrieks at me, trembling in Aicha's grip. 'Coin. As in the plural of Cu sidhe. This is the mountain of the Coin sidhe.'

As if on cue, I hear a mournful howl echoing up from down below, on the slopes we just climbed up. It carries easily, mainly due to it being approximately the same volume as an entire pack of normal wolves turned up to eleven. When it's joined by another howl, then another, then a third, it becomes so loud, the very earth trembles. At the far reaches of my field of enhanced vision, I see the first gleam of massive glowing eyes. What's much worse is that they also see me.

Chapter Five

Faerie dogs. When ordinary canines capable of tearing you
limb from limb in a second just won't do.

Aicha draws closer to me and pulls her katana out of its
sheath. 'If I put you down, Nain, will you promise not to
run?'

'It's too late, too late.' He groans, quivering so hard in
her grasp he's practically vibrating. 'They've sealed off the
mountain even for teleportation. We cannot get out.'

'Drums, drums in the deep.' Aicha drops the little fae
and draws her wakizashi, another sword, with her off-hand.

'Wrong book.' I look around wildly to see if there's a
more defensible position. Nothing. We have the high
ground. That will have to do. 'You've done a fucking Thorin
and Company, choosing to have a meeting in the Wargs'
favourite locale.' I scan round again. 'And there're no trees
to hide up or pinecones to turn into Magictov Cocktails
either.'

'Luckily, I don't need pinecones.' The ends of Aicha's swords glow with violet bale-fire, deep maroons flickering within. 'You call for the eagles. I'll burn these fuckers to the ground.'

'I don't think a quick rendition of 'Hotel California' is going to help right now. And, if I remember rightly, Cu sidhe are immune to fire. Because of course they are.'

I'd ask the Nain, but he's taken to gibbering inanely in terror while trying to hide behind Aicha's legs, which forces her to boot him in the face a couple of times to give her space to work.

'I meant more grabbing a lift to their eyries and getting the hell out of Dodge, but that reminds me. We still need to sort out some theme music.'

The glowing eyes get closer. A quick glance left and right reveals two more pairs appearing out of the dark. I move to position myself back-to-back with Aicha as I draw my own sword from my etheric storage. 'Do you really think this is the best moment to discuss that right now?'

'There's never a good time. I'm just making sure we keep it earmarked. Needs to be a priority, I think.'

'Okay, well, let's stow it until we survive the ravenous fae wolves, shall we?'

'Dogs. Dogs!' The high-pitched voice is partially obscured by the fact the Nain Rouge appears to be trying to climb up Aicha's trouser leg to hide. Which means he probably won't survive long enough to get torn apart by the approaching hounds.

'Okay, whatever particular subspecies of *canis* these *enormous and magically immune* dogs are.'

'That's easy, easy. I already told you they're Coin sidhe.'

That's it? *That's* the particular hill the Nain Rouge has decided to die on, the specific *genus* of fae dog these are?

Not counting the actual hill that we are all probably about to pop our clogs on, of course.

An ominous growl starts up. It sounds like someone has detuned an angle grinder or maybe recorded it and slowed it down to half-speed. Then attached it to the world's most powerful sub-woofer. I can feel it reverberating in my chest, throughout my whole body until it feels like my vocal cords are producing the same noise. I can taste the growl in my throat. It tastes like agonising death. Which is not my favourite flavour of Ben'N'Jerrys. Not even in the top ten.

The first of the Coin sidhe steps into view. Fae creatures are a real favourite of human authors, and everyone loves dogs, right (except cats, but then cats don't like anyone apart from themselves)? So when human writers hear about a Cu sidhe, they want to make them into these bounding loyal companions whose tongues wag as they lick their enemies to death. They basically transform them into Clifford the Big Green Dog.

What we often forget about is that we bred those characteristics into our canine companions over generations. I'd love to know how many fingers it cost to persuade the first wolf to stand guard in exchange for a share of the hunt. Go pet a wild dog, even one who comes from generations of domesticated animals, and see how far it gets you. My guess is "as far as it is to the nearest A&E centre".

There's never been a domesticated Cu sidhe. Oh, sure, they serve in the Wild Hunt, but the clue there is in the name. They aren't beagles following the bugle call of some poncy toff in a red jacket, pointing to the poor, exhausted fox, then leaving the final japes to their posh wanker of an owner. These are the harbingers of the Hunt. When Oberon blows his horn, it draws the hounds to him, then they lead the way, driving and chasing, harrying and harassing anything in the Wilds unable to fight or flee. The rest of the time, the Wilds are their playground. If perhaps there is a dominant species in this No Man's Land, until the fae lords and ladies take their sport, it's the Coin sidhe.

A creature the size of a horse stalks out of the bracken. If said horse had been jacking anabolic steroids and bench-pressing serious weight with his other horse bros at the gym every day for the past ten years. The flaming emerald colour of its eyes stands out against the shaggy seaweed-style fur, matted and tangled, that covers it all over, a green so dark as to be almost black. Its lips curl back to reveal teeth as long as my hand and as sharp as a cutthroat razor. The rumbling from its voice box makes me feel unsteady on my feet, like I'm standing in the starting tremors of an earthquake, as if the very earth is moving in sympathy with their terrible voice. Hell, this is their mountain.

Okay, diplomacy first. 'We mean you no harm. We didn't know this was your mountain. It was an honest mistake.' I hold my sword above my head, its flat side facing them, my other hand splayed wide to show it's empty. No tricks.

The gigantic canine cocks its head, a curious look on its face. Then it chuffs, a hacking laugh, as three more Coin sidhe emerge out of the darkness. An echoing bark of venomous amusement comes from behind me and to the right, but I don't turn my head. Aicha will have it covered. Breaking eye contact now is asking for the creature to attack.

'A mistake? Well, we can all agree it was a mistake.' There's a playful viciousness to his tone, like a cat inviting a mouse to dance. 'Whether or not it was honest matters little. Still, you're here.' It sniffs, a heaving snuffle drinking in our scents. Considering I haven't done more than a cursory wash in weeks, I feel almost sorry for it. 'What manner of prey are you? How are you called? I can smell so many strange and wonderfully unfamiliar scents to trail along.' It gnashes its teeth suddenly, the bass-note growl back as a harmony to its words. 'Oberon rarely brings us two-legged prey these days. And the Winter Lady isn't allowed to play anymore. You carry a strange scent, the both of you.' It breathes in deeply through its nose again, then gives another chuff. 'If I didn't know that he knows better, I'd swear I could smell a Nain Rouge who has strayed foolishly onto our territory.'

'Definitely not, definitely not!' squeaks a tiny high-pitched voice behind me. 'And if you did, if you did, it would certainly not be of my own choosing but because of these human cretins.'

We're going to have another chat about manners with the Nain if we all get out of here alive. I make one last attempt at diplomacy.

'I am Paul Bonhomme, Holder of Toulouse in the mortal realm. Is there anything we can do to make amends for our trespass?' I still hold my hand high and clear to show no immediate threat, though I can swing my sword back down into a guard in a second if he lunges. 'Anything that will persuade you to let us descend the mountain unharried and unharmed?'

The gigantic mutt grins, displaying all of his varied and vicious teeth. He lets his tongue loll. It doesn't look in the slightest bit friendly, more like he's thinking how much I look like a piece of prime rib. Being drooled over as food isn't the ego boost it sounds like, let me tell you. 'Let you descend, little prey? Of course!' He shuffles sideways, opening a pathway between him and the nearest other Cu sidhe, who regards me with equal parts fascination and delight. Not the delight of "what an interesting creature" but the delight of "oh, a new plaything. I wonder how quickly I can snap it in two?"

The Cu sidhe who was talking turns his massive shaggy head back towards me. 'Go ahead; walk on down then, little prey.'

'And you'll leave us be if we do?' I narrow my eyes. Just because it looks like a dog doesn't mean it won't act like a fae.

'Of course.' Even the creature's eyes are laughing at me. The rest of the pack is huffing away like mad. They clearly think he is some sort of comic genius, which shows you why you should never let dogs do stand-up comedy. 'For, oh, let's say a hundred wags of our tails. Sounds fair, doesn't it, little prey? Perhaps you can get enough of a lead to run all the way back to Summer. What do you think?'

I hear a brittle laugh behind me, and the Cu's mouth snaps shut. We aren't supposed to be finding anything about this situation amusing. He's never met Aicha though.

'Give up the high ground?' The level of incredulity in her voice is so brimming over, it drips out in every single syllable. 'Run ourselves ragged through your home territory, so you can pick us off one by one as we collapse from exhaustion?' The ridiculousness of the very idea is categorical. Doesn't matter the price, the flashy discount stickers, and special offers. Aicha isn't buying it.

The gigantic hound loses all of his playfulness. His muzzle pulls back in a snarl, foam flecks dribbling out of the corners, that earthquake growl once more abuzz. The tone mirrors its way through the pack. 'Run, prey!' He snaps his teeth at us, the sound like a clanging gong. 'Run or die.'

'Yes, as you wish.' Even the notes of incredulity have

gone from Aicha's voice now. It's flat, monotone. This is Aicha Kandicha in ready mode.

The growl falters ever so slightly. This isn't how the conversation is supposed to go. 'What do you mean?' The confusion is clear in the Cu sidhe's voice. 'We already said we want you to run.'

'Oh.' There's the verbal equivalent of a face-palm in the faked tone of realisation. 'I thought you just realised that *you* can run, or you can die. The choice is yours.'

The hound looks baffled now. 'No, prey, the choice is yours.'

'Oh, I don't really mind. You can run or you can die. Honestly, makes no difference to me.'

I can see his hackles rising, but he swings his cart-horse-sized head left and right, seeking reassurance from his companions. 'No, I meant *you can* choose whether you run or you die, prey.'

'Ah, I see. I understand now.'

The Cu sidhe smiles, triumphant at Aicha's words. Finally, the prey understands, and they will hunt!

'You're confused.' The smile disappears. 'You think you're the one in control here.' The growl comes back, the snarl as well. 'You're mistaken. It happens to the best of us.' There's a pause while she thinks. 'Actually, I'm never mistaken, so it doesn't happen to the best of us. It happens to the rest of the world. Particularly him. He's wrong, like, almost all the time.'

'Thanks, Aich.'

'Any time, *saabi*. Anyway, the mistake you made is you think we're going to be the ones running or dying. I am Aicha Kandicha, the Undying Druze Queen, Guardian of the Aab-Al-Hayat, and if you do not start running right now, *I will neuter each and every one of you by feeding you your own testicles and ballsacks.*'

One or two whimpers sound, and tails droop defensively over several of the Coin sidhe's private areas. Aicha isn't done.

'I'm assuming you're all boys as no girls would be so suicidal, but I will happily perform a pap test all the way to the back of your throats with my blade if there are. I'm an equal-opportunity end-ployer.'

A couple of the dogs paw at the ground before backing up a couple of paces. For a moment, I think it might work. Then the massive beast who tried to intimidate us snaps out of the funk Aicha's threats plunged him into. He snarls and snaps, twisting his head wildly to take in all the other Coin sidhe. They stop backing up and rally, the pack call stirring them, bringing their unfettered rage to the fore. The intelligence I saw there flees. Their feral nature is in full control. They are the Wilds.

The leader turns back to us, the last of his rationality slipping away, drowned out by the slathering primal madness. 'Eat…you..alive…prey.' The words get gargled out, buckets of white drool thrown clear of the ravening jaws.

'It was a good try,' I murmur out the side of my mouth to Aicha. 'What's the plan now?'

'Now?' There's no change to her inflection. She remains as cool and as calm as ever. 'Now we kill them all.'

'Oh. Right.' Simple as that.

I look at the pack of ginormous slathering fae creatures that can put the shits up a pack of sabre-tooth tigers as they advance towards us step by step.

Now we kill them all. Sounds nice and easy. No problem whatsoever.

Chapter Six

Escaping goblins to be caught by wolves! Although there's no way the Nain Rouge is escaping. And the comparison is unfair to goblins.

The pack lets out a wild unified howl for the second time this night, but this time the sound is more terrifying, more terrible than any sound I've ever heard. It swirls through my blood, chilling it, slowing it down, so that my heart beats harder than it ever has, trying to force it round the body. It feels like it has turned to water, to ice, and like every grave of every body I've ever borrowed is being danced on simultaneously, such are the shivers running up and down my back. My knees want to buckle, and my hands want to clap to my ears to dim the horrifying noise even a fraction. Anything to make it more bearable.

I don't though. Somehow, I've no idea how, I hold my ground and my sword, staying upright. A small grunt of effort sounds behind me, then a tiny *thud*.

'Are you okay, *laguna*?' I hold my voice almost steady, only the slightest quaver betraying the fear I feel.

'Fine.' The reply is only slightly strained. 'Ugly Smurf just nearly pulled my trousers down when he fainted in fear. I had to kick him in the face to make him let go.'

I swear internally. I doubt she held back when kicking him given the circumstances, and we still need him. 'Is he breathing?'

'Reckon so.' I compose myself again, and with the following relief, I feel a little of the terror thawing from my being. 'Not about to give him fucking mouth to mouth though. That's on you, dickhead.'

Well, that's a nightmare-inducing problem for later on. First, we have to survive the attack of the Terror Dogs.

'How many can you deal with?' I desperately hope the answer is all of them.

'Not all of them.' *Damn it.* 'Not all at the same time.'

They continue their slow stalk towards us. 'How many on your side?'

'Three. I count four plus the leader on your side, right?'

Of course she can count them without looking round. Show-off. 'Yep. So eight in total.'

'Can you keep two of them busy for now?'

I look up. The lead Cu sidhe's eyes are fixed on me, and he advances with menace and intense, devouring hunger. The two on each side are following the head dog's lead.

'I think I might not have a choice. Looks like they are all heading my way.'

The leader throws back his head and issues a howl that travels through my ears and down the paths of my DNA, right back to the primordial human hearing the terrors of the night, the promise of the hunt in that terrible baying.

I try to steady the betraying tremble of my limbs. I don't

want to die again. I can't. I can't go back to the dark, back to the cave, back to the unending hunger and thirst, to never see nor speak nor hear, just to suffer and die again.

In an instant, I'm back on the bridge at Graumont, watching Aicha burn endlessly; helpless, useless, broken. Then I'm back among those magically protected bodies, desperate to die, desperate to live, wanting anything but to come back again and again and again in that terrible neverending cave.

Then I'm back in the now, staring down the gaze of this Cu sidhe as he lunges towards me, and I know I'm going to die. He's going to eat me piece by piece, finger by finger, limb by limb, crunching up bone and flesh and everything that makes me me, and I'll be back there again in the dark, alone and lost forever. I'll never escape.

For a moment, I wonder if I ever really did. If this has just been a momentary lull — where my mind broke, and the madness constructed a safer reality away from the endless pain, the sightless misery. Maybe the giant dog's teeth are the Black Dog ready to pounce back onto my back and never let go, to ride me into the grave again and again and again. Tears stream down my cheeks. I'm lost, doomed. Already dead.

'Move.' A command. Simple. One word from Aicha. But it carries.

I *move*. Somehow I do, ducking under the first snapping jaws. A paw, a package of muscles and razors comes hammering down but I catch it on the edge of my blade. The shock is a cracked-bell-chime that reverberates through my leaden bones. Half my fingers go numb off that very first contact. But I've survived one. I'm not dead yet.

Try telling that to my muscles though. Three steps, a dodging half-dive and a single parry and they're burning, packed with lactic acid. I'm ignoring that though. Keeping moving. Teeth gleam in my peripheral and I'm whipping my blade up; more swinging paws on limbs the size of carthorse legs come at me and I'm dropping under them. Sweat's pouring off me and my heart is going ten to the dozen and I have no idea if it's from the exertion or the utter terror of every single second.

I'm holding my sword hand with my other now, trying to check the trembling. Another face full of knife-teeth lunges into view and I force my arms up to jab the point of my sword at it. The Cu sidhe breaks stride easily, slides to the side, tongue lolling, chuffing as it goes. The bastard. The pack of bastards. They're toying with me. Harrying me into exhausted panic. The worst thing is it's working.

I catch sight of two of them, lolloping back, heads swung round to watch me. The dogs' mouths are drawn back in razored smiles. They're enjoying my panic. No doubt they can smell my terror. The Good God knows I am terrified. I don't have long to think on that though. A paw the size of a baseball glove bats my shoulder and sends me spinning, careening towards the earth. I get a hand down, somehow maintaining my grip on the sword with the other, scrabble to keep myself from collapsing in a heap, and manage to regain my feet. My lungs are on fire, and my head is drowning in the sense that death is coming, death is all around me everywhere, that I'm mere seconds from being eaten. And the leader, who struck me, throws back his head and howls his glee at my reduction to nothing but embodied fear. The pack sings with him, and their song freezes any courage I might have. I wave my sword around at them, spinning, trying to act as though I've any belief that I might survive this, any thoughts in my head but to survive, and how impossible that is.

A burning razor line explodes across the side of my thigh. I roll away from it instinctively, following the movement of the outstretched paw that's batted across the side of my leg. I'm still standing, so the creature hasn't done too much damage to the limb. Pivoting is possible, but the soaking wet sensation tells me I'm still bleeding aplenty.

Another Cu sidhe half-lopes, half-gallops in my direction. He rears up as though to pounce on me, and I can hardly even get my sword up. I'm crying now. The dread running down my face in liquid form. There's a good chance I'm whimpering too. I can feel my throat clucking, constricting. I can't breathe. And the beast barks at me and rolls away. Apparently I'm down. I didn't even realise it. The very weight of his presence drove me to my knees and I hadn't even noticed, too lost in the horror of the giant hound. Somehow I force myself back up, despite the futility of it, ignoring the voice telling me just to lie down, accept my fate, stop this horrible fucking torturous prolonged death. They're only playing with me, enjoying my suffering. Surviving this isn't even an option.

I miss the arrival of the leader again. For a creature so huge, he's silent as he stalks, unnoticeable right up until I can smell his breath over my shoulder, until I can feel the heat of it on my neck. Legend says the Coin breathe fire. I can see why. It feels like someone's just taken a blowtorch to my shoulder blade, and he's not even touched me. Yet.

I'm trying to turn, to get my sword back up to block a mouthful of blades, and I know I'm not going to make it. The chuffing of the hound, a sound full of glee and victory, tells me he knows it too. But the following noise isn't the one I expected. Isn't that Velcro-like tearing noise of flesh leaving bone. No. It's a confused whine, and I complete my turn in time to see the creature flying backwards. Aicha has struck him a pommel strike, slamming the butt of her sword into him like a hammer. She looks like she's just taken a shower with Carrie, blood coated from head to foot. A nightmare for our enemies.

'Head in the game, dickhead.' She's not even breathing hard. I don't doubt she's had chunks of flesh, possibly whole limbs, torn from her by the dogs, but her healing is nearly instant. Looking past her, I can see two downed Coin sidhe. I assume they're dead. Unless they can survive having their heads removed from their bodies. They've paid for taking their last meal from Aicha's one.

'Stop playing defensive. You're better than this. You know it. Constant guard is just asking to be worn down.'

'Hey, I'm not *playing* defensive. I'm struggling not to die —'

'Stop struggling. Start thinking. Look for the space to strike. Then take it. Strike. Strike for Redwall, I Am That Is A Dickhead.'

The leader shakes his head, throwing off the concussion of her blow. His eyes are on me, and they burn like hungry fire where I'm fresh wood.

'Okay, right, yeah. But how about, you take this one, and I take that smaller, already wounded one —'

But she's gone, leaving me to fend on my own.

Good God damn it, it's easy to say but so hard to do. Fear tastes like iron in my mouth. The bitter taste of failure and loss. The desperate cowardly terror that the moon might turn its back on me. That I might die in the dark and wake in it again. That I might go back under the mountain and never leave.

But I cannot give up. Because even after those wrong decisions, even when others have paid, they still believe in me. Even when I turned *my* back on my best friend, she came through to save me. They've kept me safe when I've needed it, even when I didn't realise I did. Just like now. She believes in me.

That or she thinks it's going to be fucking hilarious to watch me get my ass chewed out. Again. Both seem possible.

Another whine that grates across my teeth nerves like a dentist drill issues from behind me. Another Cu sidhe just bit the dust.

And for a moment, just a single instant, the lead hound's gaze...wavers. His eyes flick from mine to whatever brutal form of bloodshed is happening behind me. And in that single second, I see it...

He's afraid too.

Maybe that's the truth. Maybe we're all afraid. The only real form of bravery instead of ignorant stupidity and all that. Our only choice if we want to keep going is to see it, embrace it, and keep walking forward.

So I do just that. Slowly, my legs trembling, lactic acid burning in every inch of muscle, I take a single wavering step forward. Towards the leader.

My sword hangs, pointed at the ground. My arms are so tired, it seems almost impossible to lift it. Again, that slight widening of eyes in the Cu sidhe's expression. He didn't expect this. I'm the prey. The weak member of the pack. The one to be teased and tormented and then torn to pieces for shits and giggles.

Dead prey walking aren't supposed to advance on you with your own death in their eyes.

Of course, it's not enough for him to give up and bolt. I'm still enfeebled, shaking with the effort of every step. Aicha is who he's really afraid of. Aicha who's mopping up the rest of his pack behind me. Who's kept me alive long enough to get my act together, flip my fear the bird, and fake it till I make it.

The huge fae hound narrows his eyes, and a growl reverberates out of him, an echoing rumble like the demon's scream from *Evil Dead*, a promise of slow and painful death until he feasts. It fills my blood with ice again, and I seize up.

He bounds forward, eating up the ground, almost a gallop as his huge claws throw up dirt clods as he passes, pounces...

And there is a sweet sound — a clang as my sword flicks up of its own accord almost. My muscles — these muscles I'm wearing might not carry the memory of how to defend me, but my mind believes they do. And that — the mental conviction, that certitude in how things should be, that determination not to allow them to be anything else...

That's the true iron. The real steel.

And fae creatures never could handle iron.

The Cu sidhe bounces off, rolls back in a moment, and lurches forward, clawing at me. Again the sword pops to guard without thinking, seemingly independent of my conscious brain. I'm weary, wounded, trembling, and bleeding, and he thought he had me beat. Instead, I'm fending off on instinct, keeping him at bay. And now the momentum is changing, turning in my direction. He can feel it, and confusion is clear in his eyes. The gigantic dog rears back in an ungainly manner as I once more advance. He swings at me with the other paw. My sword whips up and parries once more. Oh. Oh! A thought arrives at my brain, too delicious to resist. This is perfect.

I look up and let a wry smile unfold across my face. 'Hello. My name is Inigo Montoya. You killed my father. Prepare to die.'

Now it's the Cu sidhe's turn to look afraid. I don't believe for a minute it's seen the *Princess Bride*, but it knows this isn't how this whole encounter is supposed to go. He takes a small step back, and I match it with a step forward, my smile widening.

'Hello! My name is Inigo Montoya. You killed my father. Prepare to die!'

The hound is terrified now. 'I don't understand,' he whines, rubbing at his snout. 'You said your name was Paul Bonnard or something.'

Ooh, yeah, I can switch it up. I advance, swishing my blade up and down diagonally. 'Hello! My name is *Paul Bonhomme*! You killed my father! Prepare to die!'

'I've never met your father! I've never met you before!' The enormous mutt is utterly baffled, and instinctive terror kicks in, his feet skittering out from under him as he backs away, considering turning, fleeing. I dance the blade tip, making sure his eyes are fixed on it, so he knows if he turns, I'll gut him. That option gone, he growls, his teeth bared, slathering foam from his lips, trying to make himself big, his hairs bristling. The message is clear. *Turn, little prey. Turn and flee.*

For a moment, I want to. I'm not exactly in prime form. Between weeks of nutrient-lacking leaf meals and climbing up a fucking tall mountain, I am knackered.

But Aicha is at my back. So I step forward.

And he cracks, scrambling back as he whimpers. He's done, and he knows it even if he doesn't understand how or why. His attempt to mask his fear isn't going to work. I've already embraced mine. This is my time to shine. I grin at him wickedly, and he whickers his terror and confusion at the savagery therein.

'Offer me a chew toy.'

'Yes, yes!' I almost feel sorry for the Cu sidhe, except a second ago he was ready to crack me open like a juice box and slurp down my insides.

'Biscuits, treats too. Promise me that.'

'What are you talking about? I don't understand,' the hound whines, whimpering and scrabbling backwards.

I roll my eyes. 'The correct answer is, "All that you want and more". Come on, pull your weight. Now — offer me anything I ask for.'

'Anything!' His beastly eyes pivot around, desperately searching for an out. Instead, he gets my cold hard steel plunging straight down his fiery throat and sliding through the end of his oesophagus to pierce his heart. He rolls his eyes downwards to stare at the length of metal sticking out of his mouth, uncomprehending. I pull it back out. The Cu sidhe gives a small wheezing whine, like a pricked cushion full of air as it deflates. Then his legs give way under him, and he sinks to the floor.

'I want my father back, you *son of a bitch*.' I hold my sword pose for a moment, then let my body relax, the blade point dipping groundwards. 'And — scene.'

I sweep a bow, my exhaustion hitting hard, and I am more than a little surprised to hear clapping. And not sarcastic clapping at that.

I turn, surveying the battlefield. Gigantic doggie limbs lie scattered, piecemeal across the turf. Great gouts of the earth got torn up during the fighting. Black blood and almost-black tufts of fur are evident all around. In the centre stands Aicha, grime-marked and grim but with a strange look in her eye as she applauds. And not a slow hand-clap either. Genuine applause. It takes me a moment to realise it's pride in her eyes. Next to her, the Nain Rouge is bouncing up and down on his toes, applauding rapturously.

'That was brilliant — brilliant!' I forgot the Nain is a cultured movie buff. Of course he appreciated the cultural reference.

'Best. Kill. Ever.' I am gobsmacked. Aicha isn't being sardonic. It's entirely genuine.

'Um, thanks?' I have no idea how to deal with this new-and-nicer version of Aicha.

'You're still a total dickhead, of course.' Ah, that's more normal. Still, I got a Nod Of The Head, which speaks volumes. I did A Good Thing. Go me!

The truth is it isn't only a good thing. It's a necessary thing. I've been so terrified, so utterly wrecked by fear since I got out of that cave that I haven't been living. Hell, I never even really got out. My mind is so full of darkness, I might as well still be down there.

A lump forms in my throat as I sit down, exhaustion buckling my knees. The adrenaline of the fight finally wears away, and I am left to face my fears. With my head in my hands and my sword back in storage, I force myself to remember all the times I was afraid over the centuries. The times I died screaming on the rack or the pyre or the gallows. The times I had to watch friends die or see them lessen little by little, turning from masterpiece watercolour paintings into nothing but stick people, simplistic caricatures of who they once were.

I think about going to Lourdes, where I was sure I was on my way to my doom. Of watching Aicha burn, unable to do anything. Of seeing Isaac strapped on the gurney under Ben's ministrations. Of finding Susane dead, our child torn from her on our wedding night. Of meeting her for the first time and trying to find the courage to tell her how I feel.

I think about waking immobilised in the hall of Lavaur, a simple Cathar priest caught up in witchcraft and evil beyond my imagination. Of taking up the Cathar black robes for the first time, when I knew the Church, the state, and society as a whole would never forgive me for such actions. I think of how terrified I felt the first time I stepped outside of the boundaries of my tiny village, where my father and my grandfather and his grandfather had grown up and raised their families and stayed, never questioning their lot. Every step I've ever taken, from that very first hesitant one to seek knowledge and a better, more meaningful life, has been dogged by fear. It nipped at my heels every time I put my foot down on a fresh path. It snarled and snapped at my ankles every time I had to make a decision.

I've walked with fear as a constant companion for over eight hundred years, but I learned to live with it. To domesticate it so that, while it might walk with me each and every day, it isn't constantly tearing at me, hamstringing me, leaving me crippled. At some point, I became so used to my old fears, I forgot I was even afraid.

My time in the cave, this fight — both have been reminders. Now I have fresh, new fears. I just need to break them in, get used to their companionship, and eventually they'll guard and guide me rather than bite my hand off.

I turn to the Nain Rouge. He has black blood spatters on him, but I don't see any weapons in his hands. I cock my head at Aicha. 'Did he actually get up in the mix during the fight?' I ask, shocked.

She shakes hers. 'Nope. Just followed so close behind me, it's a wonder I didn't trip over him. He got sprayed when I tore that one Cu sidhe's throat out, although he danced in it like he thought he was fucking Gene Kelly.'

I picture the Nain, an umbrella under his arm, swinging

around a lamppost while blood sprays all around him. Yep. He'd totally do that. I put the mental image to the side.

'Right.' I look him up and down. 'Now then.'

He's still leaping from foot to foot, capering on the spot in excitement. 'Yes, yes! That was so much fun! What madness do you have planned next, Good Man?'

'So, the favour you owe me. We want to sneak into the Winter Court, find a certain asshole, and then leave through Maeve's portal.'

The Nain Rouge's excited bounding comes to a grinding halt. He stares first at Aicha, then at me as though trying to wrap his head around what I just said. Eventually, he comes to a conclusion.

'You are — you are insane! You're both doomed. You might as well have crawled into the Coin sidhe's throats and had done with it.'

Good. That sounds like a vote of confidence.

Chapter Seven

The two police officers in charge of the entrance don't exactly look captivated by the mystery being investigated behind them. The impression they give is bored and frustrated. Probably because they don't have anything to do with the actual investigation and are spending their whole time driving away insistent, sneaky news reporters and the weirdos who hang out at the edge of society, having come, drawn like moths to a flame, because of their fascistic political tastes or because of their unhealthy interest in stolen coffins and violated graveyards. Neither of those types make scintillating conversational partners for the poor overloaded officers, I suspect.

They're standard policemen. The one on the left looks surprisingly up-to-date, his sideburns long but trimmed and styled, running down the sides of his face to join his moustache at the edges of his chin. His partner is shorter, slender, and newer too, judging by the panic tingeing his increasingly shrill cries of instruction. He clearly considers D'Artagnan the pinnacle of facial hair revolution, having waxed and twisted his pencil thin curler of a moustache to within an inch of its life.

They hold their hands up to block our passage almost without looking. My answer is to pull a blank business-card-sized piece of paper out of my pocket that I keep for just such occasions and present it to them, pushing a small tendril of *talent* into the card and out through it, into them, linking them together.

'Detectives Steed and Peel,' I say as I hand it over. I keep a straight face, but it takes some effort.

The younger one raises a quizzical eyebrow, but the older one doesn't even bat an eyelid. Perhaps he doesn't have access to a telly or else doesn't approve of them. There's a whole swathe of the population who remain convinced it's going to give them cancer, or it's all part of some secret Russian brainwashing program. Not that it surprises me. I remember the panic when the gas lamps got replaced by electric streetlights. People thought it would make their horses keel over and die and their brains explode. Humanity's imagination has always been its greatest weapon. Sadly, we have a tendency to use said weapon to chop our own feet off sometimes.

Either way, the card shows them exactly what they expect to see. So with some careful positioning to ensure that only we get through and not the shifty-looking individual behind us with the thousand-yard stare radiating from behind lank, greasy strands of hair fallen in front of his face, who screams "future person of interest", they move aside and let us pass. As we walk on, the FPI whines that they should let him through, that it's his right to see as an uber-menschen.

'Isn't it funny how the supposed "superhumans" are

often the most pitiable specimens?' I ask Aicha as we pick our way along the paths between the graves.

She regards me flatly. 'Hilarious.'

Right. I wasn't thinking about what the last group who harboured that belief did to her. Just because their ideals are laughable doesn't mean you shouldn't take them seriously. Even a joke can be deadly if passed around enough, making its victim invisible or subhuman under "humour". Just a *thing* to be mocked rather than a *person* to be defended.

We arrive at the secondary cordon, a smaller affair marking off the approach to the tomb itself. It's lit up like daytime by halogen floodlights. The stone lid lies to the side, lifted cleanly away. Two plainclothes policemen stand to the side, cigarettes hanging from their lips. I flash my piece of paper again and make our introductions.

Both of them wear similar brown polyester suits, ensuring that they look like they're in uniform even though they aren't. It takes genuine effort and dedication to the police life to be so obviously cops. Kudos to them.

The younger of the two has an abrasive brashness to him. He has the build of someone who plays rugby in his spare time and probably enjoys demonstrating the skills he learns on the field to criminals off it. By the way he eyes Aicha and me up and down, sneering disdain on his face, he prefers it even more if they share our skin tones. The older one looks tired, with that general weariness that comes from seeing the worst life can offer presented up on a platter for you time and again. He doesn't seem fazed by how we look but nor does he seem to object especially strongly to his colleague's attitude. I suspect he's probably about twenty years and a divorce beyond caring strongly about anything at all.

The older fella introduces himself as Gaston and the

younger as Paul, which pisses me off even further. It's enough to elicit a snort of amusement out of Aicha though, at least. That alone —her attention moving off what an absolute wanknoggin he is and onto my discomfort at us sharing a name— might well save his life. The last person I saw look at Aicha like that needed a guide dog and a white stick to get to the toilet afterwards. Luckily for him, his colostomy bag meant he didn't have to make the trip as often anymore.

'So did you find it like this?' I wave my hand at the stone that's crushing the grass to the side flat as a pancake.

Gaston takes the role of spokesman, which is a good idea. It reduces the chance of Aicha shoving Twat-Paul's tongue up where the sun don't shine. I'm not talking about Finland in the winter either.

'No, it was a clean job. Well done. They opened it and then resealed it.' He leans forward, dropping his voice to a conspiratorial murmur. Personally, I doubt any of the lingering paparazzi can hear what he has to say. Although they *are* a determined bunch, and the two police at the front were close to being overwhelmed. 'They're searching for a mortician. Reckon they must have had an expert with 'em to do such a neat job of getting it off and back on again. Looked perfect when we arrived.'

'How did you know it happened then?' Aicha's happy to let me speak. Twat-Paul tried to do what he considered a surreptitious examination of her physique, which everyone else in the world would think of as staring openly at her tits. Now he's trapped in her death stare, having just looked up, and some of the realisation of just how dangerous the woman he's ogling is filters through into his teeny, tiny brain. At least, that's how I interpret his nervous trembling and the lovely ashen-grey colour his skin turns.

'Was the caretaker. Eagle-eyed bastard. Apparently, they did too good a job. He turns up this morning; the place is too blasted clean. He has a look, realises the joints look new, so runs a finger over 'em, only to find they're still wet. Should work for us rather than cleaning up round here.'

I'm impressed and have to agree. He's certainly much more observant than most law enforcement officials I've met over the years.

I ply Gaston for any information on further leads, but they're pretty much entirely out of the loop. All they know is the investigation's centring around Paris and Verdun, where the cemeteries the Petain apologists want him buried are. They've been left here to deal with any government officials who visit the site and otherwise keep it safe from visitors, protestors, and vandals. Hardly top-tier work, but then, honestly, they're hardly top-tier cops. Gaston is obviously content to have plateaued, and Paul is clearly a twat.

Once I'm confident they've nothing more to tell us, I pull rank, effectively telling them to shove off. Twat-Paul whines a bit about his previously given instructions, but I already spotted the telltale shape of a hip flask in Gaston's pocket. No doubt he's happy to nip off somewhere he can grab a sly swig without fear of the news reporters' zoom lenses. Gaston hustles Twat-Paul away before Aicha performs a twaterectomy on him, slicing him open to cut out the twat squirrelled away deep inside. The survival chances from such a delicate and painful operation aren't high.

Now we have the tomb to ourselves, all nice and cosy-like. As they set the ambient lighting to "bright enough to see your internal organs", it isn't spooky in the slightest. Aicha leans towards me.

'They're coming to get you, Barbara,' she says, her voice

strange and plummy. 'They're coming. Look! There goes one of them now!'

I know it's a quote. I know it. She knows I know it. We watched *Night Of The Living Dead* at the cinema together after she dragged me down on her umpteenth viewing. And yet, I still spin around, looking for zombies, to my chagrin and her intense pleasure.

'If we see any zombies,' I grump, 'you're dealing with them. I like this suit.'

The amusement disappears from her expression, and she turns back towards the empty tomb.

'Right, dickhead,' she says, her tone deader than most of the residents in the eternal accommodation surrounding us. 'So now we're here, where's the coffin?'

I shrug. 'Not here?'

That earns me a slow clap. 'Genius, Poirot. Know that. Where is it?'

'Oh!' Realisation dawns on me. Apparently, my role here is to use my *talent* to find out where the thieves are storing the box.

I'm not suicidal enough to tell Aicha this, but I have no idea how I'm going to pull that off.

Chapter Eight

Aicha isn't actively giving me a countdown to perform this miracle magic she's demanded I pull out of thin air, but her pacing isn't far off the same thing.

We all have our strengths when it comes to magic. Aicha is brilliant with elemental magic. If you want something setting on fire, she's your pyromaniac in a storm. What we're looking at right now is right up Isaac's, my mentor's, street — taking an unusual problem, then searching through ancient scrolls to find something that'll resolve the issue or else devising some whole new theoretical branch of magic to tackle it head on. Pity Isaac isn't here right now. We didn't expect to need him, and Aicha was in no mood to take a detour via his house by the forest of Bouconne. He's safely tucked away, probably with a glass of whisky and a good book. The lucky bugger.

I'm more of a middleman. Jack of all trades, master of none, although I'm souped-up enough *talent-wise* that, in general head-to-head scenarios, I can outgun most "masters" in their area of expertise by sheer brute force. Go, Jack. Theoretical magic isn't really my forte, though, despite Isaac's efforts over the centuries. I studied under various masters, absorbed a fuckton of different techniques, of ways of thinking about power and its application, only to jumble it all together into my own approach, which, as a rule, involves brute force and ignorance. It's the metaphysical difference between picking the locks and kicking the door in. But this problem requires more of the former than the latter.

A part of me feels tempted to give Isaac a call and ask his advice, but honestly? It gets my goat. I love the man like a father, but I want to stand on my own two feet. Don't get me wrong, I can swallow my pride, and when I need his help, I ask for it. Problem is, I end up asking too often for my liking, and it rankles. Just because I can swallow my pride doesn't mean it doesn't stick in my throat on the way down.

I stride back across to reexamine the tomb. I'm basically attempting divination magic, which isn't a strong suit of mine to start with. Sadly, none of the scumbag grave robbers were considerate enough to drop a necklace or a wedding ring or one of their fingers in the empty grave. Rude, really.

Aicha's huffs behind me intensify. Never did a huff promise so much violence so efficiently. There's no other option than to go back to scrabbling about inside the tomb, ignoring that rank mustiness that's lingering there even though the sealed air that the flesh rotted in dissipated long ago. Telling myself I'm just imagining the smell of decomposing bodies doesn't seem to make my olfactory senses pack it in.

There has to be something in here they left. A nail clipping, a cigarette butt. A business card with their name and address on it would be nice, but I doubt even the police would miss a clue that big. My teeth grind together, my frustration close to boiling over. There's nothing. I've dug through the dirt repeatedly, and there's nothing…

I stop. Nothing but dirt. A thought thrills through me, inspired by one of my favourite recent books. I consider that thought again, realising it was written seventy-five years ago. Not really that recent by most people's way of thinking.

Aicha draws closer as I climb out of the tomb, looking for a flat surface. 'Throw up a *don't look here*, will you, over the entire area?' I ask. It's a tall order —this is the place everyone wants to look at, after all— but there are plenty of distractions in the vicinity between the press, the police, and the peculiars. Hopefully, it'll be enough. Anyhow, she can handle that. I'm handling the rest.

I spot the tombstone and hurry over, pulling out our road map and flattening it onto the clean white surface. Aicha follows, weaving the illusory spell as she walks. 'What's the plan?' she asks once she pulls it into place, hiding us from attention.

'Remember *Dracula*?' I ask, and she nods. 'So, transportation of his coffin from Transylvania. What else did he send over?'

Her eyes light up. 'Boxes of earth.'

'Right.' I give a hip finger snap of appreciation that I picked up as a pretentious mannerism from some beat poets a few years back, mainly to annoy Aicha. 'He needed them. I can't remember if it was an "as well as" for his coffin or an "either/or" but that got me thinking.'

I hurry back over to the tomb and carefully scoop up some of the dirt inside in both hands. 'No coffin is impermeable. Hell, that's why they bury them or put them inside massive stone things like this. Some of what's in the coffin…'

'Will have leaked out,' she finishes, a thrum of excitement in her words.

'Precisely. Some small particles of Petain's body must have mingled with this earth over the years, even if it was just some of his essence leeching over or whatever. If I'm right, we can set this up in synchrony to the coffin, wherever it is.' I feel righteously proud of myself. I doubt even Isaac could have done a better job. He'd probably have done it *quicker* but not better.

Aicha gives me a terse nod, which is her equivalent of a round of applause, then just says, 'Get it done.' It gives me a warm, fuzzy feeling, all this positive praise.

I close my eyes and reach out with my *talent* to the earth itself. This first part is something Aicha would be better at than me, but the second is definitely more my skillset, so I need to do it from the start. I coax the soil, prodding it with my power, investing it with a small corner of my consciousness. By letting it taste conscious thought, at least for a moment, it becomes aware, even if it's only a borrowed awareness. Once this part of me melded with the earth understands itself, I imbue it with a sense of distance, of disconnect, of forced absence, and with the notion of finding, of closing that gap.

Opening my eyes, I hold out my hand over the map. Then I open it and let a few clumped grains fall down faster than gravity should make happen, weighted by the *talent* I'm investing into them. They land on the map, swirling and turning. They skitter across the surface as though carried on a stirred spring breeze, rising as the morning sun does, though it's night and there's no wind here now. They move together, almost dancing, searching out across the map. Of course, they don't understand that's what it is, but I do, and the consciousness it holds is mine. They move further in and up before coming to a stop, swirling over the top north of Paris itself, falling inert.

I carefully transfer all the remaining dirt into one hand, and with the other, I slide the map off the surface. Having cleared the deck, I reach into my etheric storage and pull out a map of Paris itself. Aicha takes it from me and unfolds it where the other one was, then I repeat the procedure with most of the remaining dirt. It concentrates on the north, dancing along the edge of Paris itself. For a moment I think it's going to cha-cha its way into Saint-Denis, but it turns slightly more north, out into the banlieue of Saint-Ouen. It circles closer and closer, tighter and tighter until it congregates on one street. The way it lingers is categorical; this is the location.

Aicha leans forward and brushes the crumbs off the map, peering at the street name. I pull a small vial out of my etheric storage, transfer the last of the magically charged earth into it, and pop it away. Just this has sapped my energy. This isn't my normal sort of magic, and we're a long way from my home turf, which acts like a battery pack. Luckily, I haven't thrown any workings around in the last few days, so I'm pretty charged up. Still, I'll be glad when we get back to Toulouse and the safety thereof.

By the time I'm done, Aicha has folded the map away with a satisfied expression on her face. It reminds me of the sort worn by a cat after a rat traps itself down a blind alley with no chance of escape. She knows where we're going. Time to trap some rats.

'Avenue Gabriel Peri, Saint-Ouen. Let's go.' Then she pauses. 'Did you see a phone box en route?'

I try to remember. 'At the port, I think?'

She nods, glad. 'I need to make a call as soon as we can. There's someone we'll want to have meet us there.'

Someone? Not that Aicha is especially chatty unless insulting me, but that is strangely tight-lipped even for her.

"Curiouser and curiouser," said Paul.

Chapter Nine

Now to survive another load of nainsense. Like nonsense,
only considerably more annoying.

The Nain Rouge has completely switched back to how he
was — agitated, nervous, clearly about to flee. Aicha seizes
him by his neck again before he can make a run for it.

'You owe us.' She points to the blood spatters all over his
crusty tie-dye T-shirt. 'Pay or spray.'

'I can't, I can't!' he whines, shifting on the spot like his
skin is suddenly too tight. 'Don't get me wrong, you're both
very scary — very, very scary!' I feel chuffed. I got an
upgrade. Last time, he was just terrified of Aicha. 'Still,
she's *Maeve*. She's a whole other level of scary. I can't go
against Maeve!'

His eyes widen. 'I can get you home though; I can! I can
get you home. We can go to my cavern, and I can take you
through a portal back to the Pyrenees. You can be safe back
in the human world.'

I'm not going to lie — the thought tempts me. It's not been a pleasant trip to the Fae Lands. They're definitely going to get a negative Trip Advisor review from me. All we have to do is say yes, and we can be done with this terrible place and its vicious inhabitants and never have to think about them ever again.

Except I know it doesn't work like that. I *will* think about them again. I'll think about Simon getting away without paying for his crimes. Chances are he's gone straight through the portal and back out to Earth. It's so tempting to take the easy way and head home, try and pick up his trail there. Problem is, if he's hiding in Winter, he can bring whatever fucked up plans he has to fruition in his own time, as easily and leisurely as he likes. Considering the meticulous centuries-long planning that went into conning Susane, getting a fae body, and trapping me, my brain keeps circling round and round as to what he might be up to, what his endgame is. Those thoughts will haunt me and break me far more than my fear ever could. My fear I can live with. Cowardice, I can't.

I shake my head. 'No deal. We'll take what's in box number two.'

The Nain looks confused. 'There are no boxes?'

Okay, apparently his cultural touchstones don't extend to *Deal or No Deal*. 'I mean we aren't interested in the offer. We're not going home without following Simon's trail. If we have to steal him from Maeve, then we will.'

'Have you lost your mind? Have you?' He hisses at me, indignant and disbelieving. 'The trail afterwards of one of those who stole from Maeve leading straight back to my home? No, no. That's guaranteed death. You can't include that in our deal.'

'So what can you do?' Aicha gives him a little shake to

help focus the mind. 'So far, you've been utterly fucking useless. Time to give us something.'

The creature thinks for a while, a process that seems to mainly involve belching, scratching itself in unmentionable places, and then sniffing said digit. It's a tribute to our collective willpower that we don't fling him off the side of the mountain in disgust.

I see the moment he comes up with a plan. His eyes narrow, and he starts to mutter and mumble to himself. Then he grins —an unpleasant reminder of his need for the number of an emergency dentist, stat— a shit-eating smile spreading across his face. 'I've got it, I've got it!'

We wait. Nothing happens. Silence reigns. 'Okay, this is the part where you tell us what it is you've got, you stupid little shit.' I can't believe I have to explain this to him.

He starts, giving a small leap. I think he went off in a reverie somewhere. Obviously, now he's come up with a solution, he feels much more relaxed. 'Ah, right, right, of course. I know how I can help you without making it too obvious.'

'Without getting yourself gutted by Maeve, you mean?' Aicha's wry tone shows she understands exactly why the creature spent so long thinking about it.

To be fair to him, the Nain Rouge doesn't deny it. He just nods eagerly. 'Exactly so, exactly so! The problem you have is that the moment you put a foot in Winter, Maeve will know. She'll know, right?'

I nod. That seems like a pretty accurate summary of the major problem. It isn't going to be easy to find Simon if we have the entire horde of Unseelies heading in our direction as soon as we cross the border.

'So what if I make it so you don't put your foot in?' I

don't know if I trust the creature's sly grin. Actually, I do know. I definitely don't trust it.

'What do you mean?' One thing is certain. I want to clarify all the details of what he's offering before we agree to anything.

The sneaky smile doesn't leave the Nain's face. 'I can create a tiny cushion of air under your feet. That way you don't touch the ground, and Winter won't feel your presence. As long as you don't touch anything, Maeve will never even realise you're there.'

I think about it. His plan seems viable. As long as we don't actually set foot in Winter's domain, we'll be safe. Obviously, it won't render us invisible from the denizens, so we can't just saunter in without a care in the world, but it gives us a fighting chance. I look over at Aicha to see if she has anything to add. She looks lost in thought, no doubt running over the offer, searching for problems with it. And of course she finds the absolutely enormous one that I missed completely.

'If our feet aren't touching the ground, Nain,' she starts slowly, as if tasting the question, rolling it around her mouth, 'then how are we supposed to walk?'

'Oh, you can't, you can't!' The little bastard doesn't look surprised by the question, though I don't doubt he hoped we wouldn't think of it. To be fair, though, he has the answer. He walks over to a silvered sapling that was uprooted during the fight, probably when a Cu sidhe got hurled into it at high speed. He picks it up and mimes pushing off the floor, first to the left, then the right. 'Like this, like this!'

I shake my head in disbelief. He's miming punting. 'You're going to turn our feet into gondolas?'

'Floating gondolas,' Aicha corrects me.

'Floating gondolas, right.'

The Nain Rouge nods eagerly. 'Yes, yes! If you take the poles from the Wilds, they won't draw the Queen's attention. You can get in without being noticed.'

'Well, that's a good thing,' I say wryly, 'as we'll look absolutely fucking ridiculous.'

'But it'll work, it will work!'

I look over at Aicha, who shrugs. We've no better ideas. I grin at her. 'Guess it's worth taking a punt on.'

She groans loudly. 'Enough. I don't need my ears to bleed.'

I turn my attention back to the Nain Rouge. 'Okay, there's just three more bits of information I need. Where she keeps her guests, where she keeps her prisoners, and where the entrance to her portal is.' Given I have no idea if Simon is sneaking through her territory unnoticed or is an honoured guest, I want to cover all my bases.

'Of course, of course! Guests, rare things that they are, stay in the main castle. She keeps her prisoners in a special area, a building where they are locked away until she can bend them to her will.'

Talk about bending prisoners to her will sends shivers down my spine. The Nain doesn't look bothered, but then he is an Unseelie, and he isn't human. His only skin in the game is the possibility of us flaying it from his bones if he doesn't help us. 'Yes, yes! They must be broken in. Of course, of course! The only prisoners she ever bothers to keep are the kidlings. No enemies last long enough to be imprisoned.'

'Kidlings?' My blood runs cold. In all the chaos, in all my own personal drama and trauma, I forgot.

Jack had already sent some kids through before I killed him.

Good God, I can't believe I forgot. I've been so wrapped up — first in the mystery of Susane and our "son", then my misery and trauma from the cave; the children he already sent across to Maeve completely escaped my mind.

Aicha's looking at me with that level of intensity that suggests I'm about to get a well-deserved slap. I suspect it's only the frailty of my current form that saves me from exactly that. 'Maeve has human children? I thought that ended hundreds of years ago?'

That's the thing. Prior to the story with Jack, we all did. The fae — or at least those from Faerie, as opposed to those who've stayed on Earth, have been pulling back from our world more and more over the centuries. The days of the Wild Hunt riding across the plains of Europe are long gone. And —as we established in Lyon, to Isaac's shock and dismay— enough kids disappear every day for very mundane reasons or very human monsters.

I nod. 'We stopped Jack. But he'd sent some through before then.'

'How many?' I'm not sure if she means how many kids, or how many slaps am I going to get. Probably both the same number.

'Five or six.'

She looks at me, fixing me with that intense gaze, watching me, studying my every movement. 'What's our priority now?'

I know what she means. If push comes to shove, if we have to choose a target, who will it be? De Montfort or the kids?

I wonder what she'd say if I chose De Montfort.

Wonder if she'd back my play. Or if that'd be the straw that didn't just break the metaphorical camel's back but picked it up and did a piledriver off the top ropes onto it afterwards as well.

Of course, that's not the answer I'm going to give. Normally, once children have been taken by the fae, that's it. They're gone. Because nobody sane would go to Faerie, would dream about storming the Court of Winter.

But we're already planning to do that. And there is no reality where I'd leave children in the ice-cold grasp of Queen Maeve to be "broken in". I'm willing to bet she doesn't win them over with sweets and cuddles. Doesn't even give them Turkish Delight, which is practically a punishment in and of itself. It says something when Narnia's Snow Queen is nicer than the real one.

'The kids. We find them, get them out. If De Montfort is there, great, but they're the priority now.'

Aicha gives me the tiniest nod, one that says *correct answer, dickhead* if I can read her at all. Then she turns her attention to the Nain Rouge.

'You said she keeps them in this building? Trains them?'

'Yes, yes! Makes sure they understand the rules, the ways, the expectations.'

'What happens to them after their training?' Aicha's jaw muscles mirror mine. Good. We both can do with a bit of righteous anger to get us through the shitstorm we're about to enter.

'After that? After that, they get given to her Court to play their games with.' The Nain grins his wicked little grin. Then he sees how I'm looking at him, and it falters. Then he looks upwards and sees how Aicha is looking at him, and it disappears altogether. 'Not me. Not me! I play my own games with mortals out in the other world. No need for me to go to the Court. Too much risk, too much. It's a dangerous place even for us fae.'

Brilliant. Even the Winter Court fae themselves fear the Winter Court. I notice he left out an important bit of the requested information. 'Okay. Where is the building they're kept in? And where is the portal?'

He nods, eager to get away from his faux pas. 'The building? Yes, the building. It's at the end of the Winter Garden, in the heart of the labyrinth.'

'Is it guarded?' Aicha asks.

The Nain shakes his head. 'No, no. The door is locked so they can't get out. And they'd have to pass the labyrinth even if they did. They're all too scared, all too scared once they've been taken through it to try and get back on their own.'

'What about the older ones? The kids of the Court?' I ask.

'They've been hers; they've been hers for at least thirty years. They're too broken, too broken to go anywhere or do anything, anything that she hasn't told them to. She sends those still left to train the new arrivals.'

I feel like one of the Coin sidhe, a growl bubbling up in my chest. I don't expect things that aren't human to act like humans. That doesn't mean I forgive them when they act like monsters.

'Anything you can tell us about the labyrinth?' Aicha keeps her emotions under control and her thoughts on the ball to make sure we get the information needed.

The Nain shakes his head. 'Never been, never. Don't get lost?'

Don't get lost in the maze. Brilliant advice. 'So where's the portal back to our own world then, Nain?' One last bit of information, and we might just have the bare bones of a plan. The chances of it working are slim, but they exist now, at least.

'Oh, of course, of course.' He nods furiously, like a puppy eager to please. 'It's in Maeve's throne room. In her throne room next to her throne.'

And just like that, we're doomed again.

Chapter Ten

There's nothing like a solid plan of action. And this is
nothing like a solid plan of action.

'So to summarise,' I start, counting the points off on my
fingers. 'We have to break into the grounds of the Winter
Palace, sneak through the labyrinth at the end of the
gardens...'

'Without getting lost,' Aicha adds.

'Without getting lost, thanks. Potentially grab Simon if
he's there or find clues if he's not, rescue all the kids,
including a load who've been there for thirty years or more,
getting tortured and brainwashed, then break *into the throne
room itself* and use the portal that's, apparently, located right
next to where the Queen of the Unseelie herself may well
be sitting. Am I right?'

'Yes, yes! That's it.' The Nain continues to do his
nodding dog impression.

I shake my head, suddenly very weary. 'It's impossible. It

can't be done even if we had a holocaust cloak.' I look over at Aicha, but she doesn't have the same look of despair on her face as I do. She's calculating something.

'Is there ever a time when the throne room stands empty?' A good question.

The Nain thinks through the question, stroking his shiny chin while pondering. 'When the queen sleeps. When the queen sleeps, the court clears, the creatures all returning to their nests or hidey-holes.'

'Is it guarded?'

'Oh yes, oh yes. A pair of her most loyal guards keep the doors to make sure none of her subjects might try and leave her some nasty surprise, eh? Eh?'

It doesn't sound like the happiest kingdom ever known, even discounting Disneyland. 'She sounds paranoid.'

The Nain gives me a look of such disbelief, I almost stop existing on the spot. 'She is the Queen of the Winter Court. *The Queen of the Winter Court*! I think you'd be paranoid too.'

Yeah. Fair point. 'Okay, recap. Beat the maze. Rescue the kids. Subdue the guards. Find where Simon went — probably out as fast as he can if he has a brain. Use the portal. Did I miss anything?'

Aicha raises a hand. 'All without touching anything and while air-skating.'

'Right. Okay. This has passed from "entirely impossible" to just "mostly impossible". What do you reckon, *laguna*?'

She shrugs, but I can see the fire in her belly. It burns so bright, it shines in her eyes. 'Those are my kind of odds.'

They are. They really are. Damn it, now I've started sounding like the Nain Rouge.

'Right.' I rub my hands together. 'Let's get this show on the road. Nain, what do we need to do?'

'Cyril. Cyril.'

I blink. 'What?'

'My name. It's Cyril. Nain Rouge is my species. It's very odd, very odd that you continually address me as such. I shall take to calling you Human Male and Human Female, I shall.'

Aicha looks him over coldly. 'We could rename you Worm Food.'

I wave my hands at them both, trying to shoo away all of this insane inanity. 'Enough! You' —I point at the Nain Rouge— 'haven't done enough to earn being referred to by your actual name. You tried to fuck us over, and you're only here because you failed miserably at even that. You did diddly squat during that last fight, and we had to pry the help out of you with a metaphorical crowbar...'

Aicha holds her hand up. 'I'm happy to use an actual crowbar. Really don't mind.'

'... a metaphorical crowbar *for now*.' The Nain Rouge, aka "call me Cyril", gulps. 'If this idea of yours works and actually helps us, and we get back out in one piece, then maybe you can work your way up to the status of being deserving of an actual name. Until then, we can call you Dickhead or Nain Rouge —'

'Or Worm Food.'

'Or Worm Food. Up to you. For now.'

I let everything lapse into a menacing silence to really underline the threat to Cyril the Nain Rouge, a name I feel ridiculous thinking, let alone saying. Then I remember I don't want silence at all as I was actually talking about something important before being so rudely interrupted.

'Right, dickhead, you made me completely lose my train of thought for a minute there. Okay, now then. What do we need to do to get your spell in action? Magic. How? Now.'

'How magic? How magic? As in, how does it work? I'm

not sure I can explain that.' I'd say he is being deliberately obtuse, but the Nain looks genuinely confused. I feel like explaining it to him in great detail very slowly. While banging his head repeatedly on a hard surface. Then I remember I already did that back when we first met and he tried to trap me in a torture-chamber escape room, and it lost its charm relatively quickly. Still, he's sufficiently annoying, I'm prepared to give it another go.

I grind my palms into my eyes. 'Right, no thanks. I don't need a theoretical lecture on the application of *talented* forces. What I need you to do is explain what we're missing in order for you to do the magic required for us to get into Winter and how long it'll take to put it in place.'

'Oh. Oh! Why didn't you say so?' Nope, there's definitely the start of a smirk on his face. I can feel my hand itching to play a slap-happy drum solo on his cheeks, but I resist the urge. For now. 'I already did that about ten minutes ago. I thought you'd have realised.'

I look down and notice I'm not actually standing on the ground. Instead, I'm hovering just above it by a couple of inches. I pick my foot up to look under it. The action causes me to overbalance completely. My other foot shoots forward from the momentum, and I tumble straight over onto my arse. Except, of course, that also doesn't touch the ground, sending me rocketing forward, towards the edge of the hill, picking up speed rapidly thanks to the lack of friction. I throw my hands out and grab desperately at a blasted tree stump, my velocity causing me to wrap around it like a cuddle-starved koala.

Aicha glides her way over to me. 'All right there, *saabi*? The judges scored you zero out of ten for execution, but you stuck the landing.'

Having already picked up a stout branch to use as a

punting pole, she keeps herself steady with it. Of course, having her normal amount of *talent* instead of my infinitesimally teeny amount, she'd have realised far more quickly than I did. Plus, of course, she's naturally far more graceful. Although that's not a difficult achievement half the time.

I look across to see the Nain Rouge doubled over and wheezing with laughter, slapping the floor with his hand at the hilarity of it all. Of course he is. His humour is stuck in the silent movies era, and I just did the equivalent of stepping on a banana skin.

'Do it again, do it again!' he gasps out between his cackling chortles.

I heave myself back up to standing, hand over hand up the stump, and accept the second tree branch Aicha somehow procured without my noticing. 'You're never going to earn the name of Cyril if you keep that up,' I growl at him.

'Come on, Paul. No one *deserves* to be called Cyril. It's just cruel and unusual parental punishment.' Aicha might have found my pratfall amusing —as she does any time I make a prat out of myself— but I know she's still ready to gut the red shitstain for it. That is the definition of a genuine friendship. Ready to laugh at you, doubly ready to kill for you.

I can't disagree. I steady myself on the rudimentary staff and practise moving backwards and forward. Then I drift myself over towards the Nain.

'How do we undo this when we want to?' Making it permanent or at least not giving us the cancellation command would be exactly the sort of shitty thing he would do. To be fair, it's standard practice for any fae but particularly our mate, Cyril.

He stops laughing, and his expression changes. Now he

looks moody, sulking, and I know that's exactly what he planned. 'Fine, fine. If you want to undo it, just say, "Cyril the amazing Nain Rouge," and it will be gone.'

I look over at Aicha. 'Well, it might flatter his ego, but at least we'll never say it by accident.' I turn my attention back to the Nain. 'Right, we're getting going. I'm sure you're rubbing your hands with glee, thinking you're done and free of us. Just understand — if you fuck with our plan, if you contact Maeve, if you remove the magic from us at some inopportune moment. Remember we've survived much worse, and we will come looking for you. And then? Then you can play some of Aicha's "little games" since you like playing so much.'

Cyril's face goes a shade of red so pale comparatively, it's almost Caucasian pink. 'No need, no need for that!' he garbles hastily. 'You've my word it will work as promised, and I'll not interfere in any way.'

I nod, satisfied. 'Good.' Nothing is cast-iron (no pun intended) in terms of the words of fae even if they can't lie, but that's as close to a promise as I'll extract from him. I feel pretty sure he'll simply run for home. I turn to Aicha. 'Ready, *laguna*?'

'Born ready, dickhead. Let's go kick some magnificent Maleficent fairy knob-mother ass.'

Looks like we're really doing this. We're going to take on Queen Maeve in her own home territory. That doesn't count as suicidal at all. We have a proper plan. What can possibly go wrong? Apart from everything. Everything can go wrong and, as this is my life we're talking about, abso-lutely one hundred percent will.

Chapter Eleven

Aicha makes her mysterious call once we get off the ferry at Fromentine. I last, to my immense pride, at least two minutes after we pull away from the port before I start badgering her for answers. Sadly, she just rolls onto her side in her seat and sleeps — or, at least, feigns sleep. I've got no idea if it's something she really wants to keep secret or if she's just trying to wind me up. Both seem equally possible. I have to remind myself her secrets are her own to keep. Even if they're dancing like clog-wearing mice up and down on whatever part of my brain deals with curiosity. It's the part that obviously ended up overdeveloped. Unfortunately, that left little space in my grey matter for things like caution or common sense. At least, according to Aicha.

The motorway from Nantes to Paris, inaugurated a few years previously, speeds things up considerably compared to our run up the coast from Toulouse. The new, still-unfinished motorway ring-roading Paris slows us down though. It's due to open in a month and is apparently a modern marvel, guaranteed to eradicate traffic problems in the Paris area. Until it does so though, it means a lot of weaving around on smaller backroads, avoiding the new lanes that all try to guide us to firmly closed slip roads onto the incomplete motorway.

Strained grainy eyes are ready to fill in a formal protest due to how long they've had to stay open by the time we pull onto Rue Ernest Renan, a smaller side road linking onto the Avenue Gabriel Peri. I pull my thermos out and take a swig of the coffee I prepared earlier. While we don't have a precise number, the dirt grains only covered a small stretch of the avenue just north of this road, so I know we're in the right area. Rubbing the sleep from my eyes, I stretch as we get out, the various muscle kinks eager to make themselves known. Aicha flows out of her side and stands, her intent awareness clear to me even in the low-grade light. She chose our parking location. Apparently, we're meeting someone. Presumably the same "someone" she was on the phone with. Whether they're friend or foe, I can't say. Though if they're foe, Aicha would have been less likely to give them a courtesy phone call. A courtesy throat punch is more her style, in that case.

A shadow detaches itself from the far end of the road, peeling off from the roll-down metal shutter it was leaning on. It heads our way, coalescing into the shape of a man. I take my cue from Aicha; she's not drawing any weapons nor on her *talent* as far as I can tell. I do my best to look nonchalant, cursing her for putting me in a situation where I've no idea what's going on and therefore no idea how to prepare for it.

She walks around the car and whispers in my ear, 'Rubbish, isn't it? Not having a chance to prepare?' Oh, right. There is a point Aicha's trying to make with all this. Of course there is. She never does anything other than deliberately.

She swats my arm to show no hard feelings, then walks towards the man slow and deliberate. Her right arm shoots forward lightning fast, and for a minute, I think I've misjudged it, that she's going to strike him down, that we're seconds from some sort of magical street brawl. But she doesn't aim to attack. His arm comes up at a similar speed, and they clasp hands, clapping each other's shoulders with the other. I follow up behind, unsure still about what precisely is going on.

Aicha turns and steps back towards me, drawing the man into a pool of light from an overhead streetlamp and letting me get a good look at him for the first time.

The man's Berber, just like her, as far as I can tell. With his blonde hair and blue eyes, he can pass as Gallic, but having spent copious amounts of time in North Africa, I bet he's from Algeria. He carries a confidence to him that's conveyed by his neatly tailored, precisely-cut suit, which is either black or a dark shade sufficiently close to it as to be indistinguishable at night. His face is warm but his eyes worn. I suspect friendship is his first response to most people and that he's paid for such a response more than once. The only jewellery I can see is worn around his right wrist, a metal clasp wide at the front and tapered at the rear, where it snaps together, covered in elegant patterns and symbols. He stands, his hands in his pockets, and looks at me curiously. I'm equally curious, so I *look* at him, then gasp.

'Djinn!' Fuck. That was rude. I avoid clapping a hand across my mouth but only because that would make me look stupid as well as ignorant. Still, I've never met one before, not in all my time travelling the north of Africa and across the Arabic world. Despite all the legends about them, the djinn keep themselves away from the populace as much as possible, particularly the Talented. There are many uses that an unscrupulous sorcerer can find for djinn. Or parts of them. I've seen a wizened, preserved djinn hand, capable of granting wishes, and it radiated the same burning, swirling, orange-red magic as the creature in front of me does.

He smiles slightly, an almost apologetic look on his face. 'Half-djinn, I'm afraid.'

Aicha rolls her eyes and steps between us. 'Paul, you're a twat. This is Al-Ruhban. He provisionally controls this banlieue. Al-Ruhban, this is Paul. He's a twat.'

The half-djinn spreads his hands out in front of him, a welcoming gesture. 'Welcome, Paul Bonhomme. I name you *saabi*, friend, and guest in this quarter. *Lalla* Aicha, *aimra'at hakima*, has spoken of your honour and integrity.'

I search through my slightly rusty classical Arabic. *Lalla* is an honorific for a woman of importance. *Aimra'at hakima*? It comes back to me. Wise woman. Whoever this Al-Ruhban is, he clearly thinks highly of Aicha.

Aicha tuts, pursing her lips. 'Don't get a big head, Paul. I mainly told him you're an impetuous dickhead.'

Al-Ruhban's smile deepens. 'An *honourable and integral* dickhead, *lalla*.'

She makes a *pfft* noise as though blowing a strand of hair out of her face. 'Maybe.'

Al-Ruhban's face grows serious again. '*Lalla* has told me of your current mission. It is…fortuitous that the coffin has arrived in my area. There has been much upheaval in Paris in recent times. It has provided opportunities for a newcomer, such as myself, but there are areas where a Talented pair arriving at such an inauspicious moment might end up viewed with grave suspicion.'

I prick up my ears at this. Paris is divided into a series of arrondissements (twenty in total) inside the boundaries now being made crystal clear by the new ring-road and into quarters and districts outside. For the Talented, these function as principalities, paying tribute to the prince at the centre. Leandre has held Paris for over two centuries now. I've heard nothing of any unrest or disturbance during that time. He runs a tight ship, and little information gets out that he doesn't allow. In other words? This sounds like juicy gossip, and I want to get all the tasty rumours on offer, like a smorgasbord of hearsay.

Sadly, Aicha has other priorities. 'The coffin's here. On the Avenue Gabriel Peri. Not sure of the exact number yet.'

I'm all ready to pull the magically charged vial of earth out of my etheric storage and brandish it like a stage magician pulling a bunch of flowers out of his sleeve. The plan is to use the last remaining crumbs to lead us to the required door. That turns out to be unnecessary though.

Al-Ruhban grins, the gleam of his teeth showing a slightly inhuman curve. Not enough to give him away but enough to unsettle the average person perhaps. To ring some alarm deeply buried in the collective subconscious about predators just outside the campfire light. 'I believe I have found your perpetrators.' The grin fades. 'Not the coffin though.'

Now I'm confused. I searched specifically for the coffin. Aicha gives me a look that speaks volumes. Entire encyclopaedias, in fact, all packed full of reasons why I'm entirely useless.

Al-Ruhban speaks again. 'I've kept them under observation. I think the coffin was here. It's just not now. To be fair, I think it was as much of a surprise for them as it is for you.'

The plot thickens. He beckons us to follow him and

leads us around the corner. The avenue we come out onto is large, clearly a principal thoroughfare down to the city itself from the north. I've not spent much time in Paris outside of the obfuscation of an opium-haze. When sober, I knew Leandre would see me as a threat, so I kept my distance. When high, he either didn't notice me or didn't care, seeing the wreck I was.

The street is surprisingly quiet, nothing but a few early workers — bakers, cleaners and the like heading wearily towards the daily grindstone. We don't go far before I see a half-circle of light spilling across the pavement. It comes from a garage door thrown open, and there's the sound of quiet but insistent murmurs from inside, suggesting a hushed but heated discussion at the very least. I can see the fire-like glow of Al-Ruhban's magic covering the mouth of the place.

I look over at him, and he tilts his head in acknowledgement. 'A little spell that's persuaded them to stay here until we arrived.'

A sensible precaution. Now to find out why my magic led me to them, to where the coffin was rather than to where it is now. I take a deep breath and step into the garage.

Chapter Twelve

Winter is coming. Although, really, that's Winter's private business.

Finding our way towards the Court isn't difficult. We just follow our shivers.

The air in the right direction grows noticeably cooler with each step, the swirling breeze carrying a freezing kiss that speaks of endless frozen eras, of a heartless icy beauty smothering all but the hardiest of life under a blanket of stillness. Anything deciduous falls away, huddling closer to Summer's domain, where even in the Wilds they might find enough light and warmth as to prosper. The few deciduous plants foolhardy enough to creep towards Winter are brittle skeletons by the time we walk a few hours, mocked for their misplaced bravery by the lush coats of their evergreen neighbours. Blood-red berries break up the greenery, but that's the limit of colour. The ground is hard and bare, already swept clear of any autumnal fallings. The air carries

89

a citrus smell of pine and a scentless clarity that tickles the nostrils, promising snow on the horizon.

'Always winter and never Christmas. Think of that!' Aicha grinds out.

'Just imagine — you might get to meet Mr Tumnus after all!' The brightness of my tone is just a Band-Aid over the creeping terror churning in my guts. A voice keeps trying to scream at me in my brain that what we're attempting is impossible, we're doomed to fail and suffer horribly, probably for eternity. I'm doing the mental equivalent of sticking my fingers in my ears and going, '*La-la-la, I can't hear you,*' which I'm fairly sure is the mature and grown-up response to such a voice.

'Brilliant,' she replies dryly. 'I've always wanted to slap the shit out of a faun.' And that's why I love Aicha and why I can effectively ignore the panicking voice screaming for my attention. Having her along makes doom a little less certain, slightly less impending.

She still makes the gliding forward movement look easy. It's like a sheen of frozen water lies layered on the world, and she's an Olympic-level figure skater. I, on the other hand, look like someone strapped blades under the feet of some poor, ungainly bear and then pushed it out onto the ice to see what would happen. I saw someone do something akin to that once in London during the Winter Fair. I made sure the bear got a chance to have a private one-on-one meeting with their owner to express their opinion about the whole malarkey before I smuggled the creature back to the wilds.

Speaking of, we've reached the Wilds of Faerie's limits. The land gives up on any pretence at resisting and allows the snow to wrap it up in crisp folds and put it to sleep forever. Silence hangs heavy across the land. The endless snow brings a uniformity to the world, only broken by the rude protruding trees and bushes adapted for this bleak form of existence. It's like the world's shittiest Christmas cake — a beautiful white external layer but underneath, nothing but the hollow cold.

We take our last rest before we cross what we judge to be the border. Night has fallen suddenly, as it tends to do here, and we've no idea how far we need to travel to get to the Court itself. Plus, traipsing across enemy territory in the pitch-black isn't the smartest of moves, when even banging into a tree might be the equivalent of stepping on a land-mine. With similarly explosive results.

Aicha buries our sticks into the hard earth as deep as her *talent*-enhanced strength will allow her, and we tie ourselves onto them. It's important to make sure we don't roll over in our sleep and just carry on gliding all the way to waking up at Maeve's feet. I suspect we'll suffer her less than enjoyable hospitalities the following night if we do.

We take turns keeping watch during the night, then set off as soon as the light allows. As we progress farther into the sterile land, it starts to snow. I wonder how that works. It's eternal winter here, always cold, so what happens to the snow underneath? Surely it never gets warm enough for any of it to melt. Does that mean the land of Winter just slowly gets higher and higher, the snow beneath compacting to form ice so dense it becomes like rock strata? I wonder, if you did a core sample, what strange things would you find preserved like fossils down in the ancient dark?

The silence feels as endless as the landscape, stretching out immeasurable distances. There's no birdsong, no chittering of small animals, no rustling of insects performing their drone-like busy work. The only sound to break it is the crunch of our sticks as they poke holes like the buttons on a snowman's line-drawn jacket, a strange and muted noise to hear when traversing snow compared to the heavy bite a boot would normally make.

When we finally sight Maeve's castle, it seems to just appear out of nowhere. One moment we're facing an infinite blankness, a white parchment that has never seen a pen scratch. The next, there is the first glisten of twisting spires, impossibly close for us to have only just noticed them. Parapets twist into impossible shapes, like MC Escher tied knots out of swan necks made of glass. The angles hurt my eyes. I guess they weren't made for mortals to appreciate. More to weep in fear and awe at the sight of.

We draw closer. I still can't tell if it's glass made to look like ice or ice that carries the refractive properties of glass. I doubt I'll know even if I touch it, though that would be a bad idea for two reasons. One, whichever it is, I don't doubt it will be cold enough to strip the skin from my palm, leaving it behind like a slapped-up band sticker in a grotty pub toilet. Two, it will let Maeve know we're here. Not the best of plans either way.

The structure is vast, stretching up and down and around and across in all directions. It looks like someone carved a Disney idea of a fairy castle out of ice and then took a strategic blowtorch to it, melting it in places, letting it fold and reconnect and reshape into bizarre, disturbing alternative forms. Looking at it feels like what I'd imagine a bad acid trip in the Magical Kingdom might.

We pick up the pace without letting our awareness slip, skirting around the grounds of the castle far enough back to be, hopefully, invisible to all observers inside while letting us see if anyone comes out. Luckily, the area in front is simply a vast flat terrain, indistinguishable really from the rest of the expanse we've crossed, allowing us a good view of the exit points despite the first signs of the brief twilight now visible in the way the shadows lengthen. For once, I'm grateful for the snow that's settled on our bodies. It helps us blend into the scenery and will hopefully make our movements harder to spot should anyone be watching through one of the many Dali-like melting windows.

As we manoeuvre our way round towards the back, the labyrinth rears into view. I think I imagined it would be one of those garden mazes from stately homes, trimmed hedgerows looming overhead. I didn't consider that it's in the heart of Winter, and even the most perennial of bushes decided long ago that there were more hospitable climates to live in. Instead, it's made of opaque ice formed five metres tall, as thick as my shoulders — although possibly not my brain. The obscured views of the other side cause uncanny reflections that seem to dance and crouch and leap across the surface as our view changes the closer we get. A clear entry point stands in the middle of the wall facing the castle. I suspect that will be the last simple thing about it.

There are no guards at the entry, which might make the next few minutes easier but isn't reassuring in the slightest. The centre is supposed to be chock-full of human prisoners.

'What's it look like?' I ask Aicha. Her *sight* for such things is infinitely better than mine these days.

'Huge fuck-off walls made of ice?' It's not the reply I wanted, but it is the reply I deserve, probably.

'Okay, and what about magically?'

The look she gives me could strip paint off a metal fence. Hell, it could probably strip metal off a metal fence, reducing the whole thing to a bubbling mess of shame and ineptitude. 'We're in Faerie, you raving dickhead. At the heart of Winter. In Maeve's own garden. Looking at her private labyrinth. Would you believe it is aglow with magic? Inconceivable, I know.'

Right. That's definitely the reply I deserve. It's just hard being practically Talentless. I find myself second-guessing everything. Not whining about it is even harder still. Only the threat of Aicha's acerbic tongue encourages me to bite mine.

We creep closer, still clinging to the elongating shadows, half-turned towards the palace to keep a watchful eye out for arriving enraged fae. None come. Small blessings. The frontmost wall of the labyrinth is now right next to us, and the undulation of shapes and shadows inside it is…unnerving. Every time my focus goes elsewhere, I sense changing forms out of the corner of my eye, threatening movements that set my Spidey senses off, fight-or-flight warnings flooding my system with hormonal instructions that keep me constantly on edge. Aicha looks the same as ever, but it'll take a lot more than obscured ice phantoms to unsettle her.

We arrive at the entry. Aicha peers inside, where a freezing mist hangs at ankle height, swirling like clouds that have forgotten where the sky is. 'What's the plan?'

I scratch the back of my head. 'Get through the maze, rescue the children, potentially find-slash-kill Simon, and escape through the portal?'

She gives a long-suffering sigh. 'That's not a plan. That's a hypothesis just waiting to be tested. I want to know the plan to stop it from blowing up in our faces.'

She has me bang to rights, of course. Wandering into an Unseelie maze without thinking it through isn't likely to work out well for us. Problem is, I haven't come up with any obvious solutions outside of the classics. There was a ball of gardening string I spotted under one of the strange, disturbing trees lining the walkway up to the garden. I wander back and point it out to Aicha.. 'Theseus and the Minotaur?'

She waggles her hand back and forth, lifting the ball with her *talent*. 'Not bad. Works to get back, at least. How about getting through?'

'Trial and error?'

She sighs again. 'It's going to be a long night, isn't it?'

It really might be.

Chapter Thirteen

FAERIE, 5 JUNE, PRESENT DAY

I swear if 1980's David Bowie turns up draped in leather, singing about what we remind him of, I'm out of here immediately.

Aicha ties off one end of the string with her power to what looks like a sundial in the shape of a flower withering and dying, its petals closing in to obscure the top surface. Reading it is almost impossible. Of course, maybe that's the point. Or perhaps the device gives some totally different indication relative to the position of the petals. I'm not about to struggle to understand how the functional decorations of the fae work. There are slightly more pressing concerns. With that in mind, we set off into the labyrinth.

If the walls caused me anxiety before, walking between them makes me feel about one jump scare away from a major heart attack constantly. Things move in the surfaces but are never there when I look for them directly. Shadows coalesce in the corner of my view, menacing and threatening like they can leap and attack at any moment. When we reach our first dead end, our own shadows elongate, stretching up the surface in front, making the surrounding walls seem to grow and close in on us too. As we back up, following the string to the previous intersection, my heart beats too fast and my breathing is too shallow. I feel light-headed and have to resist the urge to steady myself on the walls. I don't know if my hand will freeze onto them or pass straight through for something inside to bite off. Either way, I'm not in any hurry to touch them however dizzy I feel.

Aicha is, of course, a trooper. Utterly unfazed, at least externally. She works her way methodically around the twists and turns. I don't doubt for one second she's mapping it all out in her head, drawing up the ways we've come, identifying any we've not explored yet. For me, just keeping moving is doing well, the darkness of the cave I was trapped in just on the other side of a murky ice-glass window. I can't keep myself far enough away from the walls. I feel like I can fall through them, tumbling back into the shadows to be locked away from the light forever.

So when I see the exit in the wall, it takes all my willpower not to run to it but to match Aicha's calm strides as we glide out of the maze.

And back into the garden.

We're once more where we started, the string trailing both out behind us and in front, leading to the weird garden ornament we originally fastened it onto.

Aicha harrumphs, but there's little annoyance in her voice, more the sound of a theory confirmed. 'I thought so. The walls move. It didn't make sense.'

I curse internally. 'Do you have any idea how far we made it in?'

She nods, still lost in thought. 'Pretty far. Can only judge it off the side of the labyrinth I saw as we approached but almost all the way. Felt the moment we started turning back. Reckon we were almost there before it happened.'

Instinctively, I want to make some sort of joke about it being amaze-ing, but the words freeze on my tongue and die. I don't have the energy to jest. Instead, I sink down on my haunches, my back deliberately to the maze, my eyes on the castle in front. It means we have to go back in there again. I desperately don't want to.

We sit there for some time, Aicha thinking through the problem, me trying to do anything but think, blanking my brain out, fighting to get a grip on my nervous system, to make myself calm the fuck down. I've nothing to offer at the moment except to be the least hindrance I can.

She cracks it, of course, because Aicha is a freaking genius. Having been around for such a long time helps, but being razor-sharp smart is a big part of how she's survived this long. 'It's responding to our eyes.'

I zoned out monitoring the castle, calming myself somewhat, and she sparks me from my reverie. 'What? Like a retinal scanner?'

She shakes her head. 'No. It's the fact we're looking for the path. It can't be touch-based because we're not putting our feet down. If it was because we aren't fae, none of the children could get in there, and it would have either kept us there or summoned the queen. I think the idea is both to keep the kids from escaping and to keep out any of her own Court who might want to sample the goods ahead of time. The moving shapes and forms in the glass draw the eyes. Whilst we're distracted by them, the maze changes.'

'So how do we get round that?' I know I should be able to come up with a solution, but it feels like the eternal cold has crept up my spine into my servo and blocked up my neural pathways with ice. Thinking is hard. Even more so than usual.

Aicha dusts herself down, pushing some of the collected snow off her shoulders and trousers. 'Simple. We can't get distracted. I've got the original route mostly stored in my head. I guess it must reset when we leave; otherwise, it'd be a different path each time. Keep your eyes straight ahead, walk forward. If we need to backtrack, close your eyes as we turn. Don't look at the walls.'

Easier said than done, but then, if it was easy, we'd have done it the first time, and it would be a rubbish deterrent. Aicha reels the string in, pulling it out of the maze with her *talent*, then takes the reformed ball, spooling it out, pops it on the end of her stick and poles herself straight forward, her head held high.

I scurry along, trying to stick next to her, but the presence of the walls on either side means I fall back slightly, desperate to stay in the middle, equidistant and as far away as possible from each. The movements now are terrible and terrifying.

Shapes swirl just out of view on each side: monstrous shades, torn-robed hags with claws reaching for me, portals of unending night to suck me back into the empty void. I can't see them, not properly, not without looking, and my eyes water from the effort of keeping my gaze forward, of resisting the screaming urge to look at the threats amassing on my flanks. I can hear voiceless whispers full of plots and plans on how they'll torture me, take me back to that cave, and keep me there with an unending stream of corpses, to never escape, never see the sun again. The noiseless sounds don't need syllables to spell out how much they crave my destruction, how sure they are they can achieve it.

I feel like Orpheus climbing back up from the Underworld, only I know if I look, it won't be my love I lose but my nerve. If I give in to the fear scratching at the inside of my eyeballs, the walls will move again, and we'll find ourselves back at the start, and I don't think I have the courage to attempt this a third time. Aicha, of course, has her gaze fixed forward like a soldier on parade, never wavering, and a little voice keeps saying it's fine for me to look, absolutely fine because she'll never do it, so it won't hurt, it can't. The walls won't move because she will never look away.

But I can't do that either. I can't let her carry everything, more than I already do. If I do that now, if I just assume all will be fine because Aicha will never flinch and give in to my own weaknesses, I'll never get out of that cave. I'll become a shadow, a wraith of the man I once was. There's no way I'd come back from that. I have to keep moving forward without giving in to my fears.

How long it takes us to get through the maze, I do not know. Night has arrived fully now, and although the walls keep an ominous luminance that might make putting one foot in front of the other easier —if still slippery— it only adds to my desperate urge to look. It feels like hours. I'm sweating despite the freezing temperatures by the time we get to the building where the children are being held, my jaw sore and half-seized from clenching, my neck strained from being locked in place as I fought against myself every step of the way.

We arrive in a wide square, a pathway leading up to the main entrance. On either side is what looks like sand, although I suspect it's fine granules of super cold snow turning and shaping just so in strange and slightly uncanny lines and forms, like a twisted version of a Japanese peace garden. I take a moment, imitating inspecting the place to steady myself internally.

The building is barn-sized, reminiscent of a stable, although the few windows on the forward face continue that sensation of melting and refreezing, the glass seeming to drip into the breeze blocks under the ice-white scree. There are bars over the windows. They look like iron painted white but obviously aren't considering where we are. The fae loathe iron's burning touch. I wonder what they're made of. Another metal? Silver perhaps. It seems like the sort of ostentatious display Maeve would approve of. Keeping kids prisoners with precious metals, away from anyone's eyes but hers and those she brings here with her.

Huge wooden double doors stand central in the wall, barred physically by a massive wooden beam slotted in to hold points on each side. The entrance is so magically charged that even I, practically a muggle these days, can see the doors glowing when I *look*.

It's my turn to ask Aicha the question. 'So what now?'

She opens her mouth on an in-breath, then pauses, stops, *looks* again, then looks at me. 'No idea.'

'Brilliant.' I bite back an audible groan.

'Hold up, *saabi*. Didn't say I wouldn't have an idea, just not got one yet. It's fae magic. Need to work it out.'

The ball's firmly in her court now. I've not encountered this sort of power before, so I've nothing to give her on a theoretical level, and I'm a damp squib on the magical one. I huddle to one side and monitor the way back into the maze — first to make sure no one comes sneaking up on us unexpectedly, and second to make sure the maze itself doesn't creep up and swallow us back in when we aren't looking.

An interminable amount of time passes. Aicha keeps furrowing her brow, thinking hard. Theoretical magic isn't her forte, but she can stretch herself when needs must. Now and then, she appears to get a eureka moment and steps forward to hit the doors with some working to dispel or break the strange enchantment covering them. Whatever she pulls, whichever school of magic —and I see her run the gamut of her knowledge from east to west— it simply splashes across the workings and dissipates. Aicha air-stomps away, vexed, deep in thought until the next idea strikes.

No matter what she thinks of, none of it works. Enochian Runes of Entering? They sink into the surface, vanishing from sight. Teller's Slice of Destruction? Bounces off, shattering in a moment. Fagin's Gentlemanly Pilferage? The weak spots, easy to force points of ingress that should light up like a Christmas tree, somehow get cancelled out or simply don't exist. The place might look like a stable, but magically, it's Fort Knox.

When she takes to just bombarding it with fireballs for several minutes (fireballs that freeze on contact, dropping to the floor like the world's largest hailstones), I know she needs to take some time out. This is the closest I've ever seen Aicha to a hissy fit, and if she doesn't take a break, she's likely to take out her fury on the nearest thing. Which will be the maze or me. Either way, I don't want it to happen.

'Hold up, wait,' I say as she storms towards it once more, gliding across the floor on the cushions of air but still looking like she's slamming her feet down hard enough to make the earth shake. I'm genuinely worried she's forgotten the rules and is going to kick it in frustration. 'This isn't working, Aich.'

She pauses and takes a moment, composing herself,

then slides smoothly back to me. I notice she doesn't even seem to need to use the pole. It's like the magic just adapts to her...

Suddenly, it clicks. An Archimedes moment all of my own. I start chuckling, gently at first, then harder and harder till I'm bent double, tears streaming down my face — at least at first. By about half-way down, they turn into little ice balls burning the skin on my face. Somehow, that strikes me as even funnier.

Aicha is less amused. 'What is it, you massive arsehole?' I think she knows I've figured it out, and it's driving her mad, not having the answer.

I gasp out the words where I can, between the guffaws. 'You're... fucking... Gandalf...'

She blinks. 'Not last time I looked, I wasn't. Not fucking anyone.'

I wipe at my eyes, flicking the tears away. 'No, no, no. You're Gandalf himself at the Mines of Moria.'

I wave my hands at the archway of the door as if suddenly dwarven runes have appeared above it. 'Speak, friend, and enter.'

I see the realisation hit her when her eyes widen slightly. 'What are you saying? That we just have to lift the bar off to get in?'

I nod, trying not to smirk. Don't get me wrong, I'd be completely lost without Aicha. It's just good to be useful, to actually solve a problem. 'Think about it. Being locked away in a freezing cold prison on an alien world by what looks like monsters and acts like monsters too is exactly the sort of trauma that can kick-start *talent* without training. The enchantments on the door aren't to keep them closed; the plank keeps the kids already effectively barred. No, the enchantments are to stop them moving said plank by *pulling* it when they suddenly discover the power inside them. And not to mention if she puts any of her subjects in there…'

I don't mention the idea of her keeping Simon in captivity. There's a part of me, that eternal optimist who still hopes that everything is —*actually*— going to work out all right in the end despite all the evidence to the contrary that hopes he's in there. That we'll pop the bar and waltz in, and he'll be trussed up like the world's most plug-ugly turkey ready for us to roast. The rest of me — the stone cold pessimist who's well aware that disaster isn't going to just rain down on us, it's going to piss on us instead from a great height — knows full well he won't be in there. He's been too meticulously prepared thus far to just stumble into Maeve's clutches. No chance. either way, though. He's not the main priority right now. The kids are definitely in there. Getting them out is what matters.

I turn back to the matter at hand. 'It's nothing more than a nullification field, which is why your magic failed every single time.'

She groans. 'Because they set it up specifically to dispel anything that got thrown at it from any field of human magic.'

It's my turn to give her the gun fingers. Good God, they feel great. Locked and loaded. 'Got it. So all we have to do is…'

She swings back towards the door and poles herself determinedly towards it, with me just behind. 'Lift that fucking plank out of the way.'

It's easier said than done. We can't touch it; if we do, Maeve will know we're on her territory, which is a good way to end up with an Unseelie horde pouring through the maze towards us. Magic can't help thanks to the working liberally applied to the building and doors, including the barricading beam for this exact reason. We have to try to wedge our poles under the piece of wood to lever it up. Problem is, as soon as we apply pressure, it sends us shooting backwards, and I nearly fall head over heels. I regain my balance, wobbling like a kid going ice skating for the first time but don't fall. I dropped my stick by the door when I shot off though, so I have to carefully tramp back over so as not to give a repeat performance.

In the end, we stand back-to-back. I use my pole to brace us against the ground behind, and Aicha then levers up one end of the plank until it slides through both holds and clatters to the ground. Then she pushes it clear of the doorway, hooks one of the handles, and pulls.

The door creaks open, and I grin in triumph. I solved a problem! With my thinkings! Truly, it is a rare and marvellous day. One for the history books.

We slide inside cautiously. We needn't have bothered. There are no guards. There's no need. Nobody in here is a threat nor are they going anywhere in a hurry.

We're in a vast room that would make most ballroom-equipped palace owners envious, with its vaulted ceiling and intricate detailing. It's definitely not used for dancing though. The cages scattered throughout the space would get in the way.

They look like they're made of ice. I don't doubt they're as hard as steel. Square boxes that are probably two or three metres high and wide. The sight inside each of them is enough to break the hardest of human hearts, though I doubt it has any effect on the ice block in Maeve's chest.

Children huddle, their clothes stained with substances best left unidentified, but it's the other stains — the psychic ones — that hang more heavily. The room, indolent in its haughty architecture, stinks of sweat and piss and shame and terror. The children huddle as far back from the front bars as they can, as far from us as possible without touching the rear ones. At best, the bars probably freeze; at worst, they bite, inflicting pain on any brave enough to pull on them. Their eyes are wide, and I read nothing positive in them despite them being full to the brim with emotion. These kids are drowning in despair and distilled fear that's been purified into a potency no one should ever have to experience, especially not a child.

There are about six of them that I can see. Many other cages stand empty, no doubt waiting for Jack of Plate's newest delivery that will never come now. It makes me want to rewind time, to go back and kill him again but infinitely slower, to really take my time and make him suffer. The way these kids have suffered, are suffering, just so he could stay alive a little longer. I can taste bile in the back of my throat, and I don't know if it's from pity for them or disgust at him or shame at myself that I didn't get here quicker. Centuries quicker. Faerie's debauchery was horrific but abstract before. Now it's all too vividly real.

The walls are plain and perfect white. I can imagine them covered in paintings —which, based on the architectural and design preferences we've seen so far, would be as stunning as they were disturbing— and the whole place crowded with the peculiar forms of the fae nobility. This could have once been used as a ballroom or the like. The barn conversion to end all barn conversions. I wonder why Maeve turned it into her dungeon for the children she stole. Especially considering I find it highly unlikely that she doesn't have an actual dungeon under the castle.

My eyes dart around, hoping to see a De Montfort-sized cage fully stocked, knowing it's never going to happen. I'm right, but I see something else. Looking past the plantation of cages, I realise there's another larger one covering the back wall. Inside is another group of kids, this time around twenty or thirty of them. They're older and seem to be an even split of boys and girls. The ones in the individual cages look to be between about five and ten years old as far as I can tell. This group is all adolescents. I guess they're early teens up to as old as fifteen or sixteen maybe. They wear clothes that suggest they either got snatched up from a Renaissance fair or are dressed in local fashion by the fae. Their clothes are cleaner, but the terror in their eyes is somehow deeper. The kids at the front are terrified of the unknown. The older ones know exactly what there is to fear. Knowing is, apparently, even worse.

I hold out a hand like you would to a scared wild animal trapped in a snare without losing a finger. 'Please, all of you. Stay calm. We're here to rescue you.'

I see the difference yet again between the older and younger kids, and it breaks my heart. Those at the front, the newly stolen, react. They lean forward, and hope creeps into their eyes, muscling out a bit of the dread despair that has taken up residence. The teenagers at the back don't react at all. They just watch us with dark, mistrustful eyes. It tells me this isn't the first time someone has come and promised them something similar. No doubt, each time it ended up being an agent of Maeve's. What better torture than to offer freedom and then snatch it away again? I'm sure it delights the queen bitch who considers them her property.

It hurts. Somewhere inside me, in the parts that have stayed human despite outliving normal longevity by so many multipliers. A deep sympathetic pain that sings to the terror that's still clinging to the back of my brain. To be captive with no hope of escape, no chance of anything but darkness… Whether that darkness is a body-stocked cave or the heart of Winter, it is a misery no one should have to bear. Let alone a child. Children. Multiple children. The Good God knows I probably deserve what De Montfort did to me. Probably far worse. But these kids? They're innocents. Or were before Maeve marred them just as surely as she did Jack's face.

I lean closer to Aicha and murmur in her ear, 'Right now, we have to get these kids out of here. That's the only target. But trust me, we're coming back. When they're all safe on Earth, we're going to kill the fucking monster that did this. Maeve has to die.'

Aicha gives a slight sharp nod. 'Down like a clown, Charlie Brown.' Funnily enough, we may not have invoked our power or signed in blood, but it's still one of the most solemn and binding pacts either of us has ever uttered. There is no way Maeve is going to do this again. I'm coming back here to kill her before she can retrieve the next set of kids or die trying, and it looks like I'll have a very pissed off Druze warrior by my side.

Aicha sets to inspecting the locks on the cages, working out how to spring them open without touching them. I don't doubt she has a set of lock picks on her and that she'll be able to manipulate them magically without touching the locks themselves. I head towards the cage at the back, murmuring reassurances to the kids as I go. That we'll have them out soon, that we'll get them home safe. As I make my way closer, I look the group of older kids over.

Being a teenager is a horrible thing in the best of worlds. Your body changes, betraying you as it shifts form, always one step ahead of your mind that races to catch up. Limbs elongate overnight, becoming awkward and unbalancing. Hell, no one will ever understand that better than me; I've spent the past eight hundred years hopping into new bodies, adjusting to them, forcing them to adjust to me.

These kids weren't recently snatched; their clothes alone, compared to the other kids', mark them as different, but their demeanour, their abject all-consuming despair, differentiates them even more. Faerie isn't new to them. They aren't new to it. They've been here for years, stuck as teenagers for a good chunk of that time. No doubt it's to please some aesthetical preference of Maeve's, but it's also just another form of cruel and unusual punishment. Sadly, I doubt it's even close to the worst they've suffered here.

Experience has written distrust all over their faces. Words alone aren't going to reassure them, but I still have to try. 'Hi,' I start, my tone low and gentle, trying not to spook them. 'I'm Paul. I'm here to take you home.'

Most of them just stare at me, not even bothering to move. No doubt they're just waiting for the other shoe to drop, for the pain to start. I hear a bitter laugh though, and the group pulls back to reveal a girl sitting, her arms wrapped round her knees on the floor. Her clothes are green and grey, the cloth slight and fine, the cut perhaps a tad more expensive but no less dirt-marked than the others'. She has fine features, her skin a bleached paleness beyond white. I can't see her eyes because they remain fixed on the floor, but her ears catch my attention. They carry a point to them, sharper than any human ear is.

The girl raises her head and fixes me with a glare, her eyes a brilliant pale blue, like melting ice caught half-way and forced to refreeze by another cold snap. I'd say she's a Winter Court fae, yet her face still holds a certain asymmetry: the eye on the right is a miniscule amount higher than the left, there's a misplaced freckle on the side of her nose, and the curve to her sardonic, humourless grin pulls up more towards the higher eye. To me they add to her beauty, but they're imperfections no fae would accept. They're too natural. Too mortal. Half your face burnt away? Fine because that's deliberate. This? This is just too *human*.

'What does the queen want with us now then?' There's a weary resignation to her voice that speaks of the fact she knows nothing good is coming but equally that she can do nothing about it. Then she looks more closely at me. I see the moment she clocks what's caught her attention, noticing the rounded tops of my ears. For a moment, desperate hope blossoms in her eyes, but she quickly extinguishes it. That numbed, bored terror snaps back into place. I know she'd love to be insolent, to express that righteous teenage rage. She's just too clever to do so. She knows what the likely result would be.

'I don't serve Maeve,' I say. 'Neither of us do. We really are here to take you home.'

Again, the bitter laugh. 'Oh, is that so? The two of you are going to fight your way through the Unseelie Court, are you? And tell me something. When you do —' She leans forward, never looking away from me, her expression never changing. 'Can you take us back in time as well?'

She gestures to the cages, towards where Aicha is working to open them. 'We spoke to the new arrivals, you know. Tried to calm them down. Not with lies though. They still need to know the truth of what's coming.'

Jeez. I mean, I understand the logic of it but still. No wonder the kids look terrified. I know she would've been doing them no favours by hiding it from them, but that's a heavy conversation to have with a group of scared primary school kids.

She looks left and right at her companions. 'Billy there. He's done well for himself.' She waves a hand at a young boy, his scraggly afro tightly curled in. 'Survived the last four culls. When he got taken from the plantation, he thought anything would be better than the hell he'd been born in. Ask him if he still thinks that. Janey —' She nods at a young redheaded girl with freckles to match, who doesn't even look at me. She just stares away into the distance. 'Janey's one of the newest kids. She was a breath of fresh air when she arrived. Brought some light back into our lives for a little bit, singing songs from some new group called The Beatles that she loved so much she learnt all the words. Maeve heard her one day. Hard to sing when she freezes your vocal cords, then shatters them with a tiny little flick' —her finger pops off her thumb, and I can't help but flinch— 'to the throat.'

Christ. I thought these kids were the last batch, the ones from thirty years ago. Instead, some of them have been here for over a hundred and fifty years. A century and a half serving and suffering the whims of the Winter Court.

Still, she holds my gaze. 'Tell me, can you make me human again, Paul? Can you undo what she did to me? Something in the blood, apparently. Do you know what they hate more than humans here, *Paul*?' The emphasis is like a slap to the face. 'Half-humans. Fae-like humans. I'm an abomination to them, although they won't kill me. Not outright. Not in the last two hundred years, anyway.'

I can't help myself. I wince. I just about lost my mind being put through an innovative form of torture custom designed for me for about three weeks. Having that level of twisted creative ingenuity thrown at you for centuries? Unthinkable. My admiration for this young half-fae grows even more.

'What's your name?' I notice the others all look to her. Guess being the longest here probably garners some sort of automatic level of respect. Plus, based on her unbroken spirit, I guess she's earned it from them all too.

For a moment, I think she won't answer. Then, 'April.' She said it sharply, briefly, as if it meant nothing, either the name or the action of giving it to me. I suspect it cost her more than she shows to have given even such a tiny fragment of trust, to share something with a stranger full of promises she feels sure exist only to be broken.

The hubbub building behind me drags my attention away from this intriguing, damaged, yet somehow remarkably whole spokesperson of a girl. Aicha has got most of the cages open, and the younger kids mill around, grouping together, the first thawing of their frozen terror setting in with them whispering in their huddles. They've started to hope that this might be real, that they might escape and get home.

I turn back to the older group, forcing myself to address them all, though I suspect April's who I really need to convince. 'Right, this is it. In a moment, we'll get this cage open. We're going to lead you out through the labyrinth and to the throne room, straight to the portal. If all goes well, we'll be back on Earth before you know it.'

'What if it doesn't go well?' A boy thin to the point of skeletal speaks. Looping scars trace his cheekbones and whirl around his eyes. It doesn't hide his natural good looks, but it's an ugly thing to have done to anyone.

I'm not going to lie to them. 'Then we'll either die or get captured. I've got no intention of letting that happen, but I won't make you promises. If you stay here, perhaps Maeve will treat you kindlier than the others.'

April gives a sharp barking laugh. 'Hardly. If this is a trap she's set, they'll say those who stay are cowards. As always, we have to play the game.' The words say that she doesn't have even the tiniest confidence that it's anything but a trap. Her eyes, though, burn into mine. They insist, demand that I not let these kids down. I've no intention of doing so. Of course, good intentions only take you to one place.

'I need you to take responsibility for the little ones. Aicha and I' —I indicate the taciturn warrior as she arrives to pick their cage's lock— 'will concentrate on possible arriving threats. We'll need everyone to keep silent and let us do our job.' A thought occurs to me. 'When you passed through the maze, how did Maeve get you all through?'

'Blindfolds,' April answers, picking up a strip of plain material off the floor. Of course, that makes sense.

The lock springs open, and we corral them together by the doors leading out. 'Okay, listen up.' I raise my voice slightly, although I don't need to shout. None of them are talking at a volume above hushed whispers. Hope might be present, but fear is deeply ingrained as well. 'We're going to need to blindfold you all, just like you were to get here. I know —' I raise my hand, seeing panic rise in several of the faces. 'It's not what you want. Trust me, it's the only way we'll get out. If we don't blindfold you, the maze will move around on us, and we'll end up back here. We need to get to the throne room before dawn, and the night is ticking away rapidly.'

I see plenty of unhappy children, objections bubbling in their throat, only their terror keeping their lips clamped shut. I have an idea. 'April, will you please do the honours with the blindfolds?' She nods and gets to work, sending one of the other older kids to gather the fabric strips from the cages. I reckon even the newest arrival will have picked up on her leadership qualities and her trustworthiness. Hell, I only just met her, and I trust her. She has to have a core of steel, of adamantium to have survived so long and stayed sane. The fact she clearly looks out for the others speaks to her quality of character. I doubt I would've done a fraction of so well if our places had been exchanged.

As I predicted, even the youngest children submit to April tying the blindfold on. When there's only her left, she brings the last piece of fabric over to me. As she ties it over her eyes, she murmurs under her breath, 'Don't let them down,' then falls silent once more, though still straight-backed, radiating fierceness.

'We're going to need you to stay together,' I say. 'We've got a thread that leads all the way back out through the labyrinth. Aicha will take the front. I'll put the thread in each of your hands, then follow up at the rear to protect that end and make sure none of you wander off. Just keep holding the thread, pass it hand over hand so you don't pull it away from anyone else, and we'll be through in no time.'

I should probably have got them to the thread before I got April to blindfold them, but I wanted to shut off that undercurrent of terror before it got out of control. I'm not going to get them to take them back off now they've accepted the idea. Aicha and I guide them out of the door and across the grounds to the entrance of the maze, shepherding them so they don't stumble, using our poles and quiet urging whispers to steer them to roughly the right place. Aicha starts slowly into the maze, and I use my pole to put the thread in one hand after the other until they're all passing along behind her. Then I wrap up the end of the thread on my pole and, fixing my gaze straight ahead, walk back into the maze.

Chapter Fourteen

SAINT-OUEN, 21 FEBRUARY 1973

The garage is small, which is no surprise because it's Paris. Everything is small. A thirty-metre square flat is spacious. You could fit a van in here and still have space to stand, even to unload a few boxes. That's practically palatial.

Two men, clearly the ones we heard conversing, stand at the back, although they stop talking as soon as we enter. I thought about getting Aicha to lead the interview as this is something she cares so much about, but the chances of her losing her temper and stabbing one of them in the eye are too high. It's always easier to get people to loosen their tongues before rigor mortis sets in.

There's an age difference of two or three decades between the men and enough familial traits that I'm confident they're either father and son or nephew and uncle. Both men carry the bulky form that speaks of once being in prime physical form but then hiding it under layers of cheese, saucisson, and wine. From the way they both square up as we arrive, they clearly feel confident in their fighting abilities despite that.

The younger of the two looks to be in his forties. He has a permanent squint, his eyes too small for features already inflating with age and alcohol. His clothes are clean and pressed, though, and his hair neatly clipped. If he doesn't have a recent military background, I'll be a monkey's uncle. The older is less well-kept, with his face ravaged by alcohol and pock-marked by swollen skin pores as he blew up over time like the Michelin man. His nose has a reddish glow. I'm not sure if that's from arguing with the other man or from early boozing. He has a shifty, guilty look about him, but he still holds a certain something in his posture that speaks of army days before too much drinking back on civvy street.

The younger man steps forward, snatching a tyre iron off the floor as he comes. 'Who are you? What do you want?' he snarls. The cocky anger isn't quite enough to mask the fear in his eyes. This is one of our thieves then. He's terrified we are the authorities even if he isn't scared of us as individuals. Yet.

Aicha slides forward to meet him. She brings her forearm up fluidly, locking the tyre iron in place before sending it clattering to the ground. Using the forward momentum, she pivots and sweeps his leg out from under him so he follows the tyre iron to the floor. She comes down, smashing hard onto his back, pinning him with her elbow over his throat, ready to drive it into his windpipe at a moment's notice.

I turn my attention to the older fellow, who stands, shock scribbled all over his face, seeing his tough soldier son or nephew floored in a second by the tiny Arabic woman. I love seeing Aicha get that reaction. Especially out of facist scumbags.

'That wasn't very polite, was it?' I ask him gently, stepping over the winded man and advancing on the other. He tries to back up, but there's nowhere to go. It's a big garage for Paris but not that big. 'Now let's start again, shall we? Where is it?'

'Where's what?' He gets the words out, and despite the confused terror in them, there's a bellicose belligerence to them.

I tut at his terrible attempt at stalling. 'The coffin you Nazi-wannabe fucks stole. Where is it?'

He pales further. I think he hoped this was still just a robbery. Now he realises the danger is far higher than he thought. 'Are you...the police?'

I shake my head. 'Oh, no.' There's a smile to my voice, as deadly and as cold as a crocodile's. 'We're far more dangerous than they are. Now, you absolute waste of human skin, where is the coffin?'

'I can start removing that wasted skin if you want?' Aicha pipes up from her position over the prone man. 'Reckon I can flay him in one entire piece?'

I consider the question. 'It'll be difficult.' I prod the man in his swollen belly. He rewards me with an outraged grunt. 'There's a lot to get off.'

I can see the older man is itching to hit me. Anger and terror war in his expression, his eyes flicking from me to the other man on the floor, trying to weigh up his chances. I lean forward. 'Give it a go. See where it gets you,' I mutter, my eyes fixed on his, the challenge clear.

The man's a scumball, but he isn't entirely stupid. Whatever he sees in my gaze convinces him because he sags, deflated and defeated. 'Who are you people?' There's a whine to his voice, a pleading edge that wasn't there before. He's beat, and he knows it.

'The people asking the questions. Your job is to answer

them and otherwise keep your mouth shut. Now, coffin. Where is it?'

'I don't know. We don't know!' he adds the last part as he sees my attention swing to the man on the floor.

'Who are you then?' I consider pulling a knife, but I don't think it's necessary. We've done the work to intimidate him. He might consider himself a hard man, but most of that's just bluster. He broke with minimal pressure. As with a lot of these swaggering sorts, he's just a bully. He isn't used to people standing up to him.

'Garou,' he says, his eyes cast downward, unable to meet my gaze. 'Armand Garou.'

'And the other guy?' I gesture at the prone figure, which is pointless as Armand's too scared, too utterly dominated to look at me now.

'Pierre. My son.' All the ebullience is gone from his voice. He's entirely meek.

'Shut it, da*uurkh*...' Pierre started to say, 'dad,' but it transformed when Aicha jabbed him in the Adam's apple. He wisely concentrates on trying to remember how to breathe rather than interrupting us again.

'Right.' I keep my attention on the father. I don't doubt we can break the son just as easily, but it's a waste of effort. He's grounded. Budum tish. 'You were telling us where the coffin is.'

'I don't know!' he whines. 'None of us do. Hubert sent us here to check on it...'

'Hubert?' I interrupt.

I can see him cursing himself internally for dropping a name so easily, but the fight has gone out of him. 'Hubert Massol. He led the operation.'

There was a hesitation there, a slight lie or a bending of

the truth at least, but I don't really care who all the individual shitheads are, only who has the coffin. 'Okay, so Hubert sent you here to check on the coffin, but when you got here, it was gone?'

'Yes.' His whimpering tone grates on my nerves. But then, so does pretty much everything about both of them. 'They were supposed to be guarding it, but they were gone and so was the coffin.'

Ah-ha. Now we're getting somewhere. 'Who was supposed to be guarding it?'

'Gabor and Casimir.'

I wait for him to elaborate, but nothing comes. 'Last names? Addresses? Details, man, details.'

He stutters, stumbling over his words. 'I d…don't know. Didn't know them. Never met them before a week ago. Tixier…' He stops again, biting off his words.

I'm not having that. I add menace to my tone. 'Tixier?' I prompt.

'Tixier-Vignancour. He put the operation together. Massol led it, but it was his idea. He put the team in place.'

I've heard of Tixier-Vignancour. He ran for the presidency in the mid-sixties on a fascist, nationalist agenda. Came in third or fourth, if I remember correctly. Too damn well placed for a far-right shithead either way. 'You think he stole the coffin?'

Armand looks up horrified, as if I just suggested he and his son are secret lovers. 'Never!' The exclamation is indignant, that self-entitled tone of outrage creeping back in as he forgets to be scared for a moment. 'He's a true patriot! Why would he organise all of this to restore the honour of the great man so ignobly treated, only to steal him away again? It makes no sense. No, it was those bastards Gabor and Casimir. I knew we shouldn't have trusted foreigners, even if they were Foreign Legion.'

Looks like Armand knows more useful information than he thought he did. 'They weren't French?'

He shakes his head, a sneer on his face. 'No. They were from the east. Casimir's Polish, I think, and Gabor?' I can see him thinking about it, trying to remember. 'Hungarian maybe?'

Bizarre. So we have two eastern Europeans with French nationality after their time in the Foreign Legion falling in with a group of far-right ultra-nationalists and then absconding with the coffin after their comrades left them on guard duty.

I look at the other two with me. Al-Ruhban has been happy to observe, but then he's got no skin in the game, and Aicha prefers to speak more loudly with actions than words. But they've both been listening, and I want to see if I've missed anything, any obvious questions that are worth asking. From their expressions, they can't think of anything either.

I'm done, but this isn't my rodeo really. I'm operating in a support role. 'What do you want to do with them?' I ask Aicha. Killing non-magical humans isn't my bag but killing fascists is hers.

She considers it for a minute, a minute that must seem like hours for the two men waiting to be condemned. Then she stands up, taking the pressure off Pierre's neck. 'Let them go. Let them hide. Police will catch them soon enough.' She looks over at me and says, 'Fucking idiots,' as if that explains her train of thought. Perhaps it does.

I step aside and gesture for the two of them to get out. Armand half-hoists his son to his feet with the nervous strength of the completely terrified, and the two men set off at a stumbling run out into the Parisian night.

The three of us look around the bare garage, hoping for clues, but it's completely empty.

Damn it.

Chapter Fifteen

FAERIE, 5 JUNE, PRESENT DAY

I feel like the reverse Pied Piper leading the kids home.
Which reminds me of Franc, just to make a terrible
situation even worse.

Heading through the maze is no more fun the third time
than the first or second. The threatening movements, the
menacing shadows are even more violent in their dances
just out of sight, demanding I look every step I take. The
kids' heads whip left and right, and I know they must be
hearing things trying to get them to take their blindfolds off.
I wonder if it's threats or promises, monsters or those they
miss with all their hearts. Muttered words of encourage-
ment, of motivation are all I can offer them; once, I lean
forward to gently pull the hand of a young boy away from
his blindfold. Concentrating on their well-being helps me
ignore the whispers promising to take me back to the dark;
getting these children home is worth going back to the
eternal blackness. Anything to see them safe.

We make it through, breaking out into the expansive ice garden between the maze and the house. I didn't really have time to inspect the area when we first arrived, but I can see now the intricate carvings, the intense detail in the frost-coated ornamentation. The artist must be both incredibly talented and psychologically deranged. Statues of animals and birds are here but subtly wrong — eyes too wide, teeth too long, necks stretched, fur for feathers, feathers for hair, eyes containing tiny fingers clutching the irises, claws are teeth, the toes cracked maws. Some are geometric shapes that hurt the eyes and the mind. None of it helps lift the mood.

Regardless of the disturbing artwork, I get the kids to take off their blindfolds. They need to see we've been true to our word so far. They also need to see where they're going. We can't afford for them to blunder about, knocking the statues over and causing a ruckus. So far we've been lucky, but we've helped ourselves luck-wise by being careful. I'm not about to ruin that for this last and most dangerous part.

I don't really feel it needs to be said to these traumatised children, but I still remind them silence is of paramount importance. Then we set off, picking our way carefully through the garden paths that curve out and then up towards the back door of the palace, our eyes peeled for traps or tripwires. Closer in, we can see vastbay windows on either side of the doorway. The rooms inside must be enormous as the huge panes can fold back, opening fully, no doubt to allow the party to spill outside. I doubt the Unseelie are concerned by letting the cold in.

April is further back, chivvying the younger ones. I drop back next to her. 'Do you know the way to the throne room?' I ask her under my breath, trying not to spook the little ones with my lack of knowledge. She nods, so I lead her up next to Aicha. 'Show her the way. I'll make sure everyone stays together.' It's a shame we have to be so quiet. These two could be the best of friends if given half a chance. Still, I'll make sure they get the chance once we get back to Earth.

April has clocked we aren't touching anything, so she steps up to open the door. I leap forward, alarmed, but she holds out a reassuring hand. 'The palace knows me,' she says. 'I'm allowed access. It won't set off any alarms'

She pushes open the door, and we all shuffle carefully inside. We're in a long curving corridor that reflects the strange architectural shape of the building itself. The domed ceiling, several stories high, glistens like frosted dew. Balustrades show higher levels surrounding an atrium, open to the pitch-black sky above. In the middle stands another ice statue, giving us our first view of Maeve herself.

I don't doubt it's her, not for a minute. One only has to see the size of the castle and her ostentatious taste to know she'd not tolerate statues of anyone else dominating this internal courtyard. She's beautiful, of course, perfect in that alien way that humanoid fae are, her features crisp and radiant and utterly exquisite, yet still not natural, at least not to us. The eyes themselves are sharp and bright even in the statue, but they hold no compassion, no more than the rest of the face does. This is a regal being but one as cold as the material from which this tribute's carved. The sculptor has picked out the filigree of her wings in intense, excruciating detail, the fineness of the gossamer incomprehensible. It doesn't seem possible to have made anything so meticulous out of such a fragile material. I wonder how long it took the artist and whether love of craft or fear for his life drove him to such poignant perfection.

The children don't look at the sculpture with appraising eyes. Just with that subdued horror that comes from living with an abuser, with being terrified every waking second, where nights get spent reliving the horrors of the day, so you can't escape them even in your dreams. It breaks my heart and fuels my anger. I'd be tempted to drag Maeve out of bed and slap her upside the head if it wouldn't be insta-suicide for me and a slow lingering death for everyone else.

April doesn't even spare the statue a look. I guess after two hundred years of abuse, anything other than the real thing pales, even if I doubt her fear of Maeve has decreased at all over the centuries. If anything, continued exposure will probably have sharpened it. After all, she knows exactly what might, and probably will, come next.

April hurries past, down a corridor ahead, heading farther in, towards the front of the palace. The walls remain a crystal white, bowing slightly to allow the strange curving asymmetry of the building that the path mirrors. She turns right, then left, so that we should now be paralleling the previous route, but with the way the place twists, we could have done a one-eighty and I wouldn't be sure of it. Normally my sense of direction is unparalleled, so it makes me feel slightly nauseous and dizzy, my orientation lost.

I'm impressed by how silently the group of thirty-plus children have been moving down the corridor, although I'm aware it's because they know how much they have to lose rather than thanks to my inspirational pep talk. Now April flags us all down to a halt. She approaches the corner and peeks round it before pulling back and coming to join Aicha and me.

'It's round the next corner,' she says quietly. 'We've not got long until dawn. Looks clear.'

I frown. The Nain Rouge told us there'd be troll guards.

Now we can just walk in? Too easy sets my paranoia pinging. I turn to Aicha.

'Scout it out?' I'm not about to start giving her orders, but I don't doubt she'll move more silently and strike more effectively too if she encounters any enemies. Aicha doesn't even reply, just flows around the corner and is gone.

It only feels like a minute has passed before she reappears as silently as she left. In fact, even though I'm literally focused on the corner, waiting for her, her appearance still nearly gives me a heart attack. 'No guards,' she murmurs. 'No magical traps or alarms I could detect. Door looks unlocked.'

This is far too easy. I don't like it in the slightest, but time is pressing. We can't have much longer before dawn. I hesitate for a moment, but in the end, there aren't any other options, not that I can think of, at least. We herd the kids towards the door and lever it open with our scooting poles.

I half-expect to see the whole Winter Court sitting there waiting for us, but there's nothing. The room lies empty, which, considering how grandiose it is, makes it really, *really* empty. It's roofed, but it feels loftier even than the internal courtyard did, six or seven normal stories high at least. Tapestries drape down the walls from the very top, a riot of reds and greens and blues higher up. Lower down, the intricacies become clearer. There are depictions of all the different fae species I've ever heard of — and many I haven't — in tiny detail, with it divided into frames. I realise I'm looking at the faerie equivalent of the Bayeux Tapestry, that it depicts stories and legends of the Unseelie people. I'd find it fascinating if I wasn't so petrified about us all dying any second if we linger much longer.

The floor's covered in what looks like one solid piece of Italian marble, hewn entire and perfect out of the ground.

Seeing as how the room is the size of a small factory, I imagine there must be invisible seams I can't see, where pieces slot together. Either that, or they sliced the top off a mountain and took a solid chunk that had formed underneath. I'd say that is impossible, but we're dealing with the Queen of the Winter Fae. Possible is probably just a state of mind, as much as that sounds like the slogan for some sportswear company to berate the kids in their sweatshops with. I can imagine hers is mainly, 'I want it; make it so.' I doubt many people say no.

Her throne looks about as inviting as an RSVP to dinner with Jeffrey Dahmer. Situated on a three-tier raised dais, it carries on the ice/glass theme that predominates the entire estate. In fact, it seems to be a representation of the castle itself, with turreted strands jutting out and the entire structure seeming warped and twisted. I can see spikes sticking out in all directions, like someone made an ice sculpture of the *Game of Thrones* throne and then left it in the sun too long before shoving it back in the freezer and hoping nobody noticed. It definitely doesn't look designed with comfort in mind.

The far right-hand corner glows with dormant power. There's a ring of different-sized crystal structures, jagged crags jutting up towards the ceiling, gleaming dully from some internal radiance. Lower ones on the nearest side allow access by simply stepping over them. They remind me of the Fortress of Solitude from the early *Superman* movies. I don't doubt this is our ticket out of here.

It's wide enough that we can get everyone in there together, though we have to pick up a couple of the smaller kids and hand them over the lower crystal protrusions. Once everyone else is in, I step across, then turn to Aicha.

'Right, any idea how to activate this thing?' I look

around for a teleportation lever or a big red button marked PUSH ME TO GET THE FUCK OUT OF HERE, but sadly, both are lacking. I guess they wouldn't really fit in with the décor.

'Give me a minute, *saabi*. I'm trying to work it out.' Aicha's eyes are slightly unfocused, and I can tell she's *looking* at the portal, searching for how to activate it. 'I can see the key principles, but there's something missing, something we need that doesn't seem to be here.'

Suddenly my sight swims, and a vision hits me. I see the ring, the portal, and people passing through it. Payments and pain and pleasure. I can see emotional states, things human eyes shouldn't be capable of perceiving. I see the active back and forth across the portal, and I understand what is missing and where what I'm seeing is coming from.

I turn back towards the throne and watch as the air shimmers, and the perfect illusion disappears, leaving Queen Maeve and a good part of her court arrayed across the dais. The vision came from her.

What we're missing in order for the portal to operate is the queen's permission. And I don't think we're going to get it. Even if we say pretty please.

Chapter Sixteen

It sounded like true love, but what he actually said was, 'To Maeve,' which, as everyone knows, is to be a homicidal murdering fae lunatic.

Aicha swears in Arabic behind me and spits. She's disgusted, though whether with us for not spotting the illusion or the queen for trapping us or the fates for letting us get so close just to snatch victory away at the last moment, I can't say. 'She pulled a Han Solo wall decoration on us.'

Despite the terrifyingly dangerous situation we've found ourselves in, I'm too baffled to let that go. '*Star Wars* I get, but what?'

'Han Solo wall decoration. Make it nice and obvious where we want to get to, so we go rushing towards it and don't notice them all lying in wait for us. Which makes you' —she swivels and points at Queen Maeve, the Unseelie Queen— 'Jabba the Hutt, motherfucker.'

Maeve definitely doesn't look like Jabba, although

some of her assemblage wouldn't look out of place in Hutt Castle or the Mos Eisley Cantina either, for that matter. There are boggarts and bogies, gremlins and goblins. A Dullahan stands towards the rear, the eyes on the head under his arm stitched closed, his mouth sliced wide open. I wonder if he displeased the queen at some point or if this is his natural aspect. A glaistig clacks her goat hooves in glee to the side while a trio of mna sidhe, the plural of bean sidhe, cluster together, their whispering wails underlining the general hullabaloo the Court is making.

The queen is much like her statue, only *more*. More regal, more beautiful, more inhuman. More cold. To look at her is to feel the warmth of life, of joy, of hope and happiness leach away. She burns with the frost that would cover the world and smother out the sun, and she stares at us without blinking, drinking in the scene with a dark, malevolent pleasure.

Most of the children are already whimpering, terrified, and the sharp acrid tang to the air tells me at least one has lost control of their bladder. I can't blame them. I feel like pissing myself too. I'm just glad the Winter Queen has no idea who Jabba the Hutt is. Sadly, it seems she's inquisitive too.

Freezing tendrils run through my brain, and seeing how several of the kids nearest to me flinch, I'm sure she's doing the same to them. I see flickering images pulled from my subconscious of the scene from *Return of the Jedi*, except I can smell the Carbonite defrosting too, the slight trace of perfume that Jabba's pet detects on Leia, betraying her in the first place. The first hint of a satisfied smirk twitches the corners of Maeve's mouth. That disappears, though, when the images of Jabba himself appear.

Aicha swivels her attention to the mind-numbingly terrifying goddess-level powered fae in front of her.

'Yep,' she says to a creature who controls half a world, who has been the nightmare in the dark, stealing children on a whim for thousands of years. 'A giant hideous slug. That's you, that is. You're that slug. All schlurp, schlurp.' She mimes squelch-sliding her feet along the floor, having dispelled the Nain's magic on her shoes. We aren't trying to hide anymore, and it did us fuck-all good anyhow. I mutter the utterly ridiculous counter-acting phrase under my breath to do the same, getting ready for action. Talking of which, before Maeve concentrates her considerable power on obliterating us, I want to know if we were set up.

'Did the Nain Rouge come running straight back to Mommy then?' I ask, pulling her dour, weighted expression across to me, forcing her to take a break from trying to make Aicha explode with the sheer intensity of her glare. Although she probably wasn't because that's something she could most likely manage if she set her mind to it. Her expression clears, and she laughs, the first actual sound we've heard, like the tinkling of bells on a sleigh...loaded with *Mad Max* psychopaths armed to the teeth.

Again, images come flooding into my brain. I see myself walking through the falling snow of Winter. As it touches me, I feel the queen's awareness, expansive, covering all, caressing my skin through her subject precipitation. I groan at my stupidity. Of course. The snow is hers. It's a part of Winter. Not touching it with our feet doesn't help at all when it falls directly on top of us. I have no idea if the Nain was equally oblivious or sent us knowingly to our doom. I note he failed to mention we'd need Maeve's approval for the portal to operate, although I'm also aware I failed to ask him the question. Either way, it's beside the point.

Maeve knew we were here from nearly the moment we arrived in Winter.

We're totally fucked. She let this whole thing play out for her own amusement. She seems to pick up on that thought because suddenly I see the image of myself shooting backwards when trying to open the door of the building where she kept the kids locked up. It's dipped in spiteful mockery, dripping with hateful glee, and I feel a deep-seated sense of shame and failure. Which is weird because I didn't feel like that at all when it happened. I never expect myself to be graceful. Honestly, I'm amazed every day that I don't trip over and skewer myself on my sword. *Again*. But we don't talk about what happened at Cap D'Agde. Well, I don't. Aicha brings it up quite regularly.

I realise I'm feeling what Maeve expects me to feel. Not even what she feels, but what she believes is right in terms of my emotional response to the event. Forcing me to react a certain way to something I did internally? That pisses me off.

I can see by Aicha's face she's having a similar experience and is equally pleased about it. Normally, I'd feel sorry for whoever has incurred her wrath to such a degree, but as this time it's a psychotic, practically-divine fae queen, I'm more concerned about my friend's well-being than anything.

Aicha raises her eyes, burning coals deep under the shadows of her brow, and now it's a wonder that Maeve doesn't burst into flames under the intensity of her glare. 'Stay. Out. Of. My. Head. Bitch.' She grinds the words out through clenched teeth, furious rage clarion clear in every syllable.

Again I find myself assaulted by images. Now, it's just showing us Maeve. The background situation keeps changing — a ball, a banishment, a bedroom full of lovers, an execution, but none of that matters. The essence of Maeve assails us — her power, her utter and absolute control, her conviction as to her right to rule by force and might alone. The misery and worthlessness that all who look on her should feel floods through us.

'We get it.' Now Aicha sounds more bored than anything. I don't doubt it will greatly upset Maeve's planet-sized ego, which is surely the point. 'You're Galadriel if she took the one ring. A dark queen. All shall love you and despair. Blah blah blah.'

I feel Maeve rifling through my thoughts to search for what that reference means. Obviously, this one pleases her more than the Jabba comparison. Her thought-touch purrs, and that half-lip twist appears once more on her face.

Of course, Aicha isn't going to stand for that. 'Don't think you're all Cate Blanchett just because you look like someone dipped you in bleach. I'm going to punch holes in your wings, then kick you off the top of Mount Doom, you pretentious, brain-invading, cuntbungle-version of the Very Hungry Caterpillar.'

The arriving barrage of emotions and images drives me to my knees. Outrage and disbelief arrive from outside while my worthlessness and pathetic nature parade themselves simultaneously across my brain. I weep at how entirely useless I am, at the pointlessness of my existence, of ever having existed. Through the veil of tears, though, I see Aicha standing unbowed.

'Yeah, yeah, yeah. Lot of this' —she mimes an opening and closing mouth with her hand— 'but not much actual doing, is there? Tell you what. You're such a badass. I challenge you. One on one. To the death. Unless you're too afraid.'

I gawp and shake my head, trying to dislodge whatever is stuck in my ears causing me to hear wrong because it sounded like Aicha just challenged Queen Maeve to mortal combat. And not on a games console either. I dread to think what the fae royal's finishing move is. It's likely to make ripping heads off with the spine still attached look tame.

Maeve twists her head, and I can see her inquisitive insectile mind considering the problem. The challenge laid will diminish her authority if she refuses it, although I'm sure she's original and dedicated enough in her cruelty to brutally impose it again after. I can sense the waves of plea-surable anticipation washing off her though. She wants to tear Aicha to pieces. She's trying to work out if there is a trap in it or if it's simply arrogant over-confidence by the Druze warrior. The Dullahan, the headless fae, steps forward, hesitant in placing his foot but sure in his words. I don't doubt that Maeve has a direct line into his head. A head that he lifts now above his shoulders at full arm extension.

'No iron weapons, Druze,' he intones, his voice ringing out across the great hall. 'If you fight the queen, it will be without your steel blades.'

'I accept in exchange for an oath that none will involve themselves until the bitter end.'

Maeve inclines her head graciously, accepting the terms.

What the fuck? If I was shocked before, I'm entirely gobsmacked now. I've not managed to get back up off my knees, which is a good thing because that would have swept my legs out from under me. I assumed Aicha was planning on her steel katana, short sword, and knives to even the score. She can't go toe-to-toe magically, and the Winter Queen is a perfect physical specimen. I don't doubt she's highly trained in swordplay and warfare, having honed her skills over tens, if not hundreds of thousands, of years of existence. I can't see how this can end well.

Aicha starts stripping knives off, piling them with a clatter at her feet. It's quite astounding how many she carries. There's a veritable hillock of blades in front of her by the time she's finished. She brandishes a silver dagger, and I can see one or two others on her positioned for easy reach. 'Will you lend me a silver sword to replace my steel one? Or are you too afraid to face me as an equal?' Her distaste for the Unseelie carries in her voice as she stretches, limbering herself up for the forthcoming battle that she has precisely zero chance of winning.

There are no accompanying emotions or images. It looks like Maeve's concentrating on her forthcoming battle. Still, Aicha's words clearly get to her because the Dullahan draws an intricately guarded sabre from his own belt and proffers it up. Aicha advances cautiously and takes it, her eyes never leaving the queen, awareness covering the entire ensemble, then backs up to stand next to the portal again, putting herself between the fae and us.

It is horribly, terribly brave and utterly doomed to fail. Aicha is the single most badass warrior I've ever met. That doesn't mean she can defeat a millennia-old goddess of Winter and misery. I've always said before how there are no true immortals, that eventually we meet someone or something bigger and badder than us, and before we know it, it's game over, man, game over. I love Aicha for her valiant fearlessness. I just can't see her walking away from this after. Mind you, I can't see any of us walking away from this after. At least she's going to go down swinging. Perhaps that's the plan. Die gloriously rather than languish in torture for eternity. I only hope that when I die screaming at the queen's pleasure, I don't come back in

Aicha's body afterwards. I don't think my mind could handle that.

Maeve steps forward, the wings Aicha threatened to ruin fanning out behind her like a beauty pageant Angel of Death. Her dress should hinder her movement —hell, I don't understand how you can breathe in it, let alone fight — but she flows with impossible grace to the bottom of the dais. Her hand stretches out, and her sword appears. It's ethereal, glowing, and looks made of moonlight. It's got to be at least a metre long, and I don't doubt it can slice through anything and everything, up to and including titanium and probably reality itself. It makes me think of Lyra's subtle knife from the *His Dark Materials* trilogy. I wonder if this one, too, can cut through to other worlds, whether this is how Maeve opens the portal to Earth. For now, I'm more concerned about her cutting through Aicha.

The two circle each other, their blades pointed down and outwards, their guards open and inviting the first strike. The queen continues to flow, her movements unreal, impossible. That level of grace is something only normally seen in animation or CGI, and it screams that this is somehow manufactured, illusory. Aicha, on the other hand, is present in a way where she imposes herself on reality. She's entirely here, tight and coiled, so that the world fades around her. All that exists is her and her foe. These are simply the opening steps in the dance of death she's committed to.

Reality is clearly finding it all too much between the queen's uncanny agility and Aicha's condensed intensity, and probably wants to pop off for a lie down, preferably with a nice cup of tea and a hot water bottle. I wonder if there is room for one more in her cosy armchair. Who am I kidding? I know Aicha's doomed, but I still wouldn't miss this for the world. I'll watch to the bitter end, pay tribute to her bravery.

There have been many times where I've missed my *talent*. Being stuck in the endless night of that hellhole cave still holds the number one spot, but close behind it is this moment now. Obviously because it means I can't help (though I suspect if I piled in, so would the rest of the Unseelie Court, and even at my peak best, I would be far from a match for them all) but also because I can't really see what's going on now that they've both suddenly burst into action, bringing their swords clashing together.

They move too quickly, both charged up with magic and implausible skill levels. It's like trying to watch a Michael Bay action fight, only this isn't undecipherable because of terrible directing but because of the speed with which it takes place. Blades whip and shimmer, blurring into columns of light too fast to remain solid. They cut through the air so quickly, they make audible hums as they pass, and considering the speed, I wouldn't be surprised to hear a sonic boom. They seem to move faster than the speed of *light*, let alone sound. I've seen Aicha fight plenty of times against immeasurable odds, and still it feels like she's gone up another gear. I can't even really see her, just an impression of where she was a moment previous. The queen is also a blur, but somehow amid their deadly weaving of blades and bodies, I still catch sight of her face sometimes. She looks utterly composed, entirely serene, and it makes my heart sink.

When they pull apart, I literally bite my lip until I taste blood. It's better that than giving the queen the satisfaction of gasping out loud. The queen looks just as she did prior, almost bored and untouched. Yet Aicha...

Aicha looks *tired*. I've never seen her look tired before.

Sweat beads on her forehead and dribbles down her cheeks, and I can see the tremble of her muscles. The T-shirt and jeans she wears have been sliced, so that now it'd be more accurate to say she's wearing a thousand separate pieces of fabric, each held together by the tiniest of threads all dyed the darkest red. I can see the accompanying thousand cuts through the material and see them closing, healing but slower than usual. As I feared, the queen's magic is too powerful. Somehow it counteracts the Aab-Al-Hayat, the Waters of Life that gave Aicha her regenerative powers. Anger and terror tear me apart. Aicha is incredible, but Maeve is something else. And Maeve is toying with her.

They stand statue-like for a moment, then once more their rapid movements become an obfuscation. The pervasive odour of blood and sweat fills the place, and Aicha has leaked so much of both, I don't know how the two of them don't slip over the moment they move like some slapstick scene from the silent movies era. The clangour of sword against sword sounds like a Gatling gun firing over and over, and I see more than one kid press their hands over their ears at the terrible din. April moves, forcing them back and away, turning them towards the wall, using her body and the other older kids to block the view. None of them need to see this.

There's a cry, and Aicha and the queen break apart again. Aicha clutches the side of her head, burgundy spilling out between her fingers. As she pulls her hand away, I see her ear is gone. Maeve smiles, piranha needle teeth revealed, the missing appendage displayed on the point of her sword. She lifts it off delicately then pops it in her mouth like a piece of jerky, chewing it, her eyes still fixed on Aicha. My friend, the woman who saved me for the millionth and most important time from that cave, who's stepped up to save us all one more time, pulls herself straight-backed and moves her hand away to let the blood flow. She clamps her lips tight, whether to keep pain or profanity from spilling out, I don't know, and she charges once more.

I can't watch. It's just not possible between the mix of speed and my own tears. If I wouldn't dishonour her by doing so, I'd look away, but Aicha deserves my vigil as she falls. When they break away the next time, the queen has mostly sliced Aicha's nose from her face. Maeve angled the cut precisely, leaving us to stare at the nasal holes. Blood gushes down over her lips and neck. Aicha's eyes are still full of poise and fury even as the Winter Queen disfigures her bit by bit. I only keep my silence by the force of all my will, every inch I've ever had. I'll not give Maeve the pleasure of letting her hear my heart break. I'll not degrade Aicha's price-paying in such a way.

I think Maeve is tiring of her game now, like a cat who's batted the mouse bloody between her paws and is ready to move onto the next hunt. They clash and a second later stop for Aicha's blade clatters to the floor; Maeve has her sword point resting against Aicha's throat.

I can see Aicha's life bobbing up and down past the blade tip as she swallows, struggling not to choke on the blood pouring into her mouth, desperately trying to find an out, a way to get away and strike back at this evil bitch who keeps whittling her away. Maeve leans forward, leering, her perfect face ugly-twisted by the truth of her emotions. I know she's projecting her thoughts and feelings, her superiority and victory, directly into Aicha's head with all her force. She'll want her opponent to despair entirely, to read their death in her eyes before she dispatches them once and for all.

Aicha raises her left hand up, and for a moment I think she's going to slap the Unseelie Queen across the face, a last gesture of defiance to death and all who dare to be unjust. Instead, she wraps her fingers around the lethal blade. She shifts them forward, bit by bit, releasing and grabbing as blood runs down the blade. I think she means to reach the hilt, to push the guard away from her throat, an impossible act against the queen's superior strength. Maeve clearly thinks so too, watching with detached, malicious amusement like a kid with a bug under the magnifying glass watching it try to escape the burning beam they control. I'm sobbing but silently, my chest heaving without a noise. I'll not defile her final falling with my grief. The rest of my short time until Maeve makes sure I die will be spent mourning her loss. For now, I stand in tribute to her bravery. Nothing else.

Her fingers reach towards the top of the sword, grasping as far as she can reach, and I wait for them to grapple for the handle, for Maeve to tire of it and cut through her neck to finish her. As she nears the top, though, something peculiar happens. The sword suddenly flickers, dulls, then seems to diminish. It no longer looks like sharpened starlight. It just looks like a pretty silver sword. Confusion and panic arrive in an instant in Maeve's eyes, but before she can do anything, Aicha clenches her fingers and thumb tightly around the blade and severs them all off.

I gape. I don't know what I expected her master plan to be, but it wasn't that. Blood spurts out of where her fingers were, great gouts of red. But there's something else as well. The blood is darker than it should be, further down the colour spectrum than the usual purple-red, instead approaching black. In fact, I realise it is actually black-speckled, a cloud of particles mixed into it. As confusion starts to turn to hope, Aicha turns her hand towards Maeve and sprays her life fluid straight in the Winter Queen's face.

Maeve shrieks, a piercing cry like an eagle struck by a slingshot stone, and staggers backwards. She wipes furiously at the blood, not looking to devour Aicha's essence now, only to get it off her, like she's been spattered by acid. Her face steams where the blood struck, pock-marked, the skin cracking like porcelain hit with a hammer blow. Aicha's fingers reform and regrow, though her ear and nose remain missing for the time being. I guess whatever she did, when it extinguished the sword's glow, it also undid whatever power counteracted the Aab-Al-Hayat.

Aicha digs her right toes under her sword blade and flips it up to her waiting right hand as the queen screams in fury and confusion. Maeve swings her sword at Aicha wildly. Aicha parries with ease. Only not with her sword. Instead, with her left hand, letting the blade slice it cleanly in two. More blood vomits forth from the wound, and this time I see her *push* a black cloud out of her flesh to join with the geysering claret, and I understand what this incredible, endlessly inventive woman has actually done.

You can't carry iron filings in your blood. Even for someone Talented, you'd be constantly vomiting and shitting yourself, and your liver would fail in no time at all. However, if you have miraculous healing powers granted by the Waters of Life, then what you can do is embed iron filings down under the subcutaneous layers of your skin. Aicha didn't just dash headlong into Faerie as soon as she found a way across to rescue me. No, only an idiot like me would do that. She took the time to meticulously prepare a Hail Mary failsafe by implanting a last-ditch emergency option into her very flesh.

Several of the Court stir uneasily, torn between

defending their queen and their terror at what is happening. 'Your queen made a promise,' I yell to draw their attention. Their heads snap in my direction. 'If you break it, you'll break her power.' I know enough about the fae to be reasonably sure that's true. Promises and compacts are a form of truths, and the fae can't lie. Break Maeve's word? You break her power. Since none of them spring to her defence, it looks like I'm right. Either that or they're happy to use it as an excuse to hedge their bets.

Maeve backs away, still pawing at her face, still waving her sword at the advancing Aicha. Each time she does so, the Druze uses it to free more iron particles, although now everything regrows rapidly. Up comes the blade, and off comes her hand at the wrist, black clouds and blood spraying across the shrieking fae. Down goes the sword, and Aicha's arm comes up to meet it at the elbow, her arm flying free in an accompanying haze of iron that shoots up Maeve's haughty nose, down her throat, and into her ears and eyes like a thousand tiny flies biting and chewing their way towards her brain. She's ravaged now, crone-like, her face speckled with cracks and sores, her eyes opaque and crying blood. Aicha doesn't bother to meet her next unruly swing. Instead, she lops her own arm off at the bicep, severing it near to the shoulder, coating the blade in blood and iron from root to tip. Then she swivels on the spot and buries it straight through Maeve's right eye, pushing it through to the back of her head and then out the other side, placing the pommel against her shoulder to drive it all the way through and pin the immortal Queen of the Winter Court to the floor of her own throne room.

Maeve, the First of the Unseelie, Stealer of Children, Ruler of Nightmares, the embodiment of Winter itself, is dead.

A stunned, confused silence falls across the room. A grin spreads itself across my face, and I draw breath to cheer, to scream victory to the rooftops, to congratulate my best friend for achieving the impossible, but I don't get the chance. It's hard to form words when a knife suddenly sprouts from your left eyeball. I turn the other eye, confused, looking to work out what happened, only to realise Aicha threw one of her silver blades straight into my brain.

Oh, I think just before I fall to the ground. *I didn't see that coming.*

Chapter Seventeen

SAINT-OUEN, 21 FEBRUARY 1973

The two supposed far-right commandos have cut and run, and we aren't any closer to finding the actual coffin.

I glance across at the other two. 'Any ideas?'

Al-Ruhban looks blank, Aicha irritated. 'Back at square one, right?'

I'm not sure where she's going with this. 'Right?'

I can see her mentally counting down to one from a number sufficiently high enough for her to wrestle her temper to the ground. Based on how long she's taking, I reckon it's in the region of seven digits.

'What did you do the first time?' she finally says.

'Oh. Oh!' It clicks. Her frustration is entirely justified. My stupidity is considerable. 'Got you.'

I ignore the muttered, 'About time,' and take the Paris map out of my storage, along with the vial of earth. I planned to use them to lead us down the street to the garage itself. Having built that into my head as a plan of action, I completely failed to think about how I initially put it to work to find the coffin.

Once more, I sprinkle the imbued dirt across the map, starting as close as possible to where I estimate us to be right now. The last of the granular earth scatters across Saint-Ouen before coalescing, swirling like the world's smallest dust devil around the map. They break apart down side roads, join on boulevards, and move back and forth across the paper surface, seeking the coffin like a pack of earthen bloodhounds.

Suddenly, they dance back over our current location, up the avenue, and over the waters of the Seine itself, stopping at the tail of a banana-shaped island following the shape of the river. The miniature dust devil falls apart and is gone.

Aicha peers at the map. 'The Ile De Vannes,' she reads. It isn't far at all, about a ten-minute drive over the Saint-Ouen bridge. She looks across at Al-Ruhban. 'Coming?' she asks.

His smile lights up the room, seeming to chase the shadows from the garage. He gives a shallow bow. 'Wouldn't miss it for the world.'

Damn, he's a charming fucker. We hustle back out of the garage to my Citroen. Aicha snatches the keys out of my hand. I don't complain too much. I'm exhausted, and as I said, it's her party. She can cry if she wants to. Though I suspect it'll be whoever absconded with the coffin who cries in the end.

As we drive, I plug Al-Ruhban for information. 'What can you tell us about the island? What's there?'

I can see his reflection in the rear-view mirror giving my question significant thought. 'Well, first, it's not really an island. Well, it is, but it's connected to the Ile Saint-Denis. They used to be separate, apparently, but it's one landmass now. It's a green space — at the two opposite ends of the entire island, at least. There's a huge sporting complex there. Only got completed a couple of years ago. Indoor football courts, swimming pools, the lot. They even do concerts there.'

Aicha looks across at me, catching my eye, and I can see she's had the same thought I have. Mighty convenient that there's a huge brand-new building pretty much where the soil indicated. Still, I need to be sure.

'Any other buildings over there?' I ask Al-Ruhban.

He shakes his head. 'Not as far as I know. Maybe a public toilet? It's not somewhere I go regularly.'

I doubt that these Nazi fuckers or whatever they are plan to hide out in some public toilets. That means they're either outside in the grounds of the surrounding park —a brave move during a February night in Paris— or they're in the sporting complex somewhere or other.

We pull up shortly before reaching the building's car park. I want to see the park at the front first; plus, it won't do to announce our arrival. We abandon the car at the start of a footpath under a hasty *don't look here* spell. The park itself is pitch-black and away from the road, but I draw a small amount of *talent* in, enhancing my night vision, making it easy to scan the park and see what's there. I'm far from running on empty *talent*-wise, but I've not slept in almost twenty-four hours, and I'm not on my home turf. I'm pretty much constantly tapping into my power now, using it to keep myself moving, and if I piss it away, I'll end up tapped out and in need of a serious sleep before I know it. I hope this isn't going to take much longer, but the whole mission has already taken a couple of unexpected turns. It seems entirely plausible it might take a few more, seeing as this is my life we're talking about. Me and Simple aren't on speaking terms. Not even a card at Christmas. Every time I try to show up and make things right with her, her big brother Mind Bogglingly Difficult slams the door behind him as he steps out onto the porch, rolling up his sleeves.

The grass in front of La Grande Nef, the sporting complex, is a wide open space with trees dotted at the periphery. There's a running track closer to us, but it's equally exposed. Even under the cover of darkness, there aren't many places to be unobtrusive, especially if you're lugging a coffin with you. I give it a good *look* over to be sure, then drop the night vision, conserving my power.

'Nothing out there,' I say, turning to the others. That only leaves one option.

The building itself is impressively modern, a vast semi-circle of glass panels seeming to bulge out of the parabola arch. The curves and the way they dominate the horizon bring to mind a much more simplistic version of the Sydney Opera House. As we make our way around to the front, I change my opinion and mentally salute the architect. There's a curved archway entrance that makes me think of an insectile head, and the two sides holding glass become like the wings of a butterfly, the concrete between them dipping in the middle to add to that sense of separation. It's beautiful. At least *I* think so.

Aicha pulls a face. 'Too much concrete.' I'm not sure if she means this building or the modern world. Either way, I can sort of see her point even while appreciating these specific aesthetics.

The main double doors remain sealed and locked, which causes me no end of worry. They've not forced their way in, not here at least. That means either they have keys, or they've broken in through a side door, or they aren't here. The last thought, the really concerning one, disappears when Al-Ruhban pulls up suddenly. A look of concern spreads across his face.

'Sorcery.' His lips thin, drawing back, the distaste clear on his face.

I look over at Aicha for clarification. She draws closer to me. 'Half-djinn are very sensitive to magic. Makes them very useful as magical treasure detectors for sorcerers. Also makes their body parts highly sought after for spells.'

Oh yeah. Duh. If I were a go-to chop-shop for magic users, I'd probably dislike and avoid them like the plague too.

In the meantime, that complicates our situation considerably. A sleep-deprived fight with a bunch of unTalented Nazi thugs is a whole different scenario to whatever fucked up craziness we've now stumbled into. 'You didn't say anything about magic,' I hiss at Aicha.

'Didn't know anything about it. Make a difference?'

I think it through. 'Guess not.'

'Stop bitching then.'

Fair point. I look over at Al-Ruhban. 'You don't have to come, you know.'

The affronted look to his expression tells me he doesn't appreciate my concern. 'This is my area! Or will be soon, hopefully. Do you think it will impress Léandre if he hears I scuttled away because there might be sorcerers at work? Not likely to speak volumes either to my courage or ability to hold this place. If I am to have the Prince confirm my position, I need to impress. Not disappoint.'

He points a large finger at me. 'You can stay. I can handle this.' For the first time, I see his hands. Words and shapes, like tribal tattoos, cover them, but they shift like shadows flickering behind a moving light source. It's eerie, to say the least.

Brilliant. I've handled this with the same amount of tact and diplomacy I normally manage. I hold my hands up in the universal sign for "I surrender". 'My apologies, Al-Ruhban. As Aicha warned you so eloquently, I am a twat. Sometimes, anyhow.'

I scrutinise him, ignoring the muttered, 'Too true,' from Aicha behind me. He watches me back, his brow furrowed. Then the tension evaporates, his wrinkles relax, and he laughs a sharp barking laugh like an amused seal.

'I like you, Paul the Twat,' he says and then looks puzzled when I wince.

'No, sorry, Twat Paul was a racist copper back on the Ile D'Yeu; can't use that name,' I say. 'I'm Not Twat Paul Who's Sometimes a Twat, if that's okay?'

He arches an eyebrow at me. 'I'll just call you Paul then.'

'Just call him twat,' Aicha says helpfully.

'One or the other,' he agrees and turns his attention to the door itself.

It's a two-part arching door made of the same sheet metal as the wall it's melded into, almost indistinguishable. Al-Ruhban places his right hand on the handle, his thumb covering the keyhole. The black ink-like substance rushes up his hand to fill his thumb, and his thumb then merges with the lock. It's a weird effect. It just suddenly looks like his hand is a part of the door or else, the door is an extension of his hand.

He stays like that for a few moments. Then we hear a click and the door springs open. As it does so, his hand disengages. He shakes it out a couple of times as though it went to sleep and he's trying to work feeling back into his fingers, then shoves the hand in his pocket. I guess those black marks are an integral part of his magic, though I don't know if it's the same for the djinn or just because he's half-djinn. They also probably make it easy to spot him, to identify what he is. No wonder he keeps his hands in his pockets most of the time.

He nods sideways at the open doorway. 'After you, Twat,' he says with a toothy grin.

With a smile, I thank him through gritted teeth. Getting Aicha back for that one just became a priority. I brush past her and head into the Grande Nef.

Chapter Eighteen

I'm used to Aicha shooting daggers at me. Just normally it's
metaphorical rather than actual daggers.

My eye snaps open. Just the one, although it's not my left
that's closed this time but my right. Even as I think that, I
feel the reincarnation magic fixing it, repairing the damage,
and both eyes pop open to see Aicha hovering over me, a
smug grin on her face.

The first thing that hits me is the realisation. The next
thing is…*ohshitohshitttttttoohhhhhhhhhhmyyyyyyfuuuuuucckkkkkkiiii-
inggggggggggooooodddddgggggooooooooodddddddddddddd…*

Never have I felt power like this. I'm not just Talented;
I'm *talent* itself. I'm the source of all *talent* in Winter, and
Winter is nothing more than a simple expression of me.
With a thought, I can remake the castle — in fact, I do,
straightening out some of those bizarre twisted kinks that
bothered my eyes. I can make it snow; I can *feel* it snow. I
can feel the blanket it makes drape over me because I am

the land — it's just an extension of my personality. I feel everyone who moves over my skin inside my borders and know they draw breath at my allowance, that I can stop the breath of any who have pledged themselves to my Court with a thought. Omnipotence thrills through me, the sensation of being everywhere at once.

No wonder Maeve expressed herself telepathically. Words are so limited. Worlds are so limited. I'm a god. I'm...

Suddenly, I'm clutching my jaw at a sharp pain as my head snaps back. My concentration narrows, limiting itself to where my physical form is. I've been slapped! Who has dared? Who has dreamed they might lay hands upon me...

'I dared, dickhead. Chill out on the ego trip. Now.' I concentrate on the face, on the eyes I know, on the words. Pulling myself back, I throttle the *talent* flowing through me, forcing myself into the limitations of a single space, one that's physical rather than liminal.

'Okay.' I puff and pant, trying to centre myself, to hold on to who I am rather than be subsumed in Winter. 'I'm back. I've got it under control. For now.'

Aicha curves an eyebrow at me. 'Good. Between making the whole place shake when half the palace suddenly shifted and you giggling maniacally with glowing green eyes, you were making the kids nervous.' She pulls me to my feet, then scans me up and down. 'Also, you're a beautiful elfin queen. Congratulations. Best look you've ever had.'

I look down at a body that definitely, one hundred percent does not look like mine. Seems my reincarnation magic has met its match trying to force the "packed with magic down to a cellular level" Unseelie queen's corpse to match what I think I look like. Speaking of which...

I reach out to the land to interrogate every inch of

Winter. Every iced leaf, every fallen snowflake, every ice particle of the building itself. There's a certain fae-body-wearing fucknoggin I want to get my hands on. I'm ready to pour my now abundant *talent* out, to make the land pull him down into its cragged icy heart, rending him on every sharp piece of rock on the way. Let him go down into the dark...

But he's not here. Not only that, but he's not been here. Either De Montfort didn't come through Winter, or he somehow did a better job than we did sneaking past Maeve's attention. I doubt the latter, but I'll keep an open mind. Until I can get ahold of him and open his. With a buzz saw.

I swallow down my disappointment and turn to Aicha. 'That was quick thinking, *laguna*. Absolute genius. Kill me quickly, get me in the queen's corpse, make me the fairest of them all.' I try giving a twirl a go, but even wearing this body, I'm aware I look like a fourteen year old who just had an overnight growth spurt and is trying to dance for the first time in their life. Ah well, it's the thought that counts.

'Please. Don't ever do that again. Not in front of my good eyes.' Aicha sits down heavily on the floor. I suddenly realise two things. First, she's no longer mutilated. Apparently, the death by iron of the original Maeve was enough to undo that. Second, she has to be knackered. Completely kaput.

I lean closer and lay my hand on her shoulder. 'Aich?' She lifts her head to look at me, and I let her see the pride in my eyes, the awe and utter amazement at what she achieved. 'That? That was the. Best. Kill. Ever. Title is all yours.'

She smiles — a wan, sapped smile. '*Shukran*.' Aicha Kandicha saved us. Saved me yet again.

I look over at the Unseelie Court. *My* Unseelie Court

now and sweep an imperious glance over them all, waiting to see if any are foolish enough to step forward and challenge me. If it's going to happen, it'll happen now. No one moves. They look like they've all been turned into statues, like they've been touched by the White Queen of Narnia's wand. I doubt any of them thought what occurred would ever happen. Guess they need some time to adjust.

My eyes come to rest on the Dullahan, his sewed-closed eyes. 'You, sir.'

He starts, apparently sensing I'm addressing him even if he can't see.

'What was it that you did that was so terrible Maeve sewed your eyes shut?'

The headless horseman looks like he'd love nothing more than to leap onto his ghostly steed and ride at a gallop for the hills. 'Erm, if it please you, my lord — er, lady — er… Your Highness.' *Good save*, I think wryly. 'I am — well, was — well, depending on Your Grace, Your Nobleness, I have held and could still hold the position of chamberlain.'

'Riiight.' I nod empathetically before realising it's a completely wasted gesture. 'It's lovely to know your role in the Court, but why the Coraline eye surgery?'

'Oh, yes, right, of course, My Liege — erm, My Good Ruler.' It's painful watching him struggle to find gender-neutral terms, not sure which one's appropriate. But as was ever the case, there are plenty of options available. You just have to train your brain to stop thinking in such rigid, limited ways. Check it out — only ruler of the Unseelie for moments, and I've already brought them into a new, more tolerant reality. 'Well, you see, the previous queen always expected I show her full attentiveness. One time, there was a bean sidhe who came before us, a wondrous creature.'

I see one of the two mna sidhe, standing nearby, preen,

and I can't help wondering if the Dullahan has been that close to her for an age, never realising the proximity.

'Anyhow, the queen, yourself, or your predecessor, if you will, um, she judged I looked at this bean sidhe longer than I did at her. Said I'd gazed in her direction for over ten seconds and that it was an inappropriate action. I assured her I would never do such a thing, would never act inappropriately. Well, she acknowledged that, so she did, Your Nobleness. Said in which case it must have been my eyes that had acted independently, and they alone should be punished.' His shoulders droop. 'So she did this.'

I know we're in the land of the Unseelie, at the heart of the Winter Court, and human kindness isn't a trait I should expect to see. But I also understand that the land, the Court, the Unseelie themselves, are all, to a degree, a reflection of the ruler. I can hear the land telling me of times gone by.

I can hear it, and I have to quiet it down because if not, it'll drown me in the songs and histories it wants to sing in my ears. What with the room being packed full of murder-loving faeries, I can't listen to it all, but I know there were different times. When the world was still cold and cruel but with a thread of connection and love of sorts between the land and the Court, the people and the place. When the portals closed, when Maeve became limited due to the mortal realm being closed off to her, she changed, and the land changed with her. She came to see Winter as a prison of sorts, to hate it, to want to reach out and take more or break it at the very least, like a jealous kid in another's playroom, snapping and bending and ruining everything to cover up what they lack inside themselves. Any affection withered away and died, taking the joy of this place —wild and shadowy and icy as it was— and replacing it with nothing but an empty dark. Her feelings, or at least the feelings she smothered the Court in, take me back to my own recent traumas, and when I shiver, it isn't from the cold.

I feel no guilt at all about having rid Winter of Maeve. By any definition of a good ruler —and I don't mean good as in kind and loving; that's not how to define a good Unseelie ruler. I mean good as in doing the job they're supposed to do— she failed long ago. She took the children not because she needed to keep connected, to understand the mortal realm as Oberon did with the Cagots. She took them for spite, to break and bring all her petty anger at humans down on the heads of the most vulnerable. I'm glad she's dead. And by the feel of it, so is a good section of her court, probably the majority.

Relieved as I am, that's beside the point. I came here for a reason — to rescue the kids and head home. That's what I need to do as quick as possible so we can get back onto De Montfort's trail, find out where he is, and what the hell he's up to, why it was so important for him to get me out of the way. I turn to Aicha and offer her a hand up. She must be exhausted because she accepts it, letting me haul her to her feet.

'Ready?' I ask her.

'Born ready. Fuck Faerie. No offence intended.' She holds up an apologetic hand to the baffled Dullahan that he still can't see. Actually, regarding that, I make a decision.

I walk over to the fae and pluck his head out of his grasp, ignoring his squawk of confusion. Head in hands — his head, my hands— I study the craft Maeve worked on him. Then with a simple thought, it is undone.

The Dullahan opens his eyes and blinks in wonder. I pass the head back to him and give him a nod. 'Let that be a start, Dullahan. The worst of Maeve's ignominies and excesses need to be undone. You can all follow this example once I'm gone.'

I turn away, but an embarrassed cough from stomach height brings my attention back round. 'Gone, my lad.. lor…worship? You can't go.'

I sigh, a gentle smile on my face. Of course. Of course they want me to stick around, to show them the right way to behave, a new, better path. I'm already influencing them, changing them. Why wouldn't they want that to continue? 'I'm sorry, Dullahan; really, I am. I understand what a difference me being in charge is making, how it's changing your lives entirely already, but I can't stay. I've got other people who rely on me.'

The Dullahan looks shocked. He secures his head under his right arm, freeing his left hand to flap at me, shooing away my words. 'No, no, no. I think you'll be terrible as queen. You don't understand the ways of the fae at all. I meant you literally can't leave. When Maeve closed most of the portals to keep the angelic hordes out, she tied herself to the land completely. The queen can never leave Faerie however much she wishes to.'

Ouch. I notice some of the wheedling politeness has dropped out of his words, along with the gender-neutral language. Apparently, he's replaced them with blunt insults. I hear Aicha give a coughed, 'Wanker,' under her breath, though I'm not sure if it's aimed at him or me. Probably both of us, to be fair.

Meanwhile, I can feel my panic rising. I thought it a super smart move by Aicha, killing my last body, letting me hijack the dead queen's corpse so I can open the portal. Now it looks like I've trapped myself, tying myself to this freezing shithole of a country in a world I hate with a passion. It might be less dark, but it won't be any less of an eternal imprisonment than the cave was, and I can feel my heart palpitating, the sweat building in my palms. Plus, I doubt they'll allow a body-jacking human to remain in charge for long.

Fae *talent* is still alien to me, even being mind-bogglingly tooled up to the nines with it, and someone can easily slip a knife into my back at the earliest opportunity. Then I'll be back in a weaker form, fae or human, and doubtless members of the Court will take the opportunity to demonstrate exactly how displeased they were by my rule, repeatedly. Forever.

And none of this is helped by Maeve's wardrobe choices. I still haven't got used to the fact I now have breasts, magnificent or otherwise, and I keep catching sight of them out of the corner of my eye and getting distracted, wondering all over again what's stuck to my chest. Combined with a corset that has half my internal organs feeling like they're being forced up inside my throat and the rest like they are about to be squeezed out the other end and an increased heart rate like an amphetamine head keeping rhythm with some gabba techno beating on the inside of my chest with his glow sticks, it makes it feel like my entire body is not only the wrong size but about to pop from the pressure like Arnie's eyeballs in *Total Recall*.

Apparently, becoming the Fae Queen of Winter doesn't protect you from high-grade panic attacks. Good to know.

Chapter Nineteen

Trying to control the rising panic but definitely fae-ling.

I don't know if Aicha sees or senses my growing anxiety. Either way, a moment later she's by my side and lays a calming hand on my arm. I get my breathing back under control and let her take the lead.

'Okay, do they have to stay as the queen?' she asks the Dullahan. It's weird being addressed by gender-neutral pronouns —I still entirely identify as male even if my body is biologically female— but it's a good educational opportunity for the fae and might help keep the Dullahan's disconnected head from exploding, trying to work out how to address me.

'They?' he asks puzzled. 'There is only one of her... him...er...'

'They.' Aicha leans forward. 'The word you are looking for to stop the new all powerful — albeit also all dickhead — ruler from doing the kaboom' —she mimes a miniature mushroom cloud between her hands— 'with your newly seeing head is *they*. Gender neutral before you —' Her eyes flick downwards for a moment. 'Get gender *neutered*.'

'They, got it.' He bobs his head at a speed almost faster than his Adam's apple whips up and down his throat. I'm surprised it doesn't launch out of the top of his neck like a bottle rocket. 'Oh no, they can abdicate anytime. Simply select their heir and then they can pass the crown on to whoever they choose.' He puffs his chest out, trying to stand regally. He thinks, as the only one of the Court we've actually spoken to and the one we've gone out of our way to actually help, he'll be the natural choice. Thing is, he might have fucked up with Maeve, but he also served her for, well, who knows how long? Long enough that I seriously doubt he disapproved of her methods unless they impacted directly on him. Perhaps, given time, he could change, but handing over the reins to an entire reality is hardly likely to help him control his worst character traits.

But if I don't give it to him, then to who? I don't know any of these creatures, and it's a similar problem. This is the inner court, the highest ranking Unseelie nobles, the people who clustered around Maeve and didn't get destroyed in the process. I suspect they're all similarly bad or at least close enough as makes no actual difference. I consider going out into the wildernesses of Winter and finding someone at random to hand over the crown to. Problem is, it doesn't mean they will be any better. Just that they're potentially antisocial as well as homicidal. Not an improvement to add into the mix.

Thing is, I need someone who can control these insanely beautiful, insanely insane fuckers. Someone who knows who the worst of them are, who will anticipate their backstabbing and betrayal and can lead them towards... Well, not being nicer. They aren't nice; it isn't part of who they are. But they've strayed away from their own truths too, their connections with their element, being in harmony with Winter rather than dominating it. They can be cold and dark and still have their own weird joys and pleasures. This place feels like it's been drained of everything but spite and danger for a very long time. They need someone who can understand that. Who can understand them, who is part of their world, part of the fae…

I clock the answer and instantly hate myself for it. Looking up, I catch Aicha's eye and see the same thought reflected. No doubt she got there before me, but Good God bless her, she gave me the space to arrive at the same conclusion. It sucks. Totally sucks. Sadly, I know it's the only option.

'It has to be her choice,' I whisper, muted, and Aicha gives me a sharp nod of agreement. I turn back to the Dullahan who's still acting as self-appointed spokesperson of the assembled Unseelie.

'If you'll excuse us for a moment?' I smile reassuringly. It makes him rear back in sheer terror. The expression obviously isn't quite what I was aiming for when placed on the face of someone so murderously insane. I try again, keeping my face more neutral. 'I need to discuss with my colleagues. We'll be with you in a jiffy.'

We head back towards the group that's huddled together in the portal. More than one of them stumbles backwards, clearly terrified at seeing me approach. Of course. They've no idea how my magic works. I exchange a look with Aicha, and she goes first, gathering them around her and explaining what's happened in a low tone. I can tell the point when she says Maeve's dead, that they are free, and can return home because almost all of them burst into tears, even several of the older ones, although most of those still just look lost and confused. Of course, they aren't going home to their families. They're going to a world they never lived in, that might as well be an entirely different one because it will be so completely different to both what they knew and what they've lived since coming to Faerie. Culture shock doesn't even begin to cover it. That is a problem for after though. We can worry about helping them to acclimatise once I make sure I can be there to accompany them.

And then there's April.

Leaning back against the rear wall, she separated herself from the group as soon as Aicha explained Maeve was dead. I doubt she even realises she's running her hands over her ear points, subconsciously identifying her difference. From the rest of the kids, from the rest of humanity. She had that almost entirely taken away from her. Now? I'm about to ask her to give up the very last remnant.

I walk over and lean on the wall next to her. Kicking one foot back onto it casually proves to be difficult in the flowing ballgown, twisting myself up inside the folds. Giving up on trying to look relaxed, having successfully completed the "adult trying to look cool to a teenager and making themselves look like a twat" dance, I brush down the pleats and nudge her gently with my elbow. 'How are you doing, April?'

'Pretty shit considering this is what I dreamed about every day since she — you — *she* got her hands on me.' She gives that same sharp barking laugh she gave when we first met, when she was in the cage. Now I'm going to ask her to walk into a new one.

I nod, genuinely sympathetic. I know what it means to become part of the Talented world unwillingly. 'It's not easy being different, having *power*. But you won't be alone if you go back. You can weave a glamour so normal humans won't even see your differences. And Aicha and I will be around, although we've got some pressing matters to deal with once we get back to Earth. There are other Talented people, good people who'll help you out, let you get used to being more than human in the normal world.'

Her head shoots up, her eyes fixing on me, curiosity and alarm flitting back and forth across them. She's picked up on it, of course. I never doubted how much of a sharp cookie she is. 'What do you mean, *if* I go back?'

I sigh and rub my arms as though trying to warm them. A pointless action when you're the embodiment of Winter, but old habits die hard. 'There must be a ruler of Winter. Only the ruler can activate the portal, but the ruler can't leave.'

Her eyes widen further as she realises what I want. In a second, she's upright, her hands thrown up in horror, backing away slowly like I've just threatened her with a loaded gun. Which I guess, metaphorically speaking, I have. 'Oh no, no way. No chance at all. I don't want to...'

I hold a hand up to calm her, to stop her panicking. 'You don't have to. It's a choice, okay? I won't make you. Nobody will. Basically, I can send you all home, all right, and then I'll hand the mantle on to one of the fae here. If I extract an oath from...' I sigh, looking around. 'Whoever I end up giving it to, I should be able to get back safely and get them to shut the portal so no more kids ever get taken. I'll prob-ably give it to the Dullahan if you don't take it.'

'The Dullahan!' she hisses, furious. 'No way! He's worse than Maeve was. She might have taken his eyes officially for looking at another woman, but I think it was because she knew he was plotting a coup behind her back. It was only because the rest of the Unseelie knew he'd be even more vicious than Maeve as ruler that it failed. They were desperate for change, just not desperate enough to let him take the reins.'

I chuckle. 'Take the reins, good one.'

She looks at me blankly, then snorts. 'Oh right, yeah. Headless horseman, taking the reins. Totally unintentional.'

'You see though?' I press the point, ignoring her comment about my pun. For the sake of the fae we're leaving behind, I have to try. Some of them must be decent folks, and they deserve better than being subject to the whims of a sadistic, mad ruler. 'I've got no idea about Winter Court politics, about who is trustworthy, who will do the right thing.'

She laughs again, bitterly. 'None of them. None of them will do the right thing. They're all either too twisted or too conditioned by fear. None of them ever did it the whole time I was a prisoner here.'

I take a deep breath. 'So there are no good options. If I leave one of them in charge, there's two problems. If they're really motivated, however much I try to make the language of the oath watertight, they can re-open a portal later on. Fae are brilliant at twisting promises to the very limit of not breaking them. Second…'

I sigh. 'It'll never get better here. I'm connected to the land, April, although I've had to smother it a bit because otherwise I'm going to go batshit insane.' Good work, Paul. Brilliant description. I see the terror in her face and try to reassure her. 'Because I'm not fae despite what I'm wearing flesh-wise. It's too much, too far from my reality. If I let that connection really blossom, it will try to turn me into a ruler of Faerie. That can only happen if I stop being the human Paul Bonhomme, and I won't do that. Not willingly. So the battle between my will and the will of Winter will tear me apart. If someone were already fae, already connected to that part of themselves, and willingly took on the mantle of the land, it would be entirely harmonious. A proper partnership. And then…'

I look at this improbable girl in front of me, neither entirely human nor completely fae, over two hundred years old, and still a frightened kid. It feels so unfair to even offer her this, to make her choose. I hate myself for saying this, for saying any of it, but I still do.

'Then,' I say slowly, deliberately, 'whoever rules Winter can reshape it. They can heal the disconnect between the crown and the land and bring it back towards a harmonious union. They can lead the Unseelie back to where they once were. Not' —I hold up a warning finger— 'into being human. Not into a human understanding of morality. But…' I sigh again. This is harder than I imagined. 'There could be joy here again. A colder kind of happiness than you remember back on Earth, maybe, but a real one nonetheless.'

As I speak, a single tear slides down April's cheek. 'Just because I've suffered unending misery here, who told you I was ever happy before they took me?'

Automatically, I want to stutter out apologies and excuses, but I bite them back. They'll do no good and won't show due respect for her honesty. I realise I know nothing of her story, really, nothing other than my gut instinct that she's a good person, worthy of my trust. If her life was awful both before they took her and has been since, that only makes it even more impressive.

'You can change that. You can bring some justice, some understanding to this place. You can be the guiding star of Winter's night.'

'That's it! Perfect!' Aicha suddenly pipes up beside me, so close I nearly jump out of my skin.

Once I'm sure I'm not about to drop dead from a heart attack, I turn a glare in her direction. 'What is, apart from your ability to scare me to death?'

'April, do you have a last name?' There is an intensity to Aicha's demand, an insistence April delivers the answer she wants.

April shakes her head. 'Last names were for nobles and thespians, not for the likes of us.'

Holy shit. Last names came into use in the later Middle Ages. She's not just over two hundred years like she thinks. She's over four…

Aicha punches the air. 'Brilliant. So either way, if you're going to be queen here or come back to the human world, you should have a last name. The comment about being a guiding star gave it to me. We'll call you Nighte.'

'Night?' I'm baffled.

'Yeah, but with an E at the end. Nighte.'

I try to work it out. This is obviously some sort of cultural reference. I just need to work out Aicha's thought process. Then I click what she means and groan.

'April Nighte,' I say flatly, fixing Aicha with a stare. 'A half-fae forced to be nobility. No, just no.' Trust Aicha to shoehorn a cultural reference in.

'Why not?' There's an almost petulant tone to Aicha's voice. She hates being thwarted when she thinks she's being a genius.

I don't really have a good reason other than it's just a rubbish joke. However, the choice gets taken away from me.

'I like it.' April says, pulling my attention back to her, and that, as they say, is the end of that. She is now April Nighte. Job done.

'Sylvester would be very unimpressed,' I hiss at Aicha as she walks away.

'Sylvester's an arsehole. Fuck him.' Fair point, well made. Mind you, I only wish the fae were as kindly as the creatures in Ms McGuire's books. I also suspect life might be even harder for April than it is for October Daye.

I drag myself back to the matter at hand, which is considerably more important than whether or not it's a good literary reference. 'Okay, April.'

'April Nighte.' Aicha's voice carries from behind me.

'April Nighte.' I manage to grind the words out without snapping all my teeth, which is a win, all things considered. 'The decision is yours. You don't have to stay here. If you do, you'll be queen and get to rule over all these fucknuts who treated you so terribly for the last two hundred years. You can decide whether to punish them for it or guide them to a better future. Honestly? It's not my problem. All I'd need is an oath to send us home and close the portal. The rest is up to you. Or you can come back to the human world and leave them to clean up their own mess or not, as the case may be. Take a minute; think about it.'

I leave April, newly April Nighte, and head over to join Aicha. She's cleaning off the silver sword she took from the Dullahan. I don't think he's going to get it back. Sucks to be him. She looks from it to me with a calculating gaze.

'You could give her a knighthood, you know, in the meantime,' she says. 'Just while she's making her mind up on what to do.'

I massage my aching temples with my fingertips. 'I'm not doing it, Aich. Just because you want her to be Sir April Nighte. It's not happening.'

She mutters something that sounds like, 'Spoilsport,' under her breath, but other than that, she accepts it with good grace. I plump down next to her, which isn't the most graceful of manoeuvres in a ballroom gown, especially given I nearly take her eye out with my wingtip. First thing I'm doing when we get back is buying some jeans and a T-shirt. And a large baggy jumper. Having boobs when you don't expect to —and when you get attacked in weird and unexpected ways as often as I do— is a whole world of breast-induced jump scares.

'How are you holding up?' I ask, giving her a nudge with my elbow.

'Fine. Just dandy,' she says, nudging me back twenty times as hard with the sharpest part of hers. Ouch.

'You absolutely slew it out there, you know.' I bask in the moment of companionship, even if the madness is swirling all around us. I'll take this second before we plunge back in. 'You were incredible. One could say you were amaeve-ing even.'

Aicha groans. 'That's awful, *saabi*.'

'Honestly, you were mab-nificent.'

'Enough! My ears are bleeding.'

'It was an enormous victory. One could even say titania-c.'

'Fuck my life.'

It's good to have Aicha back by my side. It's even more fun annoying the hell out of her.

Chapter Twenty

If I'm going to be a fairy, can I be the Tooth Fairy? I'll
make a fortune considering how many jaws I break
regularly. And sometimes they aren't even my own.

I can hear the mutterings and murmurings of the Unseelie
nobles, can see out of the corner of my eye the Dullahan
conferring with them. I don't doubt he's calming them
down. I also don't doubt he's laying the foundations to get
them riled up again if I don't do what he wants — abdicate
and hand over control to him. Not going to happen. Whatever April's decision, that problem will need addressing.

I spend the next period circulating, talking to each of
the kids. The younger ones gravitate to the older like they're
made of metal and the adolescents are magnetic. They stick
tight, and I can't blame them. No matter how much I tell
them I'm the guy who saved them, I still look like the person
who organised their kidnappings. I suppose I should count

my blessings that De Montfort trapped me and killed Half-Marred Jack's body. Turning up looking like him, then ending up looking like this would have really done a number on them all.

As it is, they are all going to need some serious counselling. There isn't one of them, new or old, who's not traumatised by what they've been through. The older kids catch sight of me out of the corner of their eyes now and then and instinctively flinch. It's a horrible sensation, and as much as I love the *talent* it gives me, I hate wearing this body. And not only because I keep getting caught off guard by the whole "having tits" thing. I've been a woman before, of course, but only rarely and never for long. My magic has always reshaped the body to fit my image of myself. No magic is capable of that when it comes to the Queen of Winter. I just hope with the right professional help these kids, even if they've been kids for centuries, will finally get the chance to experience something of what childhood is like.

After a little while, I see April push herself off the wall. It's only a slight movement, but it's so decisive, so definite that I don't doubt she's reached her decision. I steer myself away from the groups of children and over towards her. She gives me the smallest tightest nod, and my heart sinks. It's weird. I don't know what decision I wanted her to make, but apparently for my heart, it wasn't this one. Problem is, there are no wonderful decisions. I suspect my heart would have done a downwards dip towards the pit of my stomach whichever way she'd gone. Sometimes the only way out is to wade knee-deep through shit. You can only decide which direction to start wading in.

She doesn't wait to speak to me, instead going to gather the older kids, the ones who've been with her for hundreds of years in some cases and starts explaining quietly to them after she gets them away from the younger ones. I hear the former slave cry out, a tone of anguish, and I draw a bit closer. I suspect he's a little sweet on her and is trying to persuade her to come with them.

'... you can always stay here instead, Andre,' is her response, and he closes his mouth quickly, his body language mirroring the action. I guess he doesn't have enough of a crush on her to remain trapped in Faerie for the rest of his life. I don't blame him, but I see the hurt flash across April's face before she clamps down hard on it. Good for her. She'll need to learn to mask any and all emotions from here on in if she's going to rule over half of this world.

It is really just niceties for the rest of the conversation. If Andre isn't going to stay, nobody else is, so it's about April accepting that and saying her goodbyes. She passes from child to child, tall to small, and takes a moment to whisper encouragements. They're probably just platitudes, but they work. I see smiles spread across faces. Hope passes from her lips and gets carried down to nestle in their hearts. She gives them each a gift of words to take away with them, and in a way, perhaps it's an escape for her too, a method to make sure some part of her gets back to Earth, carried by them deep inside even while she stays stuck here.

I lead her back across to the central dais. This needs to be done correctly, to be official and irrefutable. April pales slightly at the prospect of confronting so many who hurt her so much for so damned long, but she stays solid, resolute, crossing the floor with far more grace than I can manage, mainly because I'm still concentrating on walking in heels without tripping and breaking my ankle. I don't think falling is very queenlike behaviour.

There is a moment when we stop in front of the throne

and I take off the crown, when it clicks with the Unseelie what's happening. The Dullahan starts forward, stricken, lifting his head up to — well, head height to make his complaint absolutely clear.

'Your Majesty!' His shock is as clear as the disgust in his voice. I don't like him more for either of them. 'You cannot give the crown to that…*thing*. She is only half-fae. She is not a pure blood! She cannot rule over us; we will not allow it!'

'You know who talks about pure bloods?' He was so fixated on us and his outrage, he didn't notice Aicha sidling up next to him, so when she speaks into his ear, he leaps several inches off the floor, fumbling his head, struggling to catch it before he drops it, eventually managing by wrapping his arms around it and pulling it to his chest. His eyes peek out upside down between the gap in his two forearms.

'Oops, butterfingers,' Aicha purrs, bending down to be level with the inverted head's eyes. 'The only people who talk about pure bloods are fascists and inbreds. The latter are wrong'uns; the former I kill on principle. So tell me, Dummyhands, which one are you? Do you fuck your sister, or are you a National Soc*sidhe*list?'

Even if he hadn't just watched her single-handedly kill the previously unconquerable, supposedly eternal fae queen, I'm pretty sure having Aicha be that intense, that close, with the vulnerability that must come from clutching your head the wrong way up to your chest, would have made him shit his pants anyhow. As it is, I think he'd run away gibbering in terror if he wasn't rooted to the spot with fear. He stutters and stammers, trying desperately to extricate himself from the situation.

'I can't hear you. Was that, "I have no objection to Queen Sir April Nighte, none at all, and am happy to swear fealty"?'

The Dullahan's neck bobs back and forth furiously.

'That gesture only works when you have a head on top. Try using your words.' Aicha is implacable in her terribleness.

'I — I — I am delighted, ex-ecstatic to swear fealty to Lady — Queen!' The Dullahan corrects himself rapidly as Aicha darts her face suddenly closer still, reminiscent of a striking snake. 'Queen April — Queen Sir April!' He shrieks when he suddenly finds a knife millimetres from one of his newly regained eyeballs. 'Queen Sir April Nighte, and I, I, I promise to serve her loyally and faithfully.'

The knife never moves, never wavers. 'For how long?' Aicha purrs. Good work. Otherwise, it'd only be for this precise, present moment and then he'd be ready to stab her in the back the minute we're gone.

'For ever! For as long as I live! My promise and my oath!' The Dullahan gabbles out his words, his tongue tripping over itself to give this lunatic warrior capable of killing the unkillable whatever she wants. Anything to get her and any sharp objects on her person as far away from him as possible.

'Marvellous.' Aicha smiles — a Cheshire Cat ear to ear grin that vanishes just as instantly when she turns her attention to the rest of the assembled Court. 'Anyone here object to swearing a similar oath here and now? Feel free to step forward so we can discuss it in intimate detail.'

There is a shuffling of feet, and I can see several of them looking from one to the other, doubtless wondering if anyone is going to lead the way. Nobody's feeling that suicidal though, apparently. After a moment, the group stills, and no one comes forward.

'Fine. Once April is Queen, we'll stick around long enough to hear your solemn promises and oaths. Just remember one thing.' She takes a step towards them, and they all pull back collectively, like a chorus in a Greek tragedy, trying to keep that gracious fae appearance while scrabbling to get as far away from her as possible. 'I'm not fae. I don't have time for word games or politics. Anyone I even think is trying to frame their words cleverly to get out of their promise later on won't get a second chance like Dummy here.' She waves the knife at the Dullahan, dangerously close to his eyeball, so as he shrieks and leaps backwards, all his attempts at composure gone. 'I'll slit your gizzard, and you can join Maeve in pushing up the ice daisies.'

It's a masterstroke. I don't think any of them will want to risk tangling with Aicha. No doubt it will be the most clear and concise set of promises any fae has ever made. To get an entire assembled group of nobles, regardless of species, to do the same thing will be a feat previously unheard of. Still, slaughtering an ancient fae queen in her own domain has to carry some perks. Becoming the bogeywoman of the Winter Court is definitely a nice bonus.

I've taken the crown off, but I don't hand it straight over to April. 'I'm sorry, kid,' I say, looking at her. She bites her lip, and I can see the tremble still there in her fingertips, but she remains resolute. Those assembled in front of us rained misery and terror down on her for decades, for centuries, but she will not give them even the tiniest victory of seeing her nervous, of witnessing her fear. April pulls her attention back to me, though she makes sure it's a smooth, slow transition, never betraying her mental state. I have her full attention. 'I've already asked so damn much of you, but there are a couple more things I need before I give you the crown.'

She laughs bitterly. 'What now? My firstborn? A hundred years of servitude? I think you're getting a bit too invested in this "Queen of the Fae" role.'

I smile sadly. 'And that right there is what I have to guard against. For our sakes. I don't think you'll lose yourself to Winter's freeze, but...' I sigh, waggling my hand back and forth. 'It could happen. I can't take the risk. So I need your oath on two things. First, that you'll let me, Aicha, and the human kids go — all of us. That you'll open the portal for us and let us through. Second, that you'll close the portal after and keep it closed. That you'll never take a mortal child or adult from Earth however long you live.'

She rears back like I slapped her. I can see the outrage spreading across her face. 'As if I ever... How dare you? Who do you think I am? Who do you think *you* are?'

'Right now?' I reply. 'Right now, I'm the ruler of Faerie, and I nearly lost myself to that despite eight centuries of heavy-duty magical experience. I can't wait to get rid of this blasted crown, but I'm well aware of how heavy it's going to weigh on your brow. You're going to be stuck here with a whole bunch of malicious creatures who have hated you since you arrived and treated you like something they stepped in, stuck to the bottom of their shoe.' I use the sleeve of the ridiculous robe I'm wearing to mop at my forehead. No doubt this dress is a priceless piece of high fae haute couture, but nothing will please me more than to throw it in the bin and slip some casual, comfortable clothes on instead. I guess I'm just not made for ballgowns.

My uncomfortable clothing isn't the primary concern right now though. April needs to understand what she's signing up for. 'This isn't going to be easy, kid. It's going to get *lonely*, seriously lonely being the only one here with human origins, the sole Unseelie who wasn't born that way. It'll sink in soon enough, I think. So maybe you'll just want us to hang around a little longer or for your friends' —*Or one of them in particular, at least,* I think to myself— 'to just stick around while you get settled. Maybe the time you decide you need us around becomes longer and longer, and all the while, you'll be less and less willing to let us all go. Hell, perhaps you might decide to *persuade* us all to stay, that we want to stay.'

I lean forward, grim-faced. She has to hear this. 'Fucking with people's minds is ugly magic. Avoid it at all costs.'

The shock is apparent, her porcelain features paling further, but she isn't interrupting me, isn't insisting it could never happen to her. I don't know if it's because she recognises herself in what I said or just the temptation, the inherent risk, but I can see she's listening. Good. 'But let's say you do let us go. That cold is going to keep creeping inwards. One day your heart might freeze, and whether out of loneliness or —' It's my turn to bite my lip now. Good God, I hope it never comes to this. 'Other appetites, the temptation might come upon you to open up the portal again, to bring some people, willing or otherwise, across.'

She's trembling now, terrified, and I can understand it. But she survived centuries under Maeve's far from gentle ministrations. This girl is iron-hearted. That might be enough to keep off the worst of Winter's chill...if she can see it in herself. 'You've survived centuries of their games, their degradations and kept your humanity intact. It'll be a battle, but I think you'll find that balance, that harmony between who you are and who the land wants you to be. Just think of it as an insurance policy, that's all.'

She dips her head quickly, like a bird seizing a half-spotted grain on a frozen lawn, all too aware of the predatory forces stalking through the flower beds. This little bird's about to grow talons though. Those who took her for easy quarry before might find out what happens when you give prey claws.

Then it's the hunter's turn to pray.

Chapter Twenty-One

We push our way into the main foyer, where a desk, probably for tickets, sits on the right-hand side. On the wall next to it are posters advertising recently passed and upcoming sporting events and concerts at the centre. One catches my eye. Led Zeppelin are playing two dates: the first and second of April. I flick a finger out to bring it to Aicha's attention. She gives me a nod that says, "Yes, of course I want to go, but we're doing something else right now, dickhead. Get your priorities straight". It's amazing how much a woman of so few words express in a simple gesture. I tear the poster down and pop it into my etheric storage. There's a number to call to book tickets on it. Otherwise, we'll just walk in under a *don't look here*. Either way, we're going to see Led Zep! That alone makes this entire trip worthwhile.

Through a half-cracked door on the other end, I can see the main auditorium. It's more than vast. Thousands and thousands of metres in one single space. The bowing concrete ceiling creates a sense of movement to the whole place, with the slope of the glass walls feeling like an upside-down boat, where the sky is the sea, and the floor is the wooden ceiling of the galley. It looks super impressive.

We don't go that way though. Al-Ruhban leads us through a door marked "employees only", and down a corridor. It's entirely plain, and therefore totally unsuitable, to my mind, for the grandeur of the building. I guess they aren't bothered about wowing the menial staff.

He leads us to a room that's really just a glorified store cupboard, albeit on a grand scale. Thousands of tables and chairs stand stacked in neat rows, doubtless for when they hold concerts and conferences here. We weave our way through the columns until we come to a space covered by a folded, flat-packed table big enough to seat ten. I pull at it, only to be surprised by how light it is. It slides across the floor, and where it was, we find a *don't look here* spell covering what is, to those of us who can *see*, a carefully concealed trapdoor in the floor.

I look at the other two. 'Chances the local council don't know about this hidden entrance?'

'Pretty much one hundred percent.' Al-Ruhban's face is grim. He didn't know about this either. I suspect nobody does.

I study the spellwork. 'What do you reckon? If I get rid of this, will they know?'

'Depends if they thought of it.' Aicha is *looking* just as carefully as I am.

'Any other way we can get through?' They both shake their heads.

'Doesn't look like we've got a lot of options then,' I say, and very, very carefully, I unpick the *don't look here* spell strand of *talent* by strand of *talent*.

It takes me a few minutes to finish, and I have no idea if

the effort was worth it. We've not heard the psychic equivalent of alarm bells, but that might just mean the magical body thieves aren't complete idiots. Hopefully, though, they're at least partial ones and haven't laid cunningly hidden magical alarms. Certainly, after studying the trapdoor, there are no further spells on it. Aicha gives it a once over for physical traps because only morons assume magic is the answer to every question, especially if that question is "how do I kill the foolishly unwary with high-level efficacy?", but we're clear on that too. Al-Ruhban pulls his Incredible Merging Man trick with the lock again, and we lever it up to reveal a staircase descending into the dark below.

'You know, one of these days,' I say, peering into the murk, 'I'd love there not to be an ominous pathway to hell beneath a bespelled trapdoor.'

'What *do* you want?' Aicha has already summoned a small flame in her hand to use as a torch.

It's a fair question. 'A wine cellar?' I say. A wine cellar sounds pleasant right now.

'Maybe it leads to one.' The laughter in her voice, if not her face, tells me Aicha doesn't believe that for a second. We've no idea what's down there, but it isn't going to be copious amounts of booze; more's the pity.

Aicha takes point, and I follow behind, with Al-Ruhban at the rear. I'd normally feel less than comfortable with someone I've just met watching my six, but Aicha trusts him. That's good enough for me.

We head a long way down. The walls and stairs and ceiling are all simple poured concrete but well made. I don't bother saying anything to Aicha, but I'm confident she's reached the same conclusion I have. This isn't a later addition. Whoever made this put it in at the same time as they built the Grande Nef. Someone has been planning this for a long time.

The short corridor at the bottom of the stairs follows the same simple concrete motif. At the end there is a door, also concrete and set in place. This, however, carries a clear mark. The symbol of a downwards pointing sword, with what looks like a ribbon or an iron bar crossed in front and wrapped behind it to form a loop. I know the symbol, of course. So does Aicha. It was all over the laboratory I rescued her from.

'Ahnenerbe,' she hisses, and I put my hand on her shoulder. She was about to throw herself through the door. We have at least two people on the other side, one, if not both, of whom must be a magic user, and this is their turf. For once, she's being rash and I'm being the sensible one. The world has officially gone mad.

She tenses, and for a moment I think she's going to strike out, break my arm, or force me off her at least. Then it passes. She nods, and I let go. She's back in control.

The Third Reich loved occultism. Many people have heard of the Thule Society, but the Ahnenerbe were even worse. The Thule Society would do things like wonder if killing a million Jews could summon forth an Old One from the collective dark. The Ahnenerbe would be the ones who then went and put it into action.

We approach the significantly robust door itself. I *look* at it but can't see any spells. I suspect they considered their genius sufficient to keep them hidden. Nazis and arrogance go together like my fist and their nose.

There are murmuring voices on the other side, but even with my ear pressed to the concrete, I can't make out words. I'm loath to use more of my power reserves. We might need them in a second.

A gentle hand settles on my shoulder. The strange sense of immense power wriggling under his skin slightly undermines the effect of calm. It feels like it might leap across and head under mine if we stay like this too long. I resist the urge to shudder. I have a feeling that physical contact with other people isn't something he does very often. It's intended as an honour. I want to treat it as such.

'Allow me, *saabi*,' he says and gently guides me away from the doorway. Then he lays his hands on the concrete surface and touches his forehead to it.

As I watch, it seems like either the door or Al-Ruhban himself becomes putty, one giving way to the other or else, the two of them mixing together. His hands sink in like the concrete has become grey butter and then to my astonishment, his face follows.

I look over at Aicha. 'What?' she asks.

I gesture at Al-Ruhban's bizarre half-absorption into the door. 'That! That's what. What's that all about?'

She stares at me blankly. 'Have you never met a djinn before? Didn't you travel in the Arabic world?'

I hold up fingers as I answer her questions. 'No. Yes.' I love it's me who gets to be brief for once instead of her.

She shakes her head in disbelief. 'Fucking colonial tourists. Jeez.' She turns to look at Al-Ruhban. 'This here is something he inherited from his djinn side. They can merge with the elements — rock, water, fire, even air itself. Being half-djinn, he can't do all four, but he can merge into rock and water. Rock seems to cover most physical things, so concrete, metal...' She shrugs. 'He can be one with them. When he wants to be.'

It's astonishing. If I tried to do something similar, I could probably work out how to eventually. It wouldn't be exactly the same though. I'd have to displace the rock to make space for my face, liquidising it, letting it run down and pool at the bottom. It would leave evidence of what I've done. Plus, I'd light the whole place up with my magic, like the fireworks on Bastille Day. When I *look* at him, his orange-red glow has intensified somewhat, but he isn't the beacon I'd have made myself into. It's an integral part of his nature, so it carries a lower cost *talent*-wise. Truly remarkable.

I guess some of that scholarly fascination Isaac worked so hard to instil in me has stuck after all. When Al-Ruhban pulls himself back out of the concrete, he catches me studying him like a scientist after they've just jabbed a rat with a syringe marked with a big skull and crossbones. I flush guiltily, and he turns to Aicha, waving his hand up and down.

'See? This. This is why I don't like sorcerers,' he says. 'Can't help themselves, can they? They see a djinn and see a puzzle they want to solve.' He turns back to me, and I wonder if it's just my imagination that there are flames dancing in the back of his irises. 'I'm not a riddle to crack, wizard.'

I hold my hand over my heart, splayed open, and bow. 'My apologies, Al-Ruhban. I won't deny I found your *talent* fascinating. Maybe to the point of rudeness…'

'Definitely to the point of rudeness,' Aicha mutters out of a corner of her mouth.

'… but only because it's so unique. I'm not looking to learn your mysteries. Nor will I speak of them to anyone not here, upon my power.'

This seems to appease him. He inclines his head in acceptance and then turns back to the matter at hand.

'On the other side,' he says, 'is a large five-sided room. You've met Nazi occultists before?'

We both nod. Oh yes. That's a definite. I don't ask him what his experiences were. None of us have any good ones to report.

'You know what their "laboratories" look like then. Scientific equipment everywhere and pentagrams galore. On the opposite side is a smaller door. I guess it's an escape route, so one to watch when we go in.'

Damn it. They've been fairly careless so far, not laying wards of warning or protecting their arses. But I suppose if they were clever enough to build this secret occult space (underneath the Seine itself, if I don't miss my guess), I shouldn't be surprised they were smart enough to make sure they have a second way out. Still, it's one more thing to guard. The only good thing is if they run, it'll be damn hard taking the coffin with them.

'Have they got the coffin there?' Aicha asks, her mind on the prize as usual.

He nods. 'They've taken the skeleton out as well. It's set on what looks like an operating table. That's not the problem though.'

Brilliant. The extracted corpse of Marshal Petain isn't the problem. 'What is?' I ask.

'What they're planning to do with it,' he says, and his expression looks seriously bleak.

Call me a pessimist, but this doesn't sound like good news.

Chapter Twenty-Two

What do non-binary fae do with pronouns? They ban she.

While Aicha's traumatising the entire assembled nobility of the Unseelie Court, I take April off to the side and extract some carefully worded promises from her. Although she's still only half-fae, there is enough sidhe nature there that they will constrain her effectively once she picks up the crown. I want to give her the privacy, though, of not having the whole Court witness her binding herself. Let them believe everything is her decision rather than coercion.

Once that's done, we assemble back in front of the throne, and April ascends the dais, faerie creatures scattering left and right to give her space as she steps up to take her new place as their ruler. I don't know what scares them more now — the immediate threat of Aicha glowering at them or the inevitable reign of a new monarch they've all treated like shit. Little of A, little of B, I reckon. A fuckload of both, actually.

I wait to see what April does, whether she makes a speech or the like. Whatever she wants, I'll follow her lead. It's her kingdom from here on in; she can choose how she sets the tone of her first day as ruler. But she just sits there, regal and aloof, waiting calmly for me. So I take my cue and mount the steps to kneel in front of her. No simple task in a dress that wants to be an iron maiden when it grows up. Then I hold the crown up, my head bowed, and give the rule of the kingdom of Winter to April Nighte.

I feel the diminution, the lessening as the land leaves me. It's like waking from a dream, that first initial moment when you can't lay your finger quite on what reality actually is. Where for just a second you really believe you can fly or that youth never fled before advancing age or grief and loss were only abstract concepts, not real and present boon companions. Where the hardships of life seem to be the dream, and all the doors of possibility seem flung open again before you're forced back to face a corridor where they all slammed shut long ago. I feel loss, lost and have to grieve all over again, as I did when I woke from Melusine's imposed dream haze to my new low-grade *talent*. In fact, for a moment, I think it isn't going to stop, that all my fae power will leech away with the passed coronet, and I'll be back to the low-grade mortal levels I had when not wearing a fae form. Once it stabilises, however, I realise I'm still damn *talented*, far more than I was when wearing Half-Marred Jack's form. It's just nothing —a pinch, a mote, a speck of power— compared to what I wielded when wearing the crown.

As I step back out of my state of internal mourning for lost magic, I become more aware of the general hubbub around me. I raise my head. Then I have to throw a hand up to shield my eyes because April is glowing.

I don't mean in a radiant, healthy way or in a newly pregnant way or even in a "fuck thos snaykz ur glowin bb" kind of way. She's literally glowing, pouring a cold-fire brilliance out of every inch of skin, painting the throne room in an ice blue, and it hurts my eyes to look at her directly. The shocked mutters die away as the light dims, and April turns her gaze across those assembled. The luminosity might have reduced, but her intensity hasn't dropped even a notch. I'm glad I'm already kneeling — the sounds of kneecaps smacking the floor with force echoes off the ceiling as people fall, genuflecting without intending to under the weight of her regard. I risk a peek and see Aicha still standing, her arms crossed, off to the side, in front of the children, taking the full force of April's stare when it sweeps in their direction, keeping it off the kids so they aren't forced down. April pauses, a frown forming on her face, all her attention now on Aicha, who just cocks an eyebrow at her.

'Do you defy me, Druze?' Her voice carries an undercurrent of overwhelming force, kept dammed back by sheer will and self-control. It feels like it will wash us away if she releases the torrent.

Aicha regards her coolly. 'I wouldn't say defy. Not as such. Just if you give me an order, I'm going to tell you to fuck off.'

There's a momentary pause, a collective second where everyone holds their breath, unsure if we're about to see Aicha versus the Queen of Winter take two. Then April throws back her head and laughs.

It isn't the pealing silver bells Maeve's laugh was. It's a genuine, full-throated giggle, complete with a most unqueenly snort when April tries to laugh and breathe at the same time. She grins at Aicha, and suddenly that same impressive young girl is back in the room instead of the pants-wettingly terrifying embodiment of Winter.

'I'd not expect anything different,' she says, wiping a tear from her eye before it freezes. I breathe a sigh of relief. I put her there. I don't want that feisty, courageous youngster to become another monster. I've made or enabled enough of those.

Her principal duty isn't to reassure us though. Her eyes sweep across the assembled and justifiably nervous Unseelie Court. After a couple of passes, they fix on a lutin who's doing his best to hide behind the mna sidhe. As soon as they feel the queen's attention shifting in their direction, they rapidly shuffle aside, leaving the little fellow exposed and alone.

He's reminiscent in stature of the Nain but without looking like he's been dipped in red PVC. In some ways, he most resembles the sort of garden gnomes that were a trend in the 1980s, but only if they'd been moulded by a deranged sex pest sociopath. The fact his hand keeps creeping towards his groin suggests it's only effort of will that stops him from shoving it down his pants. His eyes are cunning, shifting back and forth, and I notice them settling in an unnerving way on several of the human girls, none of whom would appreciate it. My gut instinct is to instinctively gut him for it. But April's eyes are fixed on him, and she's the queen here now. I hold myself in check and watch to see what she will do instead.

April beckons him forward, and he advances slowly, nervously casting his eyes around for support from the other fae. No one looks in a hurry to speak up for him, though whether that's because he's such a nasty piece of work, or they're more concerned with protecting their own arses, I have no idea. I suspect both.

He comes to a hesitant stop in front of the throne, where April perches ramrod straight and with an unreadable expression on her face. The lutin shifts from foot to foot, which I don't feel really helps his case —being literally shifty— and keeps his eyes downcast. When he speaks, his voice is high-pitched and nasal, so that every word sounds like a whining excuse no matter what he says.

'The queen called, and I came,' he stammers. You can hear he's trying to invest his words with a confidence he clearly doesn't feel. 'What service can I offer, who has sworn loyalty and fealty willingly to my liege-lady?'

It's a clever turn of phrase. He's making it clear that he's already taken his oath, that he accepts his position, that he's loyal to the throne. I think he hopes it'll be enough to placate April. He's sadly mistaken.

The slightest smile curves up April's cheeks. It carries a cold savagery to it that would chill my blood if I were unfortunate enough to have it aimed at me. The lutin's eyes are still on the floor though, so he doesn't see it. 'Right glad am I to have such sworn fealty, Orin. And a gift I'd offer you in return for it. Hold out your hands now.'

I see fear and greedy hope racing their way around the lutin's mind, chasing each other across his face. In the end, I don't know which wins out, but he has no choice either way. He extends his hands, palms upwards-facing to receive what the queen has to give him.

April stretches out an elongated index finger like an indolent cat as it basks in the sun to hover over Orin's hands, then goes further still. His eyes come up, unsure at that movement, just in time to watch as she makes a swift gesture left to right, and his hands fall off, severed at both wrists.

Take it from me — normally when you chop off an

appendage, it's a messy affair. Blood pumping everywhere, much screaming, etc, etc. This is the cleanest amputation I have ever witnessed. The two hands just fall off, and where they were, there's a layer of fresh skin as though it was an old accident long ago. No bodily fluids pour forth. Instead, the lutin lifts his two new stumps disbelievingly to hover just in front of his eyes before looking down at the off-cast remnants on the floor. It's fair to say he wasn't expecting that. I can see his skin whitening, the tremble to his body as shock sets in. I've no idea if it hurts, but it certainly caught him off guard. Left him harmless. Well, handless, at least.

The lutin stares at his detached hands as though he expects them to jump up like Thing from *Addams Family*, perhaps scurry back up his trouser legs and then stick themselves back in place. April watches impassively, her face a closed book, frozen over. She's really getting into this whole Fae Ice Queen malarkey.

'A present to you, Orin,' she says calmly, quietly but with enough presence to carry to all who gather. 'I give you your life. As your hands could not keep to themselves when I was nothing but a courtly plaything, I think I shall keep them as a souvenir, a memento to remind me why change is so very necessary. Perhaps one day, if you change enough, if you're capable of it, you'll get them back. Perhaps.'

I'm just thinking to myself how entirely justified her actions are and that perhaps it has nothing to do with being bonded to Winter and everything to do with the fuck-knuckle in front of her, when she waves her own hand at the pair of severed ones on the floor. They glide up into the air swallow-like, then impale themselves each on one of the protruding spikes of her throne either side of her head so that they look like a pair of fleshy wings protruding from her crown, reminiscent of the wings on Hermes' helmet. I have to resist the urge to applaud. It's a lovely piece of theatre.

April raises her voice, making it clear she's addressing everyone. 'The days of Maeve are over. Winter has changed.' She pauses, then corrects herself. 'No, Winter is restored.' She leans forward, her eyes scanning them all, the heebies and the hobgoblins, the boggarts and mna sidhe, the Dullahan and the lutin, both sallow-faced from their respective disciplining. 'There is cold and dark in Winter, the danger that lurks and preys on the mind. But there is also beauty and wonder. There is the brutal honesty of the holly leaves' spines. The neutrality of the crisp and the cold. The life that survives, nurtured below the dead surface. Perfect blue skies can follow on from freezing fog, and the moon shines brightest and longest in our season.'

Her eyes wander across them all, and her voice softens. 'We lost Maeve to the dark, alone, and Winter followed her lead. Many of you here have wronged me, but rebirth is the gift that the coldest death gives, clearing and cleansing, pruning away the old to allow space for the new to come to blossom one day. These' —she gestures towards the spread-eagled fingers above her— 'are a symbol of the price of the darkest cruelty. This' —her hands gesture at Orin, who flinches at the attention— 'this life shows there is also space for mercy, for the red berries to blossom once more. But' —she turns a smile on them all, so wintery I'm amazed her courtiers aren't instantly covered in a layer of frost from head to toe— 'know that I am also the creeping ivy, subtle and stealthy, and I will strangle the life so very slowly out of any who seeks to twist their promise and stand against me.'

She sweeps her gaze imperiously over them one by one, holding their eyes until they each break away, looking down, aside, anywhere but at her. She nods, satisfied. Then I gulp because that same intense attention swivels in my direction.

'You served well in your brevity.' She smiles, and I wonder if it's my imagination that her teeth look brighter than before, sharper than before. She leans closer, and her voice only just carries to me. 'You were wise in your extracted promises, Paul. The cold seeps deeper by the second, and I'd be tempted to keep you all here to warm myself against if not.'

I shudder slightly, and it isn't from the cold. She sees, and that same strange sharp smile breaks across her lips, like the tide's last hurrah before it retreats back from the shore. 'A promise was given. No need to be afraid.' The smile vanishes. 'Though I would not be in any hurry to return to our lands if you'd ever want to leave again.'

I nod quickly and bite back a sigh of relief when she turns her attention away from me. Her eyes linger on Aicha. She tilts her head, acknowledging the warrior, and Aicha mirrors the gesture momentarily. That is communication enough between them, and I can't help thinking about their many similarities. In another life, they might have been the best of friends. Or killed each other. One or the other.

Her eyes arrive at the rag-tag group of children still standing in the portal, and her regard softens. I see her eyes linger on Billy just for a moment, but she forces them onwards, encompassing every one of them. The expression she wears speaks of warmth, of joy. Only I can see how much it costs her, the sadness that lingers, lurking almost out of sight in the corner of her eye. I wonder if my ability to spot it is because it was me who put it there.

I see the same sadness mirrored in several of the others, particularly Billy and the other older kids, a pain that they carry, that they share. I know they feel like they've betrayed her, leaving her alone in Winter. April sees it too. 'Stop it.' It's a gentle command, but there's a force, a steel core to it. 'No more beating yourselves up. You've been here in the cold long enough. I didn't expect you to stay — hell, I wouldn't have in your place.' Her laughter, supposed to speak of a shared joke, can't quite conceal the bitter tinge to her words. Still, there's a genuine depth of emotion to how she looks at each of them that speaks of a love forged in shared suffering, the unbreakable companionship of trauma endured and survived together.

She turns her attention to the entire group. 'Come now; dry your eyes. You' —she looks at the youngest ones, those who've only had the tiniest soupçon of a taste of Winter's chill— 'are going home to your families, back to your loved ones. You' —she looks at her older companions, who rode out the arctic nights side by side— 'can craft new lives. Go. Feel the sun on your face and think of me when you do.'

She turns back to me again. 'Paul, I can't lie. My emotions are mixed when it comes to you.' It takes all my effort to match her stare, but she merits it. I'll meet her eyes full on one last time. 'Still, I'm grateful that Maeve is gone and beyond grateful for my friends' liberty. And if I'm still in chains' —she waves a careless hand down the sparkling rings and robes that have formed around her, replacing her ragged mockery of courtly finery— 'then at least I am in charge inside the walls of my prison cell.'

Aicha joins in. 'Just remember. You're not locked in here with them. They're locked in here with you.'

April smiles a wicked smile, and there are definitely sharper tips to her teeth than there were before. 'Oh, I'm well aware of that, lady. I think they're realising it too.'

I look around at the group of cowering fae nobles. It brings me a grim sort of satisfaction to see the uncertainty bordering on terror that radiates from the group. Thinking about how many humans they've terrified and tortured over the years, the horrible things they've no doubt done to captured children? I can't kill them all for it; I'm not capable, for a start. And they were responding to the whims of their ruler, reflecting the season's mood, bound to Winter and her vicious disposition. But leaving April in charge is the next best thing. If they don't reform and change, she'll bury them deep under the frozen earth one by one. Looking at their expressions, I think they know it too.

I doff an imaginary hat at the new Queen of the Unseelie Court. 'I think they might just be, at that.' And if they aren't, I reckon they'll learn. Soon enough.

Chapter Twenty-Three

FAERIE, 5 JUNE, PRESENT DAY

At the end of my extended holiday in Faerie, I can give the following travel advice to those thinking of visiting — don't.

We gather in the crystal circle. April dismissed the rest of the Court to allow herself space for some private goodbyes without displaying any signs of weakness to the vultures making up her new courtiers. I'm glad for her, that she can have this last intimate moment. Court is going to be treacherous and terrifying for some time to come. I just hope she'll be able to change it, that eventually she'll find some Unseelie she can build trust in, some connection with. She'll need it if she wants to guard any of that spark of humanity she hopes to use to light up Winter's night.

The younger kids are desperate to leave, wanting to get back home to their adults, to put this nightmare behind them. Aicha and I discuss it in great depth while the others are bidding their farewells. I meant what I said — mind magic is nasty stuff. Leaving them with all their memories of Faerie is just as cruel though.

It means exposure to the Talented world from very early on with no guidance, and the small nascent spark most of them carry won't be enough to protect them when the Talented world sees them too. Their best-case scenario? They'll learn to live close-mouthed, cut off from friends and family until they're old enough to come into their power and join the world beneath the one those around them know. Worst-case? Loose lips lead them to the gentle ministrations of a psychiatric institute, with a one-size-fits-all dinner jacket that makes it hard to hold the soup spoon. Or anything else. Actually, the real worst-case scenario is their *talent* will burn like a flare in an open field on a clear winter's night and draw hungry predators in just as quickly.

So after much *umming* and *ahhing*, we agree to wipe away the parts in Faerie. Their stay with Half-Marred Jack, we'll leave in place. Their trauma is real and simply slicing it away will do them no favours. They need to heal from the darkness. They don't need to remember about magic to do that. If they can't remember, it'll lock back down inside them, away until they're ready to discover it or to stay sealed away forever.

Eventually, the older group finishes their goodbyes, and we're ready. We still have precisely zero idea what we're going to do with them. They're all *talented* to some degree or other, and all of them have been away long enough that the world has forgotten about them even if they haven't forgotten about it. Sure, we can hook them up with some fake IDs, get them back in the system, but it's going to take time. Then they're going to need someone to train them. Their time in Faerie let them adjust to the strange way magic works here, but I doubt their *talent* will let them manipulate it in the same way back on Earth. They'll need guidance, teachers, and we have neither the time nor energy for that right now. Still, one problem at a time. Today, we'll get the youngsters back to safety. We can deal with the older ones after that.

The moment's upon us. April's face is one of concentration. The room dims, falling into a dusky half-light, and the crystals surrounding us flicker to life. Inside each, a tiny cold fire springs into existence until it glows cerulean, ebbing and flowing eerily. The shadows dance up the walls, then fall, subside, and it's like we're in a crystal lifeboat floating in a sea of darkness. There's a sensation reminiscent of being caught by a wild current, and it feels as though we're spinning in place, the entire part inside the crystals moving. The shadows continue their strange surging dances, so it's like I'm inside a Victorian zoetrope being spun by a captivated child. The floor tilts, seeming to lurch under me. Several of the children sit down hard and cling to one another, and my sea legs fail me so that I join them with a stagger and a bump, tripping over the train of my dress behind me. As much as I'm sure Louis Vuitton would be ready to sign a contract in blood offering their entire staff's first-born children for just a glimpse of this outfit, I've already decided I'm going to ceremonially burn it with extreme prejudice the moment I can take it off.

Have you ever been talking to a group, and you get halfway into an anecdote when someone just cuts you off dead? And somehow, no one is shocked, the conversation pivots, and there's this sense that it's moved on, left you behind, and that shock, the suddenness of the directional shift, means you're left outside, disconnected, not able to follow? The way the circle suddenly freezes, holding in place while there's clearly still a sense of travel needed, of distance to complete before we arrive leaves me similarly disorientated. I know we haven't arrived, that we can't have stopped, but somehow that's exactly what has happened, and my brain just doesn't know how to process it.

Looking around, I see similar reactions from a lot of the kids, which only highlights how *talented* they are. They're reacting unconsciously to this one-eighty the magic has pulled, knowing it should *go* even when it has most categorically *stopped*.

Aicha, however, doesn't look like that. Her head snaps up, hyperalert, vigilant, although, at the same time, it's not like she's alert to danger; she doesn't seem worried. More wary, doubtful perhaps about which way this might go, whatever "this" is.

The arrival catches me entirely off guard. One minute I'm trying with a distinct wobble to get to my feet while trying to both monitor the group and understand what has happened. The next, she is there.

She's made entirely out of light. And I don't mean in a hologram, "help me Obi-wan; you're my only hope" kind of way. Nor do I mean like a translucent phantom, where you can see through their pale imitation of existence both metaphysically and literally. No, she is light solidified, like a sunbeam plucked as it peeked through a gap in the clouds and condensed, intensified, then flash-frozen, perfectly preserved. She doesn't really have a body, just a formless yet substantial column of radiance that tapers up towards the head itself. And yet, I know this is a woman. She radiates feminine energy, all the strength and power combined, an embodiment of matriarchy. I can't tell you her height. She seems bigger than me. Then again, she seems bigger than everything. Humanity, the planet. Life itself.

Her face is featureless, a luminescent orb balanced on

top of the frozen-light pillar, but somehow I know she's smiling at us. There is a benevolence there I can't explain. How can I read emotion without words, without an expression? Still, I know it to be true, and it seems too correct, too pure to be some glamour like the one Melusine cast on me. Although I completely failed to spot that when she did it, so perhaps I'm not the best judge.

Aicha sighs and then she seems to deflate ever so slightly, like the sound is the air escaping from her metaphysical balloon. It weirds me out more than anything else we've gone through, more than the incomprehensible glowing female entity waiting patiently in the corner because it seems to me as if she's giving up. Aicha Kandicha never gives up. It makes me distinctly uneasy.

'Is it time then?' Aicha asks the glowing form. I wonder for a moment if it might not be an angel or equivalent from the higher realms. Although the two angels inside my mentor Isaac, Nith and Nan, have assured me they would know of another's presence on Earth, we are not yet back on Earth, stopped too soon. We're somewhere in the in-between, which should be impossible.

A voice, like the last echoing words of a long dead loved one, audible but fading as one awakes from a dream, rings in my mind. 'No, not yet. Soon but not yet. Instead, child, I come to offer my help.'

I feel the narrowing of eyes in Aicha's tone. 'In exchange for what?'

A tinkling laughter that makes me think of a determined trickle of a stream eating its way through a mountain over aeons echoes around my skull. I'm not a big fan of this talking without using our vocal cords malarkey, but I don't want to be rude either. The strange, wonderful voice speaks again. 'No, no trade. Don't fear, little one. I'm not after your cargo or your friend.'

The fact that whatever this is keeps referring to Aicha, a twelve-hundred-year-old warrior mage, as a *child* and a *little one* is disturbing enough. That Aicha is letting the being say it without trying to carve open the light-pillar and see if her insides are made of neon is freaking me the fuck out, frankly.

Aicha tilts her head. There's caution on her face but no fear still. She knows who this strange female force is. 'So what help would you offer us then, White Lady?'

It all clicks into place. Of course. This is the White Lady of the Pyrenees, the Power who got Aicha through Melusine's defences, then over to Faerie to rescue me.

'The older ones you have with you, I would aid. I think they're lost between worlds now, neither fair folk nor fully human anymore after so long away. I can offer them a sanctuary.'

She's also apparently powerful enough to hijack a group mid-portal jump between realms, which is a terrifying amount of power, at least the equivalent of the angels Nith and Nan, if not even more. So for once, I choose my words carefully. The fact I feel like wetting my pants — and officially ruining this obscenity of a ballgown in the process— helps keep me focused on being civil.

'If you think you're taking any of these kids, you've got another thing coming.' I haul myself upright with only the tiniest teetering moment where I nearly fell back over, arse over tit. 'Oh, thanks for the save, sending Aicha, as well.' See? I can be polite.

The orb turns my way, and again I can feel all the emotions not expressed on her featureless visage. Surprise, pity, understanding with just a sliver of wry amusement underneath it all. 'Take them, Last Cathar? No. I only wish to save them. The choice will be theirs.'

Now it's my turn to narrow my eyes. Godlike beings rarely meddle in the matters of mortals, and when they do, it is never good news. 'Save them from what?'

'From arriving, of course. From putting foot on the green grass of home.'

I hear a sharp intake next to me and turn to Aicha, surprised. Audible expressions of shock aren't normally her wheelhouse, except in the sense of "fuck me, Paul. I'm shocked by what a complete twat you are yet again". She turns to me, her eyes hooded, her lips thinned. 'Oisin, Paul. Think of Oisin.'

It takes me a moment, then I issue out an appropriate swear. 'Fucking cocksucker fae *fuckers*.' I stamp my foot on the last word. I feel it deserves the emphasis.

Billy draws a little closer to me, though he keeps his distance from the White Lady. Since we left April, I get the impression he's taken on her previous role as spokesperson. 'Who is Oisin?' he mutters out of the side of his mouth, his eyes never leaving the mysterious creature or deity who has gatecrashed our world-crossing excursion.

I take a moment and a couple of deep breaths to get back in control, on top of my emotions. Then I turn to him. I make sure to speak loudly enough that all the others can hear. This is something they all need to be aware of, to make a choice based on.

'Have you ever heard of Fionn mac Cumhaill?' There's a general shaking of heads, which isn't surprising. If they were Irish, they would have. Bretons might well know of him too, but apparently, the kids here aren't up on the Gaelic legends of the Fianna.

I carry on. 'He was a famous war chief over in Ireland.

He's basically their King Arthur, right down to him supposedly not being dead, only asleep in a cave somewhere until he rises to defend Ireland in their hour of need. Considering how the English treated the Irish for centuries, I reckon he missed that party though.

'Anyhow, there's a whole ream of an epic poem about him, his life, his wisdom, and his fuckups called the *Fenian Cycle*. Supposedly his son wrote it, who was a great poet and scribe. In fact, he's considered the greatest poet Ireland ever produced, which isn't a lightweight title to hold. His name was Oisin.'

It's weird telling this story of mythological derring-do while an even more improbable, godlike creature hovers off to the side, glowing at you. I press on though, undaunted. 'He was seduced by a faerie called Niamh. Her father had switched her head with that of a pig...'

A hand rises. It's a tall, slender girl who uses her black curls as a curtain to peer out from. She sticks close to Janey, the girl with the shattered vocal cords. The two of them seem to draw comfort from each other; they're hand in hand right now. 'That sounds familiar. Didn't that happen in one of Shakespeare's plays?'

Colour me impressed. 'Damn close. You're thinking of *Midsummer Night's Dream*. It was Oberon, and he did it to trick Titania, giving a human the head of a donkey and making her fall in love with him. Niamh's father was supposedly Manannan Mac Lir, a sea god, but either way, he was a ruler in Tir na nOg, the Irish form of Faerie. It wouldn't surprise me if it is another name or guise for Oberon himself.'

'So he got seduced by a pig-headed fairy?' another kid asks, a boy with eyes so dark-blue they verge on purple.

'So every fairy ever?' This gets me an actual laugh. I can

feel the kids relaxing all around me. Whether it's that they've already escaped from Faerie and think whatever this creature wants can't be as bad as what they left behind or the soothing effect that storytelling has on our collective communal psyche, I can't say, but they start to unwind. Considering the female entity at the other end of the circle is several power grades above Maeve, I'm nowhere near there yet. I plaster a relaxed smile across my face though. If it helps keep them calm, it's worth it.

'But yeah, the pig head.' I turn that easy grin on each of the kids to keep them focused on me rather than the incomprehensible pillar of light woman hovering nearby. 'Niamh told Oisin the spell would break if he returned to Tir na nOg and married her, which he did. Apparently, he then ruled there and had three kids with her. Then he…' I bite my lip. 'He thought he was only there for a few years, three apparently, but it was actually three hundred. He pops back to visit his old mates, but Niamh tells him not to get off his horse. Lo and behold, Ireland has completely changed, as it will do over three centuries, and he trots about confused as hell. Something happens — in most versions of the story, he tries to help move a boulder off the road. From his horse. Which is pretty stupid for a man supposed to be this incredible warrior-poet, but what do I know?'

A round of giggles greets me. I give Aicha the side-eye to say, *See? This is how you should react to my sparkling wit.* She rolls hers at me to say, *In your dreams, dickhead.* It truly is amazing, the depth of our connection and understanding.

Now, though, I have to get to the relevant part. This is the bit that despite my calm demeanour until now, I'm truly dreading. Still, it needs to be said. 'So he puts his foot on the floor, right? And as soon as he does — wham!' I slam my fist in my other palm. 'All the three hundred years come crashing down on him in an instant, and he's an old man, which is pretty mad because actually, after three hundred years...'

I clam up. I was about to say, 'You'd think he'd just crumble into dust,' but that's a bit insensitive considering it might happen to them. I try to think of a nicer way to say it, but the older kids have already clocked why this story applies to them. The blood drains from their faces, and they aren't finding my storytelling amusing anymore.

I soften my tone. 'So that's the story of Oisin, and the only one we've ever had about what happens to someone who returns from Faerie after hundreds of years.'

Billy is aghast. 'We'll all die instantly if we go home?'

'I mean, Oisin didn't die *instantly*.' It sounds weak even to my own ears. 'He just became incredibly ancient.' I sigh. 'Then he died.' I'm not convinced that was as helpful as I hoped.

Looking at the sheer horror plastered across their faces? I'll assume not.

Chapter Twenty-Four

SAINT-OUEN, 21 FEBRUARY 1973

Al-Ruhban leans against the rough grey wall, his hands shoved into his pockets. 'Have I mentioned how much I hate Nazi occultists?'

'I don't think anyone here is about to include them in their tribute version of the song from *The Sound of Music*,' I say drily. 'Would you mind letting us two in on what it is they're up to?'

Al-Ruhban nods, pulling a hankie from his suit pocket and mopping his forehead. 'Sure, sorry.' He stands up straight again. 'Petain's body isn't the only one they've got in there.'

Fuck. 'They've been grave robbing?'

'Sort of. A very specific grave, anyhow. And only a part of it.'

Okay, I get he's a bit shook up, but dragging this out of him is becoming a pain in the arse. 'Which grave? Which part?'

'It's from Ludwig von Mull or something. But they took his rib cage. And it's packed full of magic.'

'Ludwig Muller,' Aicha speaks up behind us, her tone flat. 'Bishop of the Reich.'

Christian Nazis. Talk about cognitive dissonance. 'What do they plan to do with it?'

Al-Ruhban flashes one of his grins again, but it's weak compared to his usual flashbulb charm. 'Luckily, one of them is getting cold feet while the other berates him, so I picked up a fair bit of the plan. Remember I mentioned the pentagrams on the floor?'

I nod. This doesn't sound good.

'They're planning to switch this Muller's rib cage with Petain's, and then call forth some sort of Aryan superbeing who will lead them in a new cleansing purge, first across France and then the world.'

I groan and resist banging my head against the wall in frustration, just. What is it with Nazis and their desire to poke their fingers in the plug socket of the universe to see what happens?

Best to clarify. 'I take it from the workings themselves, for "Aryan superbeing", read some indescribable horror from the realities below our own?'

He nods. 'Give that man a gold star.'

I don't want his gold star. I want this to be the simple "locate the stolen coffin and call the authorities" job it seemed to be when we left the Ile D'Yeu. Is it too much to ask that once, just once, it doesn't end up devolving into an absolute clusterfuck with eldritch horrors terrifying enough to give Lovecraft a permanent stiffy popping through the seemingly revolving door between dimensions? Apparently so.

'How long till they start the ritual?' I want to get in there and put an end to this before that happens.

Al-Ruhban blinks at me. 'They've already started.

They've just taken a momentary pause for the Hungarian one to get the Polish one back on board.'

Fuck. That would have been useful information to have earlier rather than having a jolly old chinwag for several minutes.

Apparently, Aicha is of the same opinion. I turn to suggest to her we get moving just in time to watch her explode the door of the laboratory inwards, showering the room beyond in concrete chips and dust. She always knows how to make an entrance.

The room beyond is exactly as Al-Ruhban described it. It's as if Victor Von Frankenstein designed an underground laboratory instead of one exposed to the elements. Then took some of the brown acid with Himmler and Crowley and just layered Nazi and occult symbols over everything.

Strange machines clank and wheeze in the background. I have absolutely no idea what they're doing apart from adding to the general ambience. They're probably for measuring the effects of whatever absolute dumb-fuck Nazi sorcery these two absolute dumb fucks are up to.

The ritual is clearly underway. I can just about see in the middle of the floor what might be an operating table with what could be a skeleton on it. It's mostly obscured, though, by the glowing circle of enormous power it sits smack bang in the middle of. The floor's covered with a pentagon encased in workings, bringing the protective barrier to life. It's a fuck-ton and a half of magic, and I really wasn't expecting it from a pair of deadbeat Nazi occultists who didn't even remember to set their alarm wards.

Speaking of, I can see the pair at the far end of the bunker-style room. They've set up a dais, presumably for no other reason than dramatic effect. The problem is, the ceiling is low slung, meaning the taller of the two of them has to crick his neck slightly to the side. It makes him look deformed. His weird slightly offset face doesn't help with that.

The other is a short, rotund chap. They're both in their forties, at a guess, but he looks like he's about to keel over any day. His hair has mostly gone from the top of his head, a fact he's thought to cunningly disguise by throwing the few remaining strands dangling down the left-side across the top to the right. Of course, both he and his companion, the great hopes of the Aryan race, have brown hair. What little remains of it in his case, anyhow.

I point at the taller one, who's doing the Quasimodo impression. 'You, you're Igor; I get it. But you —' I point across at the shorter one, who looks more likely to be building model train sets than chthonic chambers. 'You aren't Victor. Loser Von Frankenstein, his even shittier brother, perhaps?'

The two of them stare at us, agape. My creative wit has that effect on people. I look around and realise Aicha has pulled her swords and is looking at them with bloody murder in her eyes. Okay, it might be more her than me.

Eventually, the shorter one finds his tongue again. 'Who are you? What do you want?' His accent is thick, almost Germanic but farther across into Europe. If I've not missed my guess, this is Gabor, the Hungarian.

'We're the shady lair inspectors. Part of the completion of the Grande Nef. Three-year checkup. Make sure all the weird Nazi hideouts with concealed entrances are up to scratch.' I mime examining an imaginary tick board. 'You just carry on destroying the universe. We won't get in your way.'

The tall one, Casimir if I'm right, can't get his head around this. Even with his eyes on a diagonal angle, I can see how hard he's working to digest what I said. More fool him. I rarely know myself.

Gabor isn't so easily confused. He's doing an incredible impression of someone turning into a tomato though. His face is a beautifully virulent shade of bright red. 'You bastards do not know who it is you are messing with.'

I glance over at Aicha with a chuckle. 'Oh, look. He thinks we should be afraid of him!' I turn back to him and put on a nasal redneck drawl. 'See, what we've got here is failure to communicate. Some men you just can't reach…' I stop and think for a second. 'Oh, wait. Yes, I can.'

I lash out a tendril of force like green balefire. There's been enough clever magic and creating spells ad hoc. I just want to throw down some brute force and ignorance now.

It hits him in the chest like a tonne of bricks, sending him flying from his pretentious little dais and smashing into the wall, crushing his rib cage simultaneously. By the time Casimir cranes his neck around to track his friend's impact, then swivels back to us, he discovers Aicha's wakizashi sprouting from his midriff.

'Oh,' he says, which is all we ever hear him say because Aicha shoves her katana blade in through the roof of his mouth and straight into his brain.

Two seconds and we've cleared the room. I look askance at Aicha. 'Well, that was easy,' I say.

This, as I should well know, is a stupid thing to say. A cough from Al-Ruhban draws my attention in his direction.

'Uh…' He points at the magical circle surrounding the mix'n'match skeleton inside. 'Is it supposed to be doing that?'

The power in it has tripled, quadrupled even maybe. It blazes with a deep, dark red that speaks of blood and hell-fire and other such cheery prospects. It was present before, sure. But now it feels *alive*. On the other side, something is coalescing. Something that carries more metaphysical weight than anything I want to tangle with.

A broken phlegmy cough of a laugh sounds from the far wall. I turn to where Gabor is wheezing away. He doesn't look too far from death. Not something I expected him to find funny.

'You're...you're all doomed...now,' he splutters, his teeth stained red in his mad rictus grin. 'Our deaths were... They were the final...component... Poor old Cass...he was losing his...nerve... Thanks to you, he didn't...he didn't have to make the...choice...'

Oh shit. Shit, shit, shit. We just pressed the "on" button for the crazy Nazi monster time. That's a show I can live without watching, let alone taking part in. I stride over and drag the dying man back up the wall.

'How do we stop it?' I shake him. 'How?'

He coughs and spits blood in my face. 'You can't. There's no stopping it. Once we die, there's no way back... The Super-Man will come... The cleansing will...begin... The Aryan...race will...rise again...'

'Rise again?' I shake the fanatical maniac harder. 'Rise *again*? You never stopped rising. If you'd taken a moment from stepping on the heads of everyone else to get even higher up, you might have realised that. How do we stop it?'

I'm practically shouting now, but it makes no difference. Even at full volume, he can't hear me all the way down in Hell. At least, that's where I hope the dead son of a bitch has gone, if the place exists.

'Fuck,' I swear and turn back just in time to see the magical circle burst into even greater power. 'Fuck!' The presence behind it is solidifying, becoming ever more real, ever more here in our world.

I fling my *talent* at it, but the circle just absorbs it, soaking it up, adding it to its own. That's not the effect I was looking for. I look at the others. 'If anyone has a genius idea how to shut this down before an unnamed, unknowable psychopathic evil tears its way into our world, now would be an excellent time to speak up!'

I'm greeted by an overwhelming chorus of absolute silence.

Fuck.

Chapter Twenty-Five

SOMEWHERE, SOMEWHEN, PRESENT DAY

If any giant poorly-concealed allegorical lions rock up, I
shall be very put out.

They know the score now, at least. The next part is finding
out what exactly this weird entity is offering in terms of
"saving" them. The fact she makes me trust her so
completely worries me deeply. If there is one thing my
recent adventures have taught me, it's that if something or
someone seems one way, they're probably entirely the opposite. Except for the Tarrasque. He's exactly as much of a
twat as he seemed when we first met. Fucking Tarrasque.

I turn back to the White Lady. 'So what is it exactly that
you're offering to do for these kids?'

I feel waves of concern tinged with love come washing
off her, and I know she's looking at me with sympathy and
pride. Which still feels utterly weird when *she doesn't actually
have a face*. It's messing my head up a bit. 'I will take them to
another world. One where they can live.'

I notice an important omission. 'Safely?'

The White Lady shrugs without moving, which is both obvious and impossible. 'As safely as they would have lived back on Earth. There are no guarantees in any plane of existence. But they will be free, and they will not age instantly and die.'

'Why did you let us take them from Faerie in the first place?' I demand, feeling my anger rising. 'At least there they had April. It was a new start!'

Again, I'm baptised by the sympathy washing from her, the benign tolerance for my temper. 'I didn't let you do anything. You came to the portal. Here, between the worlds, I can help you. There I could not. Anyway, ask them if they really want to go back to the eternal frost.'

I look over at them. None of them meet my eyes. I guess they feel ashamed that, when they can't go back to Earth, they still don't want to return there. Back to April. I don't blame them. It will be the only April they ever get. And they've been through a Winter full of a lot more than discontent for decades, even centuries.

Aicha catches my eye and tilts her head back just so. It's a slight gesture but enough to tell me she trusts this being. I sigh. End of the day, it isn't my choice. Doesn't sound like much of a choice at all.

'Okay, you heard the lady. All the younger kids — we're going to get you home, back to your parents…'

The White Lady touches my thoughts. 'I will help you with what needs to be done with their remembering.'

I'm torn by that. I don't like the idea of messing with people's memories at the best of times, and while "fucking with your head" is a speciality of fae magic, I don't feel confident in using my fae power yet. I'm also not exactly ecstatic about letting weird luminous uber-Talented other-worldly beings poke around in young human minds. Need to put that to the side for now though. The entire ensemble is looking at me wide-eyed. I try to pick up the thread of what I was saying.

'Young kids, the ones just taken, no problem, straight home. You've only been gone…a few months or so?'

I direct the question towards the White Lady and heave an internal sigh of relief when she again does the weird nodding-without-moving thing. Considering the whole "three years for three hundred" thing that happened to Oisin, I was a tad concerned how much time might have passed on Earth.

'A few months, okay. We'll put together a cover story to explain what happened, but we'll deal with that after. The priority for the moment is you lot.'

I gesture towards the gathered group of teens. There's a momentary wave of guilt when I realise I only know two of their nineteen names. I suppose "fighting for your life against the Unseelie Queen" is a pretty good excuse for a temporary lack of manners, but still. These kids trusted me to get them out, and now it's all turning to shit, and I don't know the first thing about them. It feels like a poor show considering the choice I'm about to give them.

'You've heard the story of Oisin, and you heard what the White Lady said,' I start, but Hair-Curtains, as I've started to think of her, raises her hand and interrupts again.

'Who is she?' The fact she asks at full volume and without looking entirely terrified is testament enough to the foolhardy insolent courage of youth, even if the person in question has been young for a very long time. It's a justified question though. I give her an equally blunt, honest answer.

'No idea. The White Lady, as a concept, is worldwide. No one knows if there's one White Lady or an entire football team of incomprehensible deity-level entities kicking around the globe.' I shoot a glance over at the White Lady in case she wants to enlighten us, but all I get back is a sense of indulgent amusement. Doesn't look like any answers will be forthcoming. 'Generally, she's believed to be a guardian of the portals between worlds. Some people have sought her out, seeking to journey into other realms. Most of those have never come back. But those few who have were clear that she's honourable, if unfathomable, in her dealings. If she accepts a bargain with you, she'll see it through. Anyone's failure to come back was on their heads, not hers.'

I don't think me telling them I know next to nothing about the Lady is exactly reassuring, at least based on the hardly concealed panic I see washing across their faces. As I search for the words to calm them down, Aicha speaks up.

'You can trust her,' she says, her tone flat but firm. Her eyes cut across to the White Lady, but there's no fear or anger there. Maybe the slightest hint of regret but nothing else. She isn't afraid. That does wonders for calming down the group.

Hair-Curtains continues to show more chutzpah than you'd think given she's using her fringe as a shield. 'How do you know?'

It isn't exactly rude nor exactly challenging. I think even the rashest teenager would hesitate to be brusque with Aicha after seeing what went down with Maeve. Still, she wants more information.

Aicha looks at her impassively. There's no menace to it though. 'Made a deal with her. Long ago. Always honoured it up till now.'

Although I know she made a deal with the White Lady to save me from Melusine and again to get into Faerie, this "long ago" mention is news to me, but I can't even claim to know more than a smidgen of her past story. "Long ago" might mean ten years or two hundred or a thousand. I've not got a clue. Nor does she owe me the story. If she feels it's important, she'll tell me. I trust Aicha implicitly. Considering what we've just been through, I'd be a fucking ingrate not to.

'Trust her,' she says again simply, and something about the force of her words, the utter certitude that they carry does the job. The teenagers move away from internal debates as to who the fuck this glowing woman is and instead discuss amongst themselves what they might want to do. It rapidly becomes clear none of them is in a hurry to go snowboarding soon as much as they all miss April. Everyone concentrates on the terrible times before, on all the things they hated about the Unseelie and the Winter Court, but there's more to it than that. I see it when April's name comes up. Eyes slide away, jaws clench, fingers flex into fists and back. Her name doesn't just bring up fond memories or abandonment guilt. They saw how she changed, how she handled the lutin. Her name now sparks those same fight-or-flight mechanisms centuries in Faerie honed towards fleeing. They're scared of their old friend. I'm just glad she isn't here to see it, however understandable it is. It would break whatever's still human in her and freeze her heart completely. I'm glad she'll get to hold on to the memories of their friendship rather than their fear.

It's Aicha who swayed them though. Without her, they might have decided the misery they knew was better than the utter unknown. Her vouching for the White Lady tips the balance, and a short while later, they reach a concurrence. All of them are ready to go. They stand together, nerves visible in leg tremors, in fidgeting hands, in fingers moving back and forth along the forearms like fingering a flute. Still, they remain resolute, determined, unified. There are worse states to be in before heading off to explore strange new worlds. Boldly go and all that.

The White Lady radiates love and pride towards the group. She is like the incarnation of later motherhood, once the immediate weaning and walking and constant threat of death-by-anything has passed. When the hormones are on their way out, and responsibilities are on their way in, and the wings are unfurling little by little to catch the currents of life. I guess it means she won't be there to kiss their boo-boos and stick a plaster on them, but she'll be cheering them on from the sideline. I just have to hope that will be enough.

She turns and makes a gesture without moving because of course she does. Behind her, the darkness beyond the crystals parts like Victorian theatre curtains on a pulley, and greenery shows there. It looks like a meadow — grass or something very like it covering the ground. Birdsong carries through with the smell of fresh, clean air and the warmth of a day where the sun has ejected every cloud out of the sky to make it brilliant and unblemished in its blueness. Billy grins, his teeth gleaming as they catch the sun's rays, and the others mirror his expression. I wonder how long it's been since they've felt warm. Probably since they got taken from Earth, at a guess.

The nineteen of them file through the gap. Billy goes first, scouting ahead, but turns and gives me a half-salute before he's gone. The others follow behind, with Hair-Curtains guarding the rear, her hands on Janey's shoulders, gently leading her through while her eyes dart in all directions, utterly alert and ready behind her hair's concealment.

I've not got time to delve into goodbyes though. The

gap in the black nothingness closes up, and the teens are gone. I turn my attention back to the White Lady.

'You best keep them safe.' Is there anything more ridiculous than issuing ultimatums to someone who can literally rip holes in dimensions and intercept people travelling through the in-between? I try to sound confident and threatening even if I feel like a preschooler squaring up to a professional wrestler, challenging them to go three rounds.

Again, the dominant emotion I get from her is amusement. 'Why would I do that, Cathar?'

I look askance, first at her, then at Aicha. 'You took them from us! They're your responsibility now!'

'I did not take them. I gave them an opportunity. They can take responsibility for themselves now. Their opportunities to flourish or fail are all their own.' She smiles her mouthless smile again, though a tinge of sadness carries through it. 'What sort of guardian would I be if I didn't let them live? That would make me more of a prison guard. Don't you think they've had enough of captivity?'

I open my mouth to argue, then stop and shut it. Good God damn it, she's right. It's very annoying. Only I'm allowed to be right when I'm pissed off. I'd call it getting in touch with my feminine side if it wouldn't make me a raging chauvinist. Plus, Aicha would knock me on my arse if I did. Repeatedly, till I bleed sufficiently to show she's right and I'm wrong.

The Lady carries on looking at me, laughter in her invisible eyes. 'So what now, Last Cathar? Will you challenge me to a duel to assuage your conscience? Or shall we help the children left?'

'Children left,' I grumble, refusing to meet her gaze.

'Can't hear you, dickhead.' Aicha's voice isn't exactly sing-songy (I can't imagine her hitting the local karaoke bar except in the sense of "with a large iron bar to make them all shut up"), but I can still hear the mocking rhythm in it anyhow.

'Help the children left.' I say it with as much humour and good grace as I can manage. Which is precisely none. Petulance is for life, not just for Christmas.

The White Lady turns her attention towards the group of youngsters. They're even closer to each other, and now the older ones have gone, they all look on the verge of panic, the last vestige of safety they had during captivity having been stripped away from them. Now they're stuck with two bloodied strangers, one of whom is wearing the body of the evil bitch who had them kidnapped, as well as an other-worldly being that anyone in their right mind would find categorically terrifying. Considering their own experience of "other-worldly" has been trauma and terror, I don't think the White Lady's presence is helping them to relax.

But she reaches out to them, her luminous aura surrounding them, and their terror and fear sluices off their features. Brows smooth, and the stigma that ingrained itself into their eyes, their cheeks, their souls washes away. Their eyes stare away into nothingness, vacant, no longer with us. I'm not sure what they're seeing now, but it's not the here and now. But neither is it the horrors they've just lived through. That'll have to do for the moment.

'What will they remember?' I need to know. It won't be my responsibility; we'll hand them off to the authorities, let them deal with it; even so, I need to know. Part of me will never forgive myself for not having stopped Jack sooner. Centuries sooner, even though realistically that would have been impossible; if Gwendolyne didn't know what he was up to, how were we ever supposed to find out, especially considering we all thought Maeve had stopped stealing human children? Plus, April's kidnapping shows someone was active on the queen's behalf prior to Jack's employment in her service and had we not dealt with Maeve, doubtless someone else would have stepped into his shoes afterwards. The thought doesn't help. It doesn't stop me from feeling like I failed them. I need to know they're going to be all right.

The White Lady turns her benevolent blankness in my direction again. 'They will remember being taken. Cages, a man disfigured, their captor. Two heroes —a man and a woman— who saved them. Vague descriptions. They'll remember the fear. That is theirs. I cannot take it. Will not. Still, they will not remember Faerie nor the future they expected there. It is the best balance I can offer, to let them return to the world without endless questions both from others and of themselves. It will allow them to heal and to forget with the aid of those equipped to help them.'

It's what I wanted. I can't ask for more. Doesn't mean I won't though. 'We're looking for a man —' I start, but she cuts me off.

'I know. He has his own way through. A magic from his maternal side combined with a certain stolen sceptre.'

Oh fuck, of course. Gwen is the mistress of the Cagot portal, and she mentioned Oberon used Susane to shepherd some of the Cagot across. Portal magic must run in the family, and De Montfort combined that with Melusine's uber-goth staff. He can come and go from Faerie as he pleases without ever needing to pass through the Courts. The sneaky cockgoblin.

I've one last request to make of her. 'Will you make sure we get back to Lyon? Ideally next to Gendarmerie.' Of the three different police forces in France, the gendarmes are probably the best ones to leave a bunch of freaked-out kids with rather than those connected to the military with their automatic weapons and threatening aura.

I feel the smile that I know is there but still can't bloody well see. 'Why, Good Man, we're already there.' Her gaze seems to go past me over my shoulder, and I turn to look. We're no longer in the circle. Instead, I'm looking at a load of buses row-parked in a municipal carpark underneath the uniform grey of some sort of government building. I turn back to the White Lady, only to find her gone. Where she was stands the Gendarmerie. The "Embodiment of the Seventies" pallette of pastel oranges and browns of the squat cube building isn't exactly welcoming, but hopefully the cops inside will offer a warmer reception, especially to a group of lost kids. I think about their distraught parents, wonder if the police charged them or let them go. Considering the lack of evidence, I imagine the latter, but this — getting their kids back — is the thing that will truly set them free. Free from the unbearable misery they've had to live through since they disappeared.

I look the kids over again. The Lady's radiance is still visible on them, a glow of *talent* that means they've not yet come to. Aicha looks as unfazed as ever, but then again, she just single-handedly slaughtered the Wicked Bitch of the West, Maeve herself. Sudden relocation is hardly likely to throw her.

Aicha wraps herself in her *talent*, disappearing out of normal sight. I feel around with the strangeness of my now-fae abilities and find a line of somewhat sad beech trees patrolling a thin strip of grass a little farther down the building. Fae magic runs off nature, borrowing from it when in harmony, stealing from it when not. I'm aiming for more of the former than the latter, so I draw a little of the shade from the trees' branches, wrapping it around my shoulders, cloaking me from sight. Then I take the sensation of a winter's wind gusting through their branches from deep within their slow-living collective memory.

As we walk up the road, I build up the breeze I grabbed and send it whirling towards the heavy metal gate of the Gendarmerie, making it pop free of its fastening and whip back and forth with much accompanying screeching protest. It's enough to get the attention of the police inside. The desk sergeant jogs outside, confusion clear on his features even as we draw farther away. Then he clocks the kids. The gate's forgotten as I let the wind die, and he turns towards the group of children who are just coming round, the last vestiges of the Lady's touch dissolving like morning dew. The youngest one starts to wail that thin high-pitched insistence of a child in uncomprehending distress, and as the first gendarme hurries towards them, others pop their head round the doorway, primordially drawn by that noise that triggers the protector in all of us. Well, most of us. I guess there's always a Half-Marred Jack out there somewhere.

We turn left at the top of the road and head towards central Lyon, keeping our obscuring magic wrapped around us for a few more turns, until we're sure not to get spotted by inquisitive police searching for who might have left the kids outside their premises. The authorities will take care of all the children now, reuniting them with their doubtless frantic and despairing parents. Much though it will do my heart glad to see some positive results from our actions for once, we'll leave that to the proper legal channels. Our part in the children's stories is done.

Chapter Twenty-Six

After all that Shakespearean-level drama and tragedy, I just
want to go home — Lyon, Macduff.

Being on the fucking Tarrasque's turf, which spans the city
boundaries of Lyon at the very least, we don't linger, much
as it would amuse me to watch him try to run the racist bullshit he specialises in on Aicha. After watching her beat
Maeve, I'd be willing to lay money on her making a clutch
purse and a matching pair of extremely ugly Tarrasque-skin
cowboy boots out of him in a matter of moments.
Tempting as that is, we need to get going. We have a
murdering magical maniac to get our hands on. Again.

I pull a burner phone out of my etheric storage as soon
as we drop our cover and give Isaac a call. He wants the
complete story, including every sordid detail, but honestly,
I'm knackered, and it's a lot to tell. We agree it'll be easier
to discuss over a pint of beer and a shot of whisky. Possibly
even a pint of whisky and a shot of beer. If he's not exactly

happy to leave it at that, he's able to read my voice enough to know that will have to do for now.

Isaac tells us he's had the call that his Tesla is back up and running, it having been previously damaged by the Tarrasque, and he's expecting delivery in the next few days. He offers to give them a call and organise for us to pick it up instead. Unsurprisingly, the small town of Vienne, where the incident happened, doesn't have an approved Tesla garage, so it's already in the centre of Lyon, where it was towed so it could get the required pieces to replace those melted by the Tarrasque's phlegm. We flag a taxi to the address Isaac gives us, and by the time we arrive, Isaac has already called and smoothed out any concerns they might have had about handing over the expensive sedan to us. Isaac's charm is astonishingly effective even at a distance. If I'd tried it, they'd have wanted a thousand release forms, signed in triplicate.

We drive up and over Fourviere Hill past the Basilica, the four monumental cross-tipped spires guiding us as we mount. You can see why the locals call it an upside-down elephant, its gothic feet waving in the air. I feel like waving, too, when we cross over the ring road out of Lyon — waving goodbye to all the recent memories that have left foul tastes in my mouth. The fact it means we're getting farther and farther away from the fucking Tarrasque is a bonus too.

We head northwest before turning more westerly, following the A89 in the direction of Clermont-Ferrand and the Massif Central, the mountainous central part of France. Shaped by volcanoes but cut off from the Alps by the slicing presence of the Rhone, it's a gentler, more pastoral scenery than the rugged mountains towards Switzerland. Aicha takes the wheel when we stop for coffee about an hour along the motorway, and I don't argue. When we get back in the car, I've just about enough time to wonder how long it's been since that last night we slept in the Wilds of Faerie before I'm gone, dead to the world, fast asleep.

When I wake, it's night-time, and the dashboard's purposefully dulled glow is far more in tune to my mental state than the brightness of the headlights. I recognise the strip of autoroute currently rumbling away under our tyres. We're cutting through the eastern edge of Montauban, various car garages hawking their wares among industrial units and factories. Part of me is sad to have missed the winding turns of the peaks and gorges between Périgord and Rocamadour, one of my favourite areas of France to drive through. The other is incredibly glad to have finally got some rest and even more pleased not to have woken up screaming. It might not be beating-a-faerie-queen-in-battle, but I'll take that small victory right now.

Now that we know how De Montfort's been getting back and forth to Faerie, we need to focus on finding him here. My guess is that now, having trapped me and killed Susane, he'll not risk heading back there. I grin savagely. Part of me hopes he does, and he stumbles into Winter. I'm sure April will give him a particular cold reception. Probably by encasing him in ice for the rest of eternity. Sadly, I doubt he's that reckless or stupid or that I'm that lucky.

It must be close to midnight by the time we pick up the road towards Auch, peeling off from Toulouse's ring road. Part of me wants to call it a night, head home and sleep in my own long neglected, sorely missed bed, but I owe Isaac answers to his questions. He deserves the full story as a matter of priority. We wend our way up through Colomiers, the hulking concrete barriers placed to dull the roar of traffic for the locals, as well as shield much of the city from view, before taking the turnoff sign-posted for Pibrac. A few minutes more of driving and we're at the small dirt track in the forest itself, leading us up to Isaac's cottage-castle folly, the lunatic dream of some landowner farmer with delusions of grandeur two centuries previous.

We don't bother knocking, just push the door open and walk into the warmth of pooled light around the weathered rural kitchen table. I texted Isaac an updated ETA when I woke up, so I'm not surprised to find him sitting at the table, a glass of whisky in his hand and one loaded with golden ambrosia and a single ice cube waiting for me on the opposite side. There's a glass of some sort of juice for Aicha, but my eyes are entirely fixated on the little dram of perfection he prepared for me. I sink into the nearest chair and take a sip, letting the fire build and roar down my throat to warm my belly and chase the frosts of Winter from my soul.

Aicha takes the other chair, and Isaac absent-mindedly pats her shoulder. That she doesn't stiffen or knock his hand away shows the depth of love and devotion she has for the man. It's a talent of his, inspiring that sort of loyalty, almost more impressive than his *talent*.

'Good to see you again. Glad the two of you have resolved all that nonsense over Franc.'

Aicha looks over at me. 'Not really talked about it in great detail.'

I shake my glass, watching the ice cube swirl around, eddying in the currents I create. Isaac's attempt at a subtle cough, which sounds like he's taken up gargling concrete as a recreational sport, brings my head back up. His attempt at nodding surreptitiously from me to Aicha would have been seen by the Dullahan before he got his eyes unstitched. But just in case I didn't get the message, he mouths, 'Apologise, lad,' at me, over-enunciating each syllable. I groan and rub my temple.

'Apparently, Aich' —I tip my whisky glass at my mentor — 'Isaac's going to break into apology charades if I don't tell you I'm sorry.' I sigh. 'Which I am. Basically —'

'You're a dickhead. I'm brilliant. Know all this. Isaac, you look like Dory trying to talk to a fucking whale; knock it off.' Aicha raises a warning finger at me. 'Try to hug it out, just try. Hard without any fucking arms.' Considering she already chopped her own one off to rid this body of its previous owner, I'm prepared to take her seriously on that.

And I appreciate her far too much to get up inside her personal space. I raise my whisky glass, give her the nod, and hold her gaze for a minute. Let her see it. How far beyond words my appreciation goes. How sorry I am for getting it wrong. That she came for me, saved me when any normal person would have walked away and left me to drown in my own shit. She snorts as she looks away, but she tips her fruit juice in my direction nonetheless.

Thanks, Aich. You're the best. Always have been. Always will be.

Isaac smiles. 'Brilliant. About bloody time too. Anyhow, sounds like you've got quite some story to relate. Let me just make sure Jakob is listening.' His gaze goes blank for a moment as he turns his attention inwards, talking to his brother, who resides in his body along with the two angels they've each bonded to — Jakob to Nan, Isaac to Nith. Then he's back. 'Right, we're both paying full attention. Let's start from the beginning. What happened once you went through the portal? Did your bloody, lunatic suicide-vest plan actually work?'

So I do. I go right back to the start. I tell him about arriving in Oberon's Court, blagging my way out with my dead man's switch. About tracking Susane and my supposed son across the Wilds of Faerie. When I get to Susane's death and Simon's big reveal, I have to stop for a minute. Huge tears splash down Isaac's cheeks. 'The poor lass,' he murmurs. 'Horrible. Just horrible. I am sorry, my dear boy. We both...just... I can't, lad. I don't have the words.'

My own eyes feel hot too, that burning itch where the emotions scratch like wounded, whimpering animals, demanding to escape, and once the floodgates open, I can't hold back the tears. The anger, the incandescent rage again at Simon De Montfort for what he did is still there, but it takes a backseat. This is a moment for the grief to flow, for me to mourn properly. For my twice-lost wife, the only woman I ever loved. For a child who was never truly mine and for the dream that died at the same moment Susane did, both times. For evaporating fancies of lives lost before we could live them and for pain that outweighed hope for hundreds of years, has dragged me down and made the taste of life turn to ashes on my tongue. I weep for everything and everyone that a vicious, hateful man took from me, for all the hurt he gave to so many people to satisfy his own vindictive nature and further his own dark schemes. For those two thousand and six victims, especially those extra six. Isaac stands and holds me, and I bury my head against his chest and pour my heartache out in soundless, gasping howls. I lament love and dreams left unburied, and in doing so, pay tribute to them, to their weight and worth, and unburden my soul in the process.

By the time I calm down, I feel lighter than I have in the longest time. It reminds me that, what with rescuing stolen kids and letting go of some of my own tight-cradled darkness, I need to do some serious sinning soon to put a bit of weight on my soul again. Between Susane's loss and my time in the cave, I'd have happily walked away from this painful mess of an existence at various points during my horrendous sojourn in Faerie. Now I've done my grieving though, I don't wish to disappear into nothingness on my next death — which might happen if my soul becomes too clean. That makes the next step perfect for me as the next step is bloody vengeance.

'You need to tell Gwendolyne, lad.' Isaac's words are soft but firm. 'Or else, I can do it if you prefer?'

My breathing has calmed, stopped hitching, and I shake my head. I'll call her. I owe her that much.

Isaac dials the number and passes me the phone. It connects after a couple of rings.

'Rabbi? Did the idiot pup make it back yet?' The words are harsh, but I wonder if I imagine a tone of concern behind them.

'I did. I'm here now, Gwen.' Considering the news I have to give her, I'm not going to give her a hard time for the name calling. She can have that one.

Silence holds for a moment, and it breaks my heart all over again. This time for her. Because I know what that silence feels like. The instant before a momentous question is asked, when a definite and final answer will be given. A last blissful moment of ignorance, of potential where the world might still hold the response you want it to give.

But such a moment can't last forever. She asks the question she needs to. '… and Susane?'

I swallow. 'She's…she's dead, Gwen. The bastard killed her when I tried to get her away. I'm… I'm sorry.' Inadequate words. But how can language stand up and bear the weight of giving such news to a parent? It feels like reality itself should crack and crumble before the heaviness of delivering such tidings.

I hear the hitching gulp, that tiny swallowing intake as

she struggles to grasp the unbearable load that just became hers to shoulder forever. I give her a moment, space to allow it to seep in enough that she knows the truth. Whatever she wants to know, I'll tell her.

When she does speak, it's simple. 'Did he pay?'

'Not yet, Gwen. But he will. We're after him. And he'll pay. I swear it on my soul, Gwen, he'll pay for what he did.'

'Make sure he does, Good Man. You come and see me when he has. I'll take the full tale's telling when you can give me that ending. For now...' Her voice quavers, cracks. She swallows, then comes back. 'For now I'll find him for you.'

Ah, yes. Luckily, even in her grief, in the throes of the loss of her child, Gwen can think clearer than I can. It didn't even occur to me but he wears a Cagot's body. Thanks to Oberon's gift, Gwen should be able to track him down.

Sadly. The emphasis is on should. Her voice is cold fury, dripping with frustration when she speaks again. 'I can't find the prick. You're sure he's on Earth?'

'According to the White Lady he is.'

A shrill noise distorts the tinny speaker, ear-piercing enough that I have to pull it from my ear. It's only as it fades that I realise it's Gwendolyne screaming in frustration. I hear her take two, three heaving breaths. When she speaks her iron self-control is back, her will imposed once more. 'He's blocking me somehow then. I can't detect any additional Cagot, any outside those I already know and watch.'

I can imagine how much that pisses her off. A curse of a gift, and the one time it'd actually do her good, to allow her to track down her daughter's killer, it doesn't work. Typical Fae present. I suppose I shouldn't be surprised. De Montfort has been ready for every potential threat up until now. He would have known about Gwen's gift. Of course the cunning bastard has come up with some way to nullify it.

'It doesn't matter, Gwen.' It's weird to be reassuring her, a powerhouse of a woman. I still think she needs that right now. 'There'll be other ways to find the fucker.'

'You come see me after — promise me that.'

I know what she's asking. Kill him and survive it to bring her back his metaphorical pelt. 'I promise, Gwen. His story's ending will be yours to have.'

'That'll do for now, Paul.' The phone goes dead. I didn't think my heart could hurt more, thinking of my dead love. Turns out I was wrong.

I take a moment, sipping my drink and letting the pain wash through me. Between breaking down and then the conversation with Gwen, relating the story of my time in the cave to Isaac is easier to bear after unloading those pent-up emotions, after concentrating on the pain of Susane's death. My imprisonment feels like a story now — something to tell rather than to live, to say without it transporting me back to that unending dark all over again. I'm not even close to over it, but I am gaining some distance from it. One step at a time, I'm finding my way out of that damn trap. I'll make it, however long it takes.

After telling of my reunion-rescue with Aicha, I whip through the battle with the wolves and the Nain Rouge's useless help, hurrying along to the rescue of the kids.

Now it's Isaac's turn to shed a few tears. He wipes them away with the cotton hankie tucked in his breast pocket and murmers 'bless you, bless you both for that,' when I tell him we got them out.

I take the time to give Aicha's battle with Maeve the dramatic retelling it deserves, and Isaac's eyes grow rounder and larger. He scoots to the edge of his seat, enthralled. If he were a nail biter, I doubt he'd have a cuticle left even knowing how the story must turn out considering we're both here, sitting in front of him. When I tell him of the iron filings, of Aicha's genius plan, he leaps to his feet, his chair skidding backwards under his enthusiasm, and bursts into rapturous applause.

'*Chapeau*, lass. Incredible. Bloody incredible! A battle for the songs of the bloody Valkyries, that one, my goodness.'

It takes quite some time to get him to calm down and sit again. Aicha rolls her eyes, but I see their slight crinkle, and if I didn't know better, I'd say she has a small glow to her cheeks. She loves Isaac as much as I do, and even Aicha isn't immune to his charm or unappreciative of his praise.

I pick up the story again, telling him of my brief reign as the ruler of Winter, of passing it off to April and our interrupted portal ride. When I tell him about the White Lady, his eyes slide over to Aicha, consternation clear in his thinned, drawn lips, but he holds his tongue. It's an understandable reaction; I'm just as worried what deals or promises she's made with this ineffable, incredible Power, but Aicha is a big girl. We have to trust her decision, back her play, just like she's done for all the idiotic sketchy plans I've got her mixed up in. It can't be worse than getting your magic munched because of an unnecessary promise to the Mother of the Sistren of Bordeaux. The fact she doesn't spend every second of every single day taking the living piss out of me for that shows exactly what a good friend she is.

'… and then she dumped us outside the Gendarmerie and fucked off. So here we are.' I finish, both the story and my whisky, giving my glass a hopeful waggle, the pathetic sliver of ice left too reduced to even make a tinkle against the sides.

Isaac takes both my entirely unsubtle hint and my

tumbler, heading to top us both up with whisky and ice. Then he slumps back into his chair, mopping his brow with his pocket handkerchief.

'My goodness, lad. I thought we went through some tumultuous adventures of recent times, but that's…' He stops, searching for the right words. 'That's quite a bloody escapade, to say the least. Hold on. Jak wants to say something.'

The micro-shift of features rippling across his face lets us know Jakob has taken up the body's reins. 'Well, my dear boy, my dear girl, it sounds like you've been through the wringer. I know you're both going to want to go charging off full steam ahead after this blackguard, De Montfort.' He turns his eyes my way, sympathy clear in his regard. 'Is that the best option right now though? I know there is some time limit, but sixteen years is quite some stretch, is it not?'

'I appreciate it, Jak, but even though he tried to make it so I was gone for sixteen years, time really is of the essence. We don't know what he's up to, and I won't be able to relax until we do.'

'But will you be in a fit state to do battle with him? Not simply physically but mentally as well? This' —his features screw up in distaste— 'disgusting so-and-so has proven himself quite the clever bounder. He's been playing you for hundreds of years, intent on causing you misery. Are you really in tip-top shape right now?'

I hear the doubt in his voice, and I reckon it's well merited. I'm grimy, covered in this body's previous owner's blood, and as much as this conversation has helped ease away some of my suffering, I'm not foolish enough to think one big cry is going to resolve the sort of trauma I'm now carrying. My damage pokes out from behind my eyes, present in my posture and poise, easy enough for someone as empathetic and aware as Jakob to spot. However, thinking about how I look brings an even more important realisation to the forefront of my fatigue-clogged brain. I'm still wearing Maeve's torture-chamber of a dress in a house that contains T-shirts and jogging bottoms. This will not stand. I, on the other hand, do.

'Sorry, Jak. Hold that thought,' I say grimly. 'I've got a bonfire to build. Be right back.' Then I sweep out of the room, which is really the only way you can leave a room when dressed like a fairy queen. Good God, I'm done with wearing anything that trails on the ground behind me ever again.

Chapter Twenty-Seven

Is this entire outfit getting ceremonially burned? Of
corset is.

Here's something I never thought about before. Modern
casual clothing isn't designed with wings in mind.

I practically shred the ballgown getting it off, especially
as I have no idea how to pass it over my extra appendages.
There's no way I'm going to ask for help; it's weird enough
being in a body that doesn't look like mine in the slightest.
Normally, I'd get naked around either Aicha or Isaac
without hesitating. Wearing a form most would hold up as
the pinnacle of female perfection makes me feel distinctly
uncomfortable. My issue, not theirs. Recognising that
doesn't make it go away though.

I eventually get dressed by cutting a large section out of
a T-shirt and folding my wings in tightly to my back. That
also helps to accommodate my breasts, which I studiously
avoid looking at while naked. It's quite an accomplishment

to make yourself both uncomfortable and slightly aroused. It's also deeply unsettling.

I head back downstairs and sink into the wooden chair with an enormous sigh of relief. Isaac topped my glass back up. I tip it in acknowledgement at Isaac/Jakob and sink half of it in one go. I'm more interested in getting the alcohol out of the tumbler and into my stomach than working out who's in charge of their body at this particular moment.

After I burn away some of my completely unnecessary awkwardness with the drink's dragon breath, I look back across. Apparently, it's still Jakob in charge, waiting patiently for my answer. Aicha leans back in her chair, savouring her juice. She's earned it. Two juices, even. Hell, go wild. Pour her a well-merited third.

I peer thoughtfully at Jakob, trying to recall where we were. 'Right. So let me get this straight. Question is, am I in a fit shape to be going toe-to-toe with De Montfort?'

Jakob nods. I pause for a moment. I gave it some thought while struggling with clothing and making myself feel like a hormonally overcharged schoolboy. It's a question asked with love, out of genuine concern, and Jakob warrants a proper response.

'Probably not,' I say honestly, looking down into the ripples of my glass rather than at Jakob's borrowed eyes as I lay myself even barer than I was a minute ago upstairs. 'Thing is, I'm not sure I'm going to get any more ready, and he certainly is. He's had centuries to plan, to lay the ground-work to trip me up and beat me down, and let's be honest; if Aicha didn't save my ass —'

'Again.'

'— again, yes. Thanks for that essential interjection, Aicha. Then he'd have broken me entirely. Problem is, if I rest, yeah, I might get a bit more mentally sharper. Or I might start finding excuses.'

I suck at my lips, concentrating on the sensation of them rubbing over my teeth's peculiar sharpness rather than the pain of the humiliating truth. It has to be said though. 'Maybe I'll think, *Oh I can take another day*. Then it might become another week. Another month. I have sixteen years until he expects me to be out, why not next year? Thing is —' I force myself to look up, to meet his gaze, to let him see the raw wounds inside of me. 'I'm terrified, Jak. I am so damn scared of what else he might have cooked up. De Montfort doesn't strike me as the kind of man who sticks all his eggs in one basket full of torture implements. He's wreaked misery and suffering on me and broken me already, twice. Once each time he killed the only woman I ever loved. Sure, I want my revenge. I want to make him pay for what he's done. But anger isn't the overriding emotion. Not if I'm honest. Fear is. And the longer I wait, the more I'm going to let that take root and blossom in my mind. And you know what the Bene Gesserit said.'

'No? Who is this Benny? A philosopher, perhaps?'

Oh, yeah. I forgot the whole "trapped in a skull for centuries by my ex-BFF and missing out on literature and popular culture" thing with Jakob. 'Of sorts, yeah. Basically, they said fear is the mind-killer, a form of small death —'

'Ow. My ears.' Aicha winces like I've just burst her drum with a rusty screwdriver. 'Ignore the philistine. "Fear is the mind-killer. Fear is the little death that brings total obliteration." Want me to go on?'

'I think that's enough to give Jak the general gist. Point is, if I stop still now, try to heal with this hanging over me? I won't. I'll just let it kill me step by step, let it break me and make me a slave to that fear. So the only option for now is to keep going. I recognise that there is some serious self-building to do when we get to the other side. But if we don't get to the other side, I can't start laying the foundations. Honestly?' I make sure he can read the truth, the desperate plea for support in my gaze. 'If we don't, I'll never rebuild. I'll just crumble.'

Jakob dabs at his eyes with the hankie, then leans forward to pat my arm awkwardly but affectionately. 'Of course, my dear boy. I fully understand.' He blinks and then he's gone, and Isaac's back in his place. 'Right, lad. So we've established the game plan is to go after De Montfort. Question is, how do we manage that if Gwendolyne can't locate him? Where is he? What on earth do you think he's actually after?'

I tap my glass on the table, keeping myself from smashing it into a million frustrated shards through sheer force of will. 'I don't have a clue. Looks like he'd learnt from Ben's example not to give me his whole master plan just because he had me trapped. Did I mention that he fucking orchestrated that whole skull shitshow, by the way? Fucking absolute bastard.' I nudge the glass towards Isaac hopefully. He obliges and goes to fetch us both a top-up like the saint among mortal men that he is. I make a mental note to splurge on something really special spirits-wise for him in the near future.

Thinking about Ben and what happened brings me back to that weird shack. The one in those strange endless sands apparently outside of Life itself. Both Aicha and Isaac (and by extension, I assume, Jakob as well) know about my visits there after my first death and after Ben killed me in his lab and of my recent visits in between my agonising deaths in the dark of that cave in Faerie.

'What about the thing the voice told me?' I say slowly, rolling the words around my tongue, tasting them like wine.

Aicha peers up at me from under her hooded brow. 'Want to specify which particular schizophrenic episode you're referencing? Was it a giant, freaky-looking bunny rabbit? *Drop Dead Fred*?' She leans closer. 'Did God talk to you through the neighbour's dog?'

'While I don't think anyone will rush to label me as sane,' I start, but Aicha interrupts.

'Agreed.' We both stare at each other for a moment in silence before she graciously waves her hand like a passing monarch. 'Do go on.'

I eye her suspiciously. 'As I was saying,' I continue, waiting for her to interrupt again. 'I'm not claiming perfect sanity, but I haven't started hearing random voices yet. Only when I die horrendously, apparently.'

A thought occurs to me, triggered by the last part of Aicha's sardonic interruption. I look over at Isaac. 'Could it be an angel? A Bene Elohim or someone else from the higher dimensions trying to give us a hint?'

An expression crosses Isaac's face —a certain rumpling of the skin above his nose, his eyes pulling together, a flare to the nostrils— that tells me not only is he giving it serious thought, but he's majorly annoyed with himself that he didn't think of it first. Then his brow softens slightly, his eyes lose focus, and I know he's gone to ask a higher authority on the subject.

'Nith doesn't know. Neither does Nan,' he says when he comes back to us. 'They both seem pretty sure it won't be one of the Elohim but can't discount it could be someone else from higher or lower up the dimensional ladder.' That answer seems to satisfy him about as much as it does me.

It isn't really the point right now though. 'Fascinating

and frustrating though it is in equal measures, that wasn't why I brought it up. The voice told me to remember the key, then her hand did a striptease all the way down to the bone.'

It was weird, her skin turning translucent so I could see the bones underneath. I mean, even more weird than the whole being in a crazy shack in another dimension with some unidentified being who's been dropping occasional cryptic hints at me for centuries. So, pretty weird.

'There does seem to have been an inordinate amount of skeletal parts involved of late,' Isaac says, rubbing his chin.

'Two super powerful skulls,' Aicha puts in. I can see her thought process whirring behind her eyes. 'Plus, Melusine's staff.'

'Which was a whole mix of arm and hand bones imbued with some pretty heavy-duty magic.' I think back to that last showdown with De Montfort. 'He seemed to think the staff was a big key part of his plan. If everything in his fucked-up scheming until my capture was Phase 1, it really felt like having that allowed him to progress to Phase 2. At first, I thought it was because of the wish-granting power in it, but I'm not so sure now. He didn't use it in that capacity even though he could have. It allowed him passage to and from Faerie to set his trap, but otherwise, it seemed to be more what it represented than what it could do.'

It's distinctly puzzling and feels a bit like the whole shit-show with Ben all over again — a cunning, well-informed foe several steps ahead of us while we stumble about groping in the dark. The mental image brings back unpleasant recent memories. I shudder and push them away, my stomach dropping as I struggle to stay in the present.

I look over at Isaac. 'You still got Almeric's skull?' The original plan was he'd hang on to it while I went after Susane and my son in Faerie, but I was gone for a lot longer than planned. He might have dropped it back into Lou Carcoilh's safekeeping over in Hastingues. Lou's natural ability to shield magic thanks to his *talent*-proof shell makes him a more secure guardian than even the farmhouse's angelic wards. However, Isaac gives me a slightly abashed grin and leans around behind him to the wooden bread bin on the kitchen side. When he lifts the hinged front, I see the cold gleam of bone. Which is a poor substitute for toast, unless you're a giant prepared to grind it down to make your bread first.

I heave a sigh of relief. 'Okay, so we're good on that count. I suggest we gather up the other one from Lou and then we can try and work out what the hell is the connection between the bones.' A sudden thought hits me. 'What about the whole thing with the Nain Rouge? Y'know, his habit of biting his own fingers off and the skeleton key thingy where he made me pull out all my right arm bones to get out of his escape room? She said remember the key. There was the key right there!'

Aicha looks at me with a flat expression. 'Paul, you've cracked it. The Nain Rouge is the criminal mastermind behind the whole thing. De Montfort is his henchman. He's clearly an evil genius.'

I look at her for a minute, equally blankly, nodding slowly before we both crack up. The escape room he trapped me in just before the shizzard got his grubby mitts on me was a pretty cunning and twisted setup, but he also made some basic errors, like using his own home to spring the trap on two highly Talented, highly destructive magicians. All the resultant damage was nobody's fault but his.

I'd say his chances of a successful insurance claim were slim to none.

'Mind you,' Aich adds after a moment. 'It seems to suggest the "bones as key" idea is good. Plus, if he is involved, I'm going to use him as my personal Bop-It. We already owe him for his absolutely shit plan of infiltrating the Winter Court. He should have known about the snow.'

'True, but we should have thought of it as well.' I'm pissed off about that whole scenario, but I feel some of the fault at least lies with us for that particular fuck-up. 'Right.' I push myself up to standing. 'Let's get on our way to Hastingues.'

Nobody else moves. Aicha and Isaac just sit there, a look of patient tolerance on Isaac's face, a look that says, "you're a massive twat" on Aicha's.

'What?' There's something I'm missing. That much is clear. The problem is, I don't know what because of the aforementioned missing it.

'What time is it, lad?' Isaac asks gently.

I shrug. 'I don't know. Midnight? One?'

'It's three in the morning. When did you last sleep?'

I start to say, 'A few hours ago,' but Aicha interrupts me. 'A proper night's sleep, dickhead. Not two or three hours dozing in the car. Not with half an eye open in case a boggart bites your foot off. Proper sleep.'

I close my mouth again and think it through. 'How long were we in Faerie?' I ask Isaac.

'Nearly five weeks, all told.'

I do the mental maths. 'Then about…five weeks? Give or take a day or two.'

Aicha sits back victorious while Isaac stands and lays a comforting hand on my shoulder. 'I get what you said, lad, about needing to crack on and heal up later. You still need to sleep. Not just that body you're currently porting around, which is —' A grin spreads across his face that is dangerously close to a smirk. 'A significant upgrade from your normal look.' The grin vanishes, and serious Isaac is back. 'Your mind, your spirit both need rest, or else you're going to burn out rapidly. You can't hold back the demons, let alone even dream about conquering them if you don't recharge your batteries.'

At his words, I realise just how weary I am. Not just physically, although I am exhausted, but mentally, spiritually. I've been walking through fire so long, I've forgotten what it feels like not to burn. Being on the edge of a nervous collapse has become my normal modus operandi, but I'm not in imminent danger anymore. Now I need to be able to think clearly, to see a way for us to track down De Montfort and make him pay for all he's done. That isn't going to happen if I'm constantly wandering around on the edge of burnout only fought off by terror and caffeine.

Isaac claps me on the arm. 'Right, lad. There's no point rushing off when you're half dead and about to keel over any second. Get some sleep, get back on form, and we'll deal with it all in the light of day.' He guides me towards the stairs, where I can trudge up to one of the guest rooms and pass out. 'One night isn't going to make any difference, is it?'

I hear the words, but I don't really pay attention to them, which is a clear indicator of exactly how exhausted I am. If I were capable of any form of rational thought other than putting one foot in front of the other in order to get to the nearest comfortable surface to pass out on, I'd recognise just how much he's tempting fate by saying such a thing.

And Lady Fate never misses out on an opportunity to kick me square in the bollocks...

Chapter Twenty-Eight

Six o'clock on a Tuesday morning is a time designed for drinking a cup of tea, perhaps perusing the newspaper. What it isn't designed for is standing about helplessly while dead Nazis birth an eldritch nightmare into our plane of existence.

The circle's power isn't diminishing, and the malevolent force inside it will come tearing into our reality any minute. We've tried various things, and nothing has worked. Al-Ruhban tried hitting it with everything from a sword he made appear apparently out of nowhere (I didn't see him access any sort of etheric storage) to Casimir's dead body. Our *talent* bounces off it, as did the body, and as far as we can tell, the dead arseholes carefully set the magic up to repel all attempts to cross it until whatever is inside arrives fully in our world. The two knuckleheads who pulled this off might not have remembered to set alarm wards, but they knew what they were doing regarding configuring this circle of power.

I'm fresh out of ideas, and to make matters worse, brain

fog's setting in like marshland mists on an autumn morning. Burning my *talent* to keep awake isn't an option. I need to keep every single drop in reserve for when we battle whatever is coming out of there. Reaching into my own storage, I grab my coffee thermos and take a huge swig. The caffeine does precisely nothing. I'm fast approaching burnout, if I'm not there already.

'Good God damn it,' I scream, then hurl the thermos in frustration. I scream even louder when I watch it just bounce off exactly like everything else did. Not that I'm surprised, but I've reached my limit. Keeping calm and in control was for yesterday's Paul. Today's Paul is all about losing it completely and having a shit fit simultaneously.

I stomp back towards the body of Gabor. I don't expect to find anything new —I've searched it at least ten times— but maybe kicking it repeatedly will help me feel better.

'Paul?' There's a strange tone in Aicha's voice. It almost sounds like hope. I stop kicking Gabor and turn around to see she's pointing at where the thermos fell.

The coffee inside is spilling out, and where it's doing so, it's unstoppable in its march, pouring inexorably forward...which involves crossing the magic circle. Which it does. No problem at all.

I scramble over and fall to my hands and knees next to the dented thermos flask. 'Liquids. It doesn't stop liquids.' I crouch lower, trying to see as clearly as I can the runes that created the spell. The trickle of coffee hasn't erased any, but if I'm not wrong, the writing looks ever so slightly fainter.

'I think they did this in chalk.' I stand up, excitement practically radiating off me. 'If we get enough water on it, it'll wash the whole spell away. Now, who's got water?'

We look around. There's all this amazing electronic equipment, power sockets everywhere, gadgets to fill the craziest of mad scientists with glee but no faucet. No mop and bucket. Not even a stash of drinking water that we can see. These guys really didn't understand the importance of hydration. Or else they knew it was a potential flaw with their plan and didn't want to take the risk.

'Fuck, fuckery, fuck,' I yell and kick the concrete floor. This, you'll be unsurprised to hear, is entirely stupid and only results in me hopping around with an exceptionally sore and probably broken big toe on my right foot. In a battle between my tiny breakable bones and poured set concrete, the floor wins. Who'd have imagined? Nope, apparently, it'll take more than a kick of frustration to break the floor or walls or ceiling...

I stop dead. Aicha picks up on it, of course. I flick my eyes upwards. 'The Seine,' I say.

Her eyes widen, and she looks close to swearing herself. It must annoy the hell out of her to have missed that. The frustration passes though, and she gives me an appreciative nod. 'How do you want to do it?'

I think for a moment. 'You've got more brute force than I do, unless you've got something up your sleeve?' I look over at Al-Ruhban, but he shakes his head. 'Okay, you smash the fuck out of the ceiling, Aicha. I'll stand ready to throw up a barrier and hold back the water at the doorway, okay?'

She nods. Al-Ruhban and I step outside the door while she positions herself just inside the doorway itself. I see her concentrating, thinking it through. Then she summons all the *talent* she can draw. I feel her soaking it up through the floor, from the earth itself. She's pulling on power that can topple a mountain, the pressure that makes a diamond out of coal, the weight so heavy it keeps the moon locked in orbit around us. Then she surges all of that upwards and hits the ceiling with a blast of elemental force.

The cement roof pulverises, and for a moment it's like some strange Christmas scene, like the room's inside a snow globe that someone has just picked up and shaken hard. But only for a moment. A second later, the earth the blast smashed through comes tumbling down in huge sods, raining down and bouncing off the energy ward over the working. I grab Aicha by the shoulder, hauling her backwards and throwing up a barrier. Just in time.

Water explodes downwards, filling the room in seconds. It smashes into my barrier with an answering force to that thrown upwards by Aicha, as if it wants to demonstrate its own elemental power, to prove itself the equal of the earthen *talent* that came tearing up at it from its underbelly. It takes all my remaining power to hold the line.

While I do so, we watch the liquid obliterate the circle of chalk scrawls in a moment, and the malevolent force inside it disintegrates back out of our reality with a loathsome caterwaul that makes the hairs on my neck stand on end. Then it's gone. As the circle dissipates, the concrete opening where the door was shrinks and, before I know it, disappears completely.

I look across to my right. Al-Ruhban has merged with the concrete wall and is moving it across like one of those sliding tile puzzle toys. He brings the two sides together and then smooths it shut. With a sigh of relief, I release my shield and plonk myself down against the wall of the corridor. The other two join me.

'This was a terrible idea for a holiday,' I say to Aicha. 'Next time I'm choosing.'

She raises an eyebrow at me. 'Like when you took us to Prague?'

Ouch. 'Valid. We're both shit at holiday destinations.'

We sit there for a while, just catching our breaths both magically and physically. After a bit, a thought occurs to me.

'It's a damn shame we didn't get Petain's body back,' I say.

Aicha leaps to her feet. 'Fuck. No. No, no, no.'

It baffles me. It wasn't our finest moment, but we stopped the terrible occult evil getting through. I'd put that in the win column. 'What's the matter, Aich?'

'No. Can't have that. It'll become a folk legend for the far right. The missing coffin. The never recovered body. They'll go fucking King Arthur about him. Inspire the fuckers. A fucking already dead martyr. Got to do something.'

For a moment, I think she's going to smash her way back through the now closed wall. Instead, she turns to Al-Ruhban. 'You. Open sesame. Chop chop.'

Okay, she's not going to madly bust her way through and drown us. She's going to calmly open the doorway back up and drown us. I'm about to argue the toss with her when Al-Ruhban raises his hand.

'I can get it for you.' He stands up, dusting his trousers off.

I blink and wrack my totally overloaded and wiped-out brain. 'How?'

'My elements are earth and water. I can pass through and get the skeleton and the coffin. Anything I'm holding I can bring back through with me.'

'Good,' Aicha snaps. 'Less exposition. More moving from there. Ex position.'

He raises one of his weird fingers, the tattoos moving like an ink-black aquarium under his skin. 'On one condition.'

Aicha narrows her eyes, but I feel that's a tad unfair. I've no idea what the deal is between the two of them, but the guy's played it super straight so far in my book. He's let us rock up in his territory, for starters. Then he came along and helped us even though he could have just left it all to us to handle. I raise a calming hand to Aicha. 'Let's hear him out.'

'The rib cage. From the Nazi priest. The thing they used to power the ritual.'

Man, he loves dragging things out. 'I am aware of the rib cage you're talking about.'

'Let me have it.'

Now it's my turn to narrow my eyes suspiciously. 'Why?'

He looks at me, his arms spread wide, his body language open. 'If I give that to Leandre, it'll prove my worth and be fitting tribute enough that I'll get to keep this territory I've taken. Probably expand it even.'

I think it through. I don't know much about the Prince of the Lutins other than he's a fae who hates fae. All who've met him, though, speak of his fair nature. He's a political beast, of course, but he's kept Paris at peace with both his *talent* and his intelligence for longer than I've ever known it.

There's one final clincher for me. I turn to Aicha. 'Isaac said he liked him, that he's the most honourable fae he's ever encountered,' I say. I meet her eyes and make sure the message is clear. Despite that, the decision is hers. Whichever way she goes, I'll back her play.

Aicha considers it for a minute. Eventually, she turns to Al-Ruhban. 'Okay, but' —she raises a finger of her own— 'if you suspect even an inkling that he plans to use it for something nefarious, like summoning fucking demons, you call us, we get it back. No "he has my loyalty" bullshit. Agreed?'

He nods his head, and the two of them clasp palms. Then Al-Ruhban turns and trudges through the concrete like it's viscous oil, back into the room we just left. We settle down to wait, trying not to pass out while we do so.

By the time we manhandle the coffin up to the Citroen, day has definitely broken. Al-Ruhban gives us a hand getting it up, which is appreciated considering how exhausted we are. We drop the back seats and shove the coffin in gracelessly. Al-Ruhban stays behind to go rescue the drowned magical rib cage of a Nazi priest because that's how fucked up the world I live in is. Aicha throws a *don't look here* on the coffin and drives us to the nearest hotel. I'm so tired I don't even see what it's called. Aicha hurls a wodge of cash at the receptionist, who makes the room keys appear with such rapidity that what little of my brain is still functioning upgrades the amount thrown from a "wodge" to a "major chunk". Then I'm being guided down a slightly twisty corridor by my friend, into the ever-present lingering smell of stale smoke that hangs in every hotel room everywhere. Next thing, I've progressed from vertical to horizontal without clocking how and proceed to pass from awake to asleep similarly miraculously.

When I surface once more, it's early evening. I gave my body clock a similar kicking to the one I gave my *talent*, but they'll both recover. I can live with that. Stumbling down the shag-carpeted stairs, I find Aicha studying the food menu and nursing a Virgin Mary.

'Anything vegetarian?' I ask hopefully.

'Mushroom soup starter,' she replies. 'Caesar salad. Hold the chicken.'

I groan. '*Et tu, Brute?*'

'Hold the amateur dramatics too. Going home soon.'

We pass our order, and I force myself properly upright in my chair. 'What are we going to do with the you know?'

'Coffin?' she asks blandly. I resist the urge to *shh* at her and flap my hands, well aware she's right; no one is listening, but they will be if I do that. Instead, I give my tiniest secret agent nod.

'I've been listening to the radio. Authorities picked Pierre up.' She pauses as our starters arrive, and she spreads her pâté over the crusty fresh bread. 'Massol is giving a press conference right about now. Trying to negotiate for a new burial site for the coffin.'

'Press conference about what?' I slurp my soup, which manages to deeply satisfy me and massively piss off a snooty guest over the way. Success on both fronts.

She cuts her bread into neat slices. 'He's setting out the demands for where the coffin should be laid.'

I snort. 'So he doesn't know the coffin disappeared?'

'Nope. Nor does he know Pierre's been nabbed and his dad's in the wind. Though not for long, I'd think. Reckon we scared them both too thoroughly so there was no one to tip Massol off.'

I agree. Neither struck me as the sharpest or sneakiest tool in the box. A sudden thought strikes me. 'What if we pop the coffin back in the garage, then let the cops know where it is?'

She stops spreading her bread, puts the slice down, the knife too, and looks at me wide-eyed. 'That is…that is brilliant. An amazing idea.' Her eyes go back to normal, and she picks up her food again. 'So brilliant I obviously already thought of it. Dropped it back and called the hotline half an hour ago. They should be… Ahh, there we go.'

She looks over my shoulder, and I turn to see a small black-and-white telly attached to the rear wall. Aicha makes a surreptitious gesture, and the volume increases loud enough we can hear it. Some of the other diners start, but I don't give a fuck. They've not been battling demonic forces under the Seine in the early hours of the morning. They can live with listening to a news report.

I can't see Massol properly at this distance, but his voice has an unpleasant, triumphant grate to it. He's taking full responsibility for the theft, entirely unrepentant. The coffin, he crows, will never be found unless he shows the authorities where it is, and he will never tell if yada yada yada, blah blah blah. And then, amid all this arrogant posturing, the police arrive. Massol has obviously been expecting them and looks pleased as punch, but then the commanding officer leans forward and whispers something in his ear. No doubt, he's just revealed that he knows the exact location of the super cunning lockup where the coffin's hidden. Massol visibly deflates, and his speech dries up entirely. The police lift him to his feet and slap the handcuffs on before they march him away.

'That —' I wave my spoon in the telly's direction. 'That was fucking satisfying.'

I hear a gasp, and a mutter of, 'Language,' from someone behind us. I turn. 'French. The language was fucking French,' I explain to the middle-aged, middle-class pearl-bedecked woman.

I turn back to Aicha. 'So that takes care of Massol. With Garou Jr banged up, it's only a matter of time before they get Senior.'

'They got the mortician too,' she adds. 'Yesterday afternoon.'

'Great. And the Fabulous Fascist Freak Brothers aren't coming back. That only leaves…'

'Tixier-Vignacourt.' Aicha's lips tighten. She's not happy.

I sigh. 'Of course. The money man, the one with status, the one who'd have actually benefited off all this if it had gone right, kept his fucking hands clean and stayed at a distance.' I look at Aicha directly, making sure I catch her eye. She needs to know I mean this. 'Do you want us to go after him?'

I see the two options warring it out in her. Then she sighs and shakes her head. 'No. Truth will come out. He's done politically, whatever he thinks.' I can see her thinking of how to put it. 'People like him? Little fascists and wannabe fuhrers? There will always be more of them. Kill one, another takes their place. Long as they don't get the power? Long as they aren't marching people to the train station? Can't kill them all. I'd have to kill ten percent of the population.'

I think she's being generous, but she isn't done. 'That'd make me as bad as them in a way.' She sinks back slightly in her seat. 'Killed as many as I could find. Those with actual blood on their hands. Malathion canisters in their back pockets. I'm done killing Nazis for now. Until the next ones come along who get power and start killing people again.' This is probably the longest spiel she's ever given in our decades of friendship. She looks dejected, really down, though of course it might just be she's feeling as worn out as I am.

A relevant idea comes to me. 'Course doesn't mean we can't punch any we come across in the face in the meantime, eh, *laguna*?' It's an old Occitan word meaning friend. It seems like a very long time since I've used it for anyone.

A smile spreads across her face, and I can see the pep

enter back into her metaphorical step. 'Good point, *saabi*.
An excellent point.'

Chapter Twenty-Nine

'I love sleep. My life has a tendency to fall apart when I'm awake.' — Ernest Hemingway

Apparently, either Isaac or Aicha put the Tesla on charge while I was dead to the world because we have the electrical equivalent of a full tank of gas when I wake up and wash the sleep out of my eyes with slightly less than Lichtenstein's yearly water consumption. The grit really doesn't want to be dislodged. Showering is no more comfortable than getting changed was yesterday. Apparently, after over eight hundred years, I've just discovered I'm a bit of a prude. Every day provides a learning opportunity.

The trip to Lou Carcoilh's home under Hastingues, a trip I've made far too often recently to drop off or retrieve the skulls, is about three hours each way. Normally more when the gigantic snail-dragon insists we pound a couple of bottles of beer and shoot the breeze before I can slip off. We bundle in, with me getting relegated to the back seat on the grounds of it being Isaac's car and Aicha's best stabbing knife getting waved in my face when I make a move to call shotgun. I sulk, sprawling across the admittedly spacious faux leather seating in the back. I can't even reach the radio control, although I have a devious plan to hijack the Bluetooth connection and inflict a heinous selection of music they both hate on them in revenge. But the moment the first droning notes of 'Yellow' by Coldplay come on, Aicha leans back, plucks the phone out of my startled hands, and deposits it neatly through the small post-box crack of her window, then watches it bounce and shatter off the road surface. The song stutters and dies. Despite my faux indignance, I'm actually pretty relieved. There's a good chance I would've suffered a brain aneurysm if I listened to Chris Martin sing.

The nice thing about starting from Isaac's house rather than mine is we take a different route towards Hastingues for once, following the motorway we pick up from the ring road to the forest, carrying on out to the west. We skirt along the top end of Auch, the cathedral Sainte-Marie dominant even from a distance, imposing itself on the landscape from its vaunted seat in the middle of the town. The road narrows to a single lane, and we settle in to playing leapfrog with lorries in between clear stretches where Isaac can open up the speed. The sun is shining, the sky is blue, and everything feels like it's coming up Paul. Which should be a warning if ever I needed one.

As we drive, we brainstorm what De Montfort could be up to. Isaac's of the opinion he plans to super-charge the wish-granting sceptre somehow, perhaps plunging it into the heart of an enormously powerful magical creature like Melusine did to her sister. Aicha's response is that she doesn't care where he sticks it, more where she's going to stick it once she takes it off him the moment she gets her hands on him. I keep silent. Not because I'm sulking, whatever Aicha says. It's because we're missing something. I'm sure of it. I just don't know what. Which makes logical sense because if I knew, we wouldn't be missing it. It's an irritating itch at the base of my brain that makes me want to put my entire hand up my nose so I can scratch it. That probably wouldn't be hygienic though.

It's midday by the time we take the turning signposted for Peyrehorade and Hastingues. 'Fancy stopping at the same café for lunch after?' I ask the two in the front. The server's horror at our food and beverage choices last time caused me no small amount of amusement.

Aicha shrugs, non-committal. 'Unless we can find something better.' Guess she wasn't as amused.

I rub the back of my neck, twisting to crack the bones. 'I doubt we'll find many options.' It's hard to get comfortable. My lower back's bizarrely sore. I guess it's the different anatomical arrangement and additional front weight on my chest. My already colossal respect for women and their capability to succeed despite everything in the universe being set up against them goes up another notch. Breasts are hard and heavy work, even unnaturally perky Elven ones. If it wouldn't mean losing all my stolen fae magic, I'd ditch this body in a hot minute.

We park up outside the old tower gate at the foot of the main hill and meander up towards the church. It's beyond words to express how nice it is to enjoy the feel of the sun on my face after my time stuck in Winter. I make a mental note to buy some decent sun cream as a matter of urgency. Ice-queen skin probably doesn't have much in terms of sun tolerance.

It's as we near the church that we get our first sign

something is wrong. The houses seem somehow drabber, less authentic. There's always been a sense of living history to them, but now something seems to have drained away, making them seem like pale imitations rather than preserved and lived-in originals. A couple of locals huddle together in a corner of the square — a tall, middle-aged rake-like man with a cigarette that matches his frame hanging from his lips, and an older woman, blue-rinse hair set in curlers that look like they're a museum piece from the 1950s themselves. They both wear worried expressions as they mutter. When they see us, their features brighten, and the man strolls over, although as he gets closer and takes in our strange varied garb, particularly my homemade T-shirt alteration, his expression falters. Luckily, I'm glamoured, so my absolutely bloody useless decorative wings aren't in sight, but we obviously aren't who he was expecting to see. Still, he presses on gamely.

'Are you the people from the gas company?'

The alarm bells that were ringing quietly in my subconscious suddenly increase in volume, going from Casio watch alarm to air-raid siren in a moment. 'No,' I answer slowly, torn between the sudden urge to run to the church and to get more information from the guy. 'Why? What are you waiting for the gas company for?'

'Ridiculous,' the old woman pipes up from the back. 'Gas company! Won't do any blooming good. It were an earthquake!'

'All the more reason to get the piping verified then, ain't it, Dominique?' The man rolls his eyes at us conspiratorially, then turns back to the woman.

'Don't you roll your eyes at me, Malcolm!' If I wasn't Talented and able to see the power of others, I'd believe her to be a witch. That isn't the matter at hand right now though.

'What happened?' I prompt again, trying to stay polite even though my subconscious is now screaming at me, panic setting in.

'Last night,' Malcolm says, 'there were terrible rumblings. Under the town itself. Some sort of gas explosion…'

'It were an earthquake!' Dominique shrieks insistently.

The two of them bicker about what might have caused such a terrible noise and made the earth under their feet shake that way. I stop listening though. Isaac, Aicha, and I share a look, then head towards the door of the church, restricting ourselves to a fast walk until we pass the nave, then accelerating down the stairs to the basement. Reaching the bottom, we screech to a halt.

The tunnel down to Lou's lair is covered by a *don't look here* spell, but it isn't the one I left here over a hundred years ago. This is a different working, a yellowing scab of a spell that makes my skin crawl. Mine just stopped people seeing the hole. This is so unpleasant, I doubt anyone who isn't Talented will want to get within twenty metres of the cellar.

I want to shred it, to run past it, to find out what is waiting for me on the other side, but I have a good idea who might have made this working. I look at Isaac. This is his area of expertise. 'If I break this,' I ask, 'will he know?'

Nobody has to ask who I mean by "he". Isaac looks grim-faced. I can't read Aicha. She's positioned herself, looking up the stairs, guarding our rear. Wise move.

Isaac examines the spell. 'Give me a minute, lad.' I can see him *look* at the working, studying it, deciphering what each part of the knitted together magic does. Magical theory is a bit like smelling your own farts for me. It's something I can do and survive, but it's not something I really want to do. Especially not in public. I leave Isaac to it and wander over to Aicha. Hopefully she can keep me distracted from the feeling that's crawling like ants dipped in itching powder all over my skin, screaming at me to burst through the spell like the Kool-Aid jug. *Oh yeah.*

'How are you holding up?' I ask her. There's been a lot of focus on my trauma over our last escapade. I can't help thinking that purposefully cutting off various parts of your arm on an enemy's blade and weaponising your own blood counts as kind of traumatic too. Not to mention the memories it must have pulled back up about her time with the Nazis.

'Fine,' is the short shrift response I get. It isn't because she's pissed off with me, just that she has other things to concentrate on. Aicha radiates readiness, and her attention's entirely focused on the narrow gap where the stairs twist back on themselves, towards the door out into the church. I don't know if it's because she's worried De Montfort is going to come back or if it's because she's desperately hoping he will. Knowing Aicha, I suspect the latter. Either way, if it happens, she's going to make sure we aren't caught unawares, so doesn't have time to spare to get touchy-feely over her emotions. So much for that as a distraction tactic for me.

Luckily for my blood pressure, Isaac finishes quickly. I'm not sure if fae can suffer from cardiovascular disease, but I've certainly been putting this heart under strain. When he calls me over, I'm by his side before he finishes saying my name.

'You were right, lad,' he says, which catches me a bit off guard because I don't remember expressing an opinion one way or the other. 'He's tied it to himself to know if anyone comes poking around. Nith has cobbled together a work-around so that when I take it down, it'll stop the message getting to him.'

While the image of an insanely powerful Bene Elohim angel cobbling together magic like some wannabe mad scientist tinkering in their garage is as odd as it's mind-blowing, I don't have the patience for it at this precise moment. 'Less theorising, more actualising. Shut it down. Shut it down forever.'

Aicha doesn't turn but gives me a whistle of appreciation for the *Dark City* reference, especially considering how stressed I evidently am. Isaac takes the hint. There's a moment of muttering, which might be him talking to Nithael or might be him doing a Muttley, grumbling at my lack of appreciation for his genius, but either way, a few seconds later, the *don't look here* spell is down. Approximately half a millisecond after, I head down the tunnel, a will-o'-the-wisp of bobbing mage-light leading and lighting the path. I'm so hoping we're going to come and find a tentacle slapped up against the wall, goop dripping left and right. Maybe a slime-encrusted six pack of beer waiting for us as the gigantic creature burbles excitedly about the latest nature documentary he overheard by listening in through his sucker pads at the villagers' windows. Perhaps he'll have captured De Montfort. Perhaps he'll be trussed up, wrapped up like a Christmas present waiting for us. He'll be a whole lot more pliant after a night with Lou chewing his ear off. Hopefully literally.

I keep on hoping. Keep holding on to that desperate hope as we plunge down the tunnel, once more into the dark.

Chapter Thirty

HASTINGUES, 6 JUNE, PRESENT DAY

There are no witticisms for this moment. It hurts enough.
More than it should.

We aren't even halfway to the cavernous chamber where Lou holds audience before the stench reaches us. It smells like the aftermath of a battlefield, when bombs have torn up earth and hearts. Thin tendrils of smoke float up to meet us, carrying both their own odour and the acrid bite that lingers after the usage of modern weaponry. We're already moving at a jog. Without a word, when we smell that, we break into a full-on sprint.

The sight that meets us is so terrible, I don't even stop at the lip of the tunnel but just launch myself out into the air. Tree roots uncurl themselves, pulling loose from the soil to form trapeze-like steps for me down to the floor. By the time I arrive, Aicha has already hammered into the ground like a meteorite, relying on her healing rather than her *talent* to get her down, and seconds later Isaac lands behind us, his fall transformed into a graceful descent when Nithael spread his ethereal, neon-electric wings.

I remember once seeing a video of a giant squid that washed up on some far-flung beach and slowly died, unable to drag itself back to the salty depths it came from. The floor looks like its considerably more gargantuan kraken cousin suffered a similar fate. Limp tendrils cling to the floor, some bunched together, others splayed their full length. The ones that cause the lump in my throat to harden, making it feel impossible to swallow are the severed tentacles still stuck to the walls, trailing parts dripping dark viscous fluid — the same fluid that lies pooled, pond-like in every place the uneven floor dips. And there, in the middle of it all, is what remains of Lou Carcoilh.

His shell looks like a roc flew in carrying a boulder and hurled it down on his intricate spirals. There's a hole the size of a bungalow smashed in the top side, the edges jagged and sharp. Dust and black residue clings to the normally gleaming surface surrounding it. It's a sorry sight. I know how much pride Lou takes in his polished carapace. Or rather, took because Lou himself lies stretched across the floor.

His fur is no longer wet with the secretions that coat his appendages but with the same internal fluid that liberally coats most of the cavern. His elongated, snake-like neck lies sprawled, his head turned sideways, his eyestalks crossed and flaccid on the cavern floor. We landed near to where they lie, each the size of a wind-farm fan, and I rush over. I don't hold out much hope he's still alive, so I nearly jump out of my skin when one eyelid cracks open the tiniest bit, the eyeball blearily focusing on me.

'Thnack? Mithter…Thnack? Ith…that you?' His voice is croaky, cracking. The words are even more obscured and mumbled than normal. I can't imagine how hard it must be dragging his lips into word shapes with all those dead-weight tentacles still attached.

'It's me, Lou. I'm here.' I rest a hand on his enormous, tube-train of a neck, feeling the rings of muscle under the hair quivering and pulsing. I don't even care about the gunk I'm getting on me. He deserves this moment of communion.

'Lou...Carcoilh.' He rasps out each syllable despite the obvious pain it causes him. 'My name ithn't...."The"... you...bloody...philithtine...'

I laugh, a half-hiccupped noise that feels dangerously close to a sob. 'Right, of course. Lou Carcoilh. The world's greatest gastropod.'

'Too...bloody...right.' His eyelid flickers, almost closing, and for a moment I think he's gone. It stabilises though, and I can still hear his rasping breathing. 'Better than...that... bloody...African losther...'

I nod, patting him. 'You're right. That giant African snail always was an imposter.'

'Withh...I got...to meet...Thir Attenborough...' I can hear the wistful regret in his tone. 'Kept...my promithe... though...didn't I, Mithter Thnack? Didn't leave the caveth...again... Kept my...word.'

'You did, Lou Carcoilh.' I have precisely zero idea of the details of whatever promise kept him here, under Hastingues, or who he made it with, but I know he honoured it. 'You're a snail of honour. Sir Attenborough would be proud of you.'

He brightens slightly, but his words are still weak. 'Do... you think...tho? Really?'

I wipe at my eyes with the back of my one compara-tively clean hand. 'Really, Lou Carcoilh. I really do.'

He gives a half-chuckle, half-cough that carries up, vibrating through my hand. 'I alwayth...thought...I'd...thtay here... Never thought...anyone would...get me.' A sucker pad pulls itself incredibly slowly off the floor and lays itself over my hand. 'Bazookath...Mithter...Thnack... He had...bazookath...'

He doesn't have to tell me who. I know perfectly well. I hold the sucker pad and squeeze it. 'Hold on, Lou Carcoilh. We're here with you. Isaac and Nithael can help, I'm sure...'

He cuts me off. 'Too...late for...that...Mithter Thnack. I'm...bloody...done for.' An enormous tear, big enough to fill a bucket, drips out of the gigantic eye, rolling down the eye-stalk to splash on the ground. 'I'm...tho thorry...he took...the thkull... Couldn't...thtop him... Bloody bazookath...'

'Shh.' I pat his side, feeling his anguish, his shame at having failed to protect the skull. 'Don't worry about that right now. Guard your strength. We'll get it back, don't worry.'

'And slice your name through his core like rock candy.' Aicha's voice is low and throaty, full of dangerous promise.

Lou Carcoilh gives a cough, a spluttering chuckle. 'Tho...bloody...fierthe. I'd feel thorry...for the...poor...bugger...if he...hadn't...bloody...killed...me...'

The tendril I'm holding between my hands pulls away and drags itself back along his serpentine neck. I want to help, but I get the impression this is something he wants, needs to do on his own. The sucker pad inches and squirms until it reaches the mouth of the shell itself, then creeps inside. When it pulls back out from the aperture, it's holding something. The tentacle flops to the floor, exhausted. Then it drags its way over to me and unfolds, revealing the Veil of Veronica half-stuck on the sucker.

'Didn't…even…bloody…take that…' Lou's rasping breath hitches, and for a moment I think he's stopped breathing. It's only when he wheezes an out-breath that I realise I did too. 'Took…the bloody…thkull…but…left… the bloody…veil…'

I try to close his sucker pad, to wrap it back around the veil, but it keeps flopping open. 'Keep it. You need it to heal. To stay alive. You need the magic to feed on.'

The whistling rattle reflected in the heaving muscles of Lou's neck isn't a good sign. '…don't…bloody…think tho… Mithter…Thnack…' A harsher grating noise, like he's breathing through sandpaper, accompanies each word now. 'I…alwayth…liked the…dramatic…endingth… I heard… ath I lithtened…to filmth…the dramatic…latht wordth… Alwayth wanted to…thay them…'

I keep trying to make him take back the veil, but he won't. There's no force left in his grip. 'Next time I come, I'm…I'm bringing a projector. I'm bringing a projector and a player.' I shove my hand into my etheric storage and pull out a new phone, jabbing at it desperately, pulling up YouTube. 'C'mon, Lou. Let's…let's watch some trailers. Pick a few greats, hey? Start with them yeah? And…and we're going to watch everything. All the films you ever wanted to watch, Lou. You and me together, okay?'

I wrap my hand around his sucker pad again, squeezing it tight, trying to force some of this strange fae *talent* in to heal him. But whether because Maeve's body's magic isn't geared towards healing, only hurting or whether because even fae magic is just a drop in the ocean compared to what's required to heal such a massive creature basically made of *talent*, it does nothing at all. Lou waggles his sucker pad, wraps it weakly around my fingers, and gives me a light squeeze.

'I alwayth thought...I'd live forever...you know... Mithter Thnack... Thought I'd live... to thee...the thtarth...burn out...and fade...away...Inthtead...itth me... who...fadeth... like tearth...in the rain...'

His one half-cracked eyeball rotates to look at me. 'I alwayth...loved that...Thounded... tho...bloody... dramatic...Did it...look magnifithent? Did...I...look... magnifithent...'

The gentle pressure of his pad on my hand disappears, and the tentacle goes limp as the last light leaves his eye. I feel my way along his neck, checking for a pulse, a muscle movement, any sign of life, but all in vain. There's nothing there. One more loss added to the tally of the score I need to settle with Simon De Montfort.

Lou Carcoilh, The Snail, one of the strangest and most wonderful creatures I have ever come across, is dead.

Chapter Thirty-One

Raise a glass to Lou Carcoilh. A snail who put the Great
African to shame. Who put us all to shame in many ways.

It is a slow walk back up the slope to the church basement. I
don't feel like Orpheus this time. I don't want to look
behind me. I don't even want to think about what I've left
down there all alone in the dark forever. I suppose, of
anyone in the world, in any worlds, I should feel the least
attachment to simple vessels emptied of the spark that
makes them anything other than flesh destined to be worm
food. Someone needs to tell my heart that. It clearly didn't
get the memo.

I wanted to leave the veil with The Snail, like an
Egyptian cephalopodan pharaoh surrounded by his prize
possessions. Isaac pointed out what happens to such graves
after comparatively little time. Hell, ancient Egyptians by
our standards were already robbing tombs of even more
ancient Egyptians in turn. Leaving a huge and powerful

artefact sitting there without Lou Carcoilh's magic-proof shell to protect it would lead to his burial chamber being disturbed sooner rather than later.

So I took the veil, although I gave it to Isaac for safe-keeping. His house is far better warded than mine is, plus I have a tendency to lose things in my pockets regularly. Usually along with the clothes. And the body wearing them.

When we come back out, I seal up the entrance again with a strong *don't look here* enchantment and ensure it's strong enough that even if I die and lose my fae powers again, it will stand the test of time. We discuss caving in the doorway, but after the multiple bazooka fire and resultant tremors through the soil, I'm genuinely worried about what effect that might have on the town above.

Once we get back to the car, we pull off and head straight to the motorway. None of us feel like heading to a restaurant now. We've lost our appetites. There's no music, no banter. I'm the only one who spent much time with Lou Carcoilh, and even then not that much, but we all recognise this was a grand passing. There aren't many creatures as magical as he was left still sharing this plane with us. It's like witnessing a mass extinction of species happen instantaneously right before your eyes. The world is a blander, less interesting place for Lou Carcoilh's leaving.

Slowly, my sorrow drops back, muscled into the background by my growing anger and frustration. Most of it's aimed at that bastard De Montfort, but I've enough left over to spare for us as well. 'We should have gone last night —' I start, but Aicha karate chops the air to cut me off and stop me dead.

'Enough. If we had some bread, we could make cheese sandwiches. If we had some cheese. Ifs and maybes. You were dead on your feet. *I* was dead on my feet. A battle last night? When De Montfort had enough power both magically and weapon-wise to take down Lou?' She shakes her head. 'Can't know how it would have ended up. Doubt well though.'

I grind my teeth together. 'It might have saved Lou.'

She shrugs. 'Might have. Might not. Maybe he'd have died, and the veil got destroyed. Maybe you'd have died. Lost any magic you had. Maybe that meant next time we confronted De Montfort, we lost, and Lou died for nothing. I don't know. Neither do you. So stop it. We did the right thing. Came at the problem fresh. You were fucking useless to Lou last night.' She pauses, then corrects. 'Even more fucking useless than normal, dickhead.'

It catches me off guard, just as she intended, and I can't hold back the snort of laughter. I keep the smile on, but the laughter dies quickly. It isn't a warm smile, but it's a real one. 'Not Lou. Lou Carcoilh. Lou just means bloody "the", doesn't it?'

He deserves his full title. The Snail. He really was *The* Snail.

I feel slightly better, although even one of Aicha's to-the-point and efficient pep talks isn't enough to entirely assuage my guilt at not being there for him the night before. I can see the sense though. At least we were there for him at the end. He didn't go alone. I wonder what he believed in, where he thought he'd end up next. Did he think he'd end up in some form of snail heaven, worshipped by legions of adoring giant African snails? Or did he believe in reincarnation? Is there a tiny, little gastropod popping into existence right now somewhere, entirely unaware that it was probably once the biggest creature ever to crawl across the lands of France? Whichever way it is, wherever he is, I hope he's happy.

By the time we reach the outskirts of Toulouse, the practicalities of hunger win out over the sense of grief, and my stomach rumbles, although I don't think any of us are ravenous. We stop at Maison Curtet, a seriously cosy bakery-cum-café on the edge of Pibrac and stock up on sandwiches, patisseries, and their incredible coffee. I'd prefer a half bottle of whisky, but I already drank my share last night, and I've been down that path recently enough to know I need to be wary of getting drunk for a while at least. Coffee will do for now.

Afterwards, we schlep our way back to Isaac's. The mood is downbeat, dejected. Even the sight of Hubert making Isaac nearly fall over — the local enormous owl dive-bombing his head, wheeling left and right to no doubt strike at the looming angelic presences does little to lift our spirits.

We gather around the kitchen table and raise our recyclable coffee cups in a silent toast to the giant snail-dragon of Hastingues. He was truly unique, entirely individual. Life is lessened by his absence from it.

After a moment's quiet contemplation, Aicha brings us back to the subject at hand. 'Didn't deserve that. Susane? Not her either. What he did to you?' Rage fills the deep blackness of her eyes. 'Payback, *saabi*. Payback.'

Oh man, I want payback. So much. So very, very much. Sadly, it doesn't look that simple. 'With you one hundred percent. It seems easier said than done though.' My head feels a mess between the shit I've lived recently and the grief for Lou's death that's hitting me surprisingly hard. I guess it's maybe a hangover from having to watch Susane die again, being helpless to stop it. I am done with feeling futile, with seeming to be incapable of stopping people from dying for others' stupid selfish reasons. Somehow, I need to get ahead of the game. Lou's a painful setback after an against-the-odds win, but the way I see it, if Aicha can defeat fucking *Maeve*, the immortal queen of the fae, then surely between the three of us, we can beat that fuckwit De Montfort. Thinking about that makes me realise something.

'Hey, did you notice,' I say, a slight tone of wonder leaching from my thoughts and into my voice that makes the others lean forward. 'De Montfort is incredibly close to Demon Fart.'

The silence hangs in the air as the two of them stare disbelievingly first at me, then at one another. Then the three of us break, cracking up into cackles of laughter until tears run down our cheeks.

'You've...you've...cracked the puzzle,' Isaac wheezes, wiping his eyes on the back of his hand.

Aicha nods in agreement. 'It's like the world's shittiest version of *The Da Vinci Code*.' She pauses and then adds, 'Since *The Da Vinci Code* itself, anyway.'

I feel infinitely better. I think we all do. We've taken a loss, sure. We're still on the back foot. No one really has any idea of where to go next. But we've come up with an incredibly childish insult nickname for our enemy. That's progress in my book.

Isaac takes a moment, communing with Jakob. No doubt he's explaining what *The Da Vinci Code* is. I'm jealous that anyone can live in a world innocent of the knowledge. It's almost worth being locked up in a skull for hundreds of years for. When he comes back, he rummages around under a pile of what looks like priceless, irreplaceable manuscripts stacked high on the side of the table. When he comes back up for air, he waves a piece of yellowed paper. He squints at it suspiciously, both sides, no doubt making sure there are no hidden spells or secrets on it, then grabs a nearby pen with a flourish.

'Right,' he says, 'let's recap what we do know. Maybe that'll help us with where we go next.'

'Okay.' I stand up. If ever there was a moment for pacing, it's now, despite Aicha's disapproving glare. 'We have some sort of other-dimensional helper who's tried to give me guidance a few times over the centuries…'

'Most of which have been recently,' Aicha interrupts. I can see her brain kicking into an analytical gear, enough so she can ignore my attempt to wear a groove into the floorboards.

'Right. So either they're getting stronger…'

'Or the walls are getting weaker.' Isaac looks dour at the thought. He scribbles that down on the paper. 'Jak, Nith, Nan, and I will get on to that as a matter of urgency. There are points where the veils are thinner. When time allows, we'll take a little road trip up to the mountains. If there's anywhere the walls between the worlds are cracking, it'll be in amongst their peaks. We'll see what we can find.'

'Good plan.' It's worth looking into. Fucking up De Montfort is the short-term plan, but there's the bigger picture to consider. I can't shake the feeling that this is larger than just our hidden feud.

'Can we trust Mysterio?' It's a valid point from Aicha. I stop my marching and consider it.

'I think so?' It's hard to give a hundred percent certain answer about the being who keeps helping me. 'I've got no actual evidence for it, just my gut feeling. Nothing set my teeth on edge or made me suspicious. Doesn't mean we should trust them blindly, but for now at least, I feel like they're not a threat, that our aims align.'

Isaac makes a note. 'Okay. This mysterious being in the

afterlife world you've popped into a few times pointed you towards all the bones and suggested that was the key. So let's look at that.'

I've been running that one over in my head quite a lot. 'Okay. De Montfort had Torquemada's skull in the first place. It was him who gave it to the shit wizard to put it in Ben's hands. Why?'

Isaac runs his hand through his hair absentmindedly, ruffling it. 'He wanted Ben to succeed?'

I nod. 'Has to be. He came bloody close to doing just that. There was no way he was banking on us taking down Ben at the last moment. What did Ben want?'

'Break the walls.'

'Right, *laguna*. So we foiled that, and next thing, we're being railroaded into going to tangle with Melusine, and we've got Susane along for the ride.'

Isaac's eyes go wide. 'You think he engineered that somehow?'

I shrug. 'It's possible. Fae magic lends itself towards being persuasive, and he already had Susane in his back pocket. It wouldn't take much to nudge either Franc's magic scout towards the Mother's daughter or vice versa.'

Isaac flops back in his chair. 'Bloody hell, lad. Really?'

I resume my pacing. 'I've no proof of it, but it seems to make sense. We go charging off to Lourdes, once again do all the hard work, and then he swoops in and grabs the sceptre...'

'Made of bones.'

'Made of bones, got it, Aich. So we know the sceptre let Melusine grant wishes in exchange for feeding it *talent*. First from her sister, then from her bespelled lovers, but De Montfort hasn't used it for that as far as we know, just as a portable portal between Faerie and here and *maybe* as a way to avoid Oberon's gift Gwendolyne has. We said last night maybe he was waiting to supercharge it, but that doesn't stack up now.'

'No.' Isaac sees where I'm going with this. 'If that was the case, he'd have used it on Lou Carcoilh. There'd have been enough magic in him to get it topped up with *talent* for some time to come.'

I give Isaac the gun fingers. 'Right. That means either he can't use the wish magic, it's exclusive somehow to Melusine, or else that's not what he's interested in. So, question. Why has he left us with Almeric's skull?'

'Doesn't know we've got it.' Aicha's head snaps up, her eyes bright. She's solved this part. 'Susane knew we'd left the skulls with Lou. Demon Fart knew you'd try to get to Faerie to chase them down. Didn't realise you'd use the skull going after Half-Marred Jack.'

Isaac slams his cup down on the table, but as his cup is made of recyclable cardboard, it has the slightly-less-dramatic-than-intended effect of just crumpling somewhat, letting out a sad half-groan as the air rushes away. 'He didn't need to get the skulls straightaway. As far as he was concerned, they were safe with Lou Carcoilh, and he could go pick them up anytime. His priority was getting you out of the way.'

I nod. 'Got it. He traps me in the cave. As far as he's concerned, he's now taken me off the board. He hops back over to Earth, where he lays a plan on how to take out a magic-proof enormous monster with a fireproof shell.'

'Bazookas,' Aicha says grimly.

'Bazookas. Exactly. Even with fae magic, not the easiest thing to procure. Plus, as far as he knows, I'm locked away, gone for good. He's in no hurry. So he puts the plan together, picks up his supplies, then last night...' I can't finish the sentence. My teeth are gritted so hard. We missed him by a matter of hours. It hurts almost physically, a pain in my side like a stitch that he won again.

Aicha, however, shines her rare, joyful smile on me. 'Didn't get what he wanted though. Not all of it. Bet that pissed him right off.'

That helps. At the thought of how utterly vexed the cocky shit must feel, having been totally certain he'd roll up and just scoop up both the super powerful magical skulls, only to find one missing with no idea where it might be, puts a smile on my face too. 'Oh, I'd have loved to see that. I bet he was raging.'

Isaac chuckles. 'Pisses on his bloody parade.' He raises his slightly collapsed coffee cup. 'That's one in his eye for you, Lou. Just the first of many, hopefully.'

I take a swig of my own coffee. I'll drink to that. 'Okay, so we know the shit weasel is after the bones for some reason. Magical, powerful bones. Do we have any idea why?'

Aicha taps her fingers rhythmically over the table, deep in thought. 'Dragon's teeth?'

It takes me a moment to decipher that. Then I clock the *Golden Fleece* reference. 'Magical skeletons?' I ask doubtfully.

She shrugs. 'Best idea I've got at the moment. Bet if he makes them, they look shit compared to the Ray Harryhausen animation.'

I can't argue with that. 'Everything looks shit compared to Ray Harryhausen animation. Real life looks shit compared to Ray Harryhausen animation. Who wouldn't want the world to look more like *Clash of the Titans*?' We're getting slightly off the point though. 'So what's his next move?'

Aicha lazily flicks her thumb back and forth, pointing at herself and Isaac. 'Us.'

I stop, confused. 'What?'

She shrugs. 'Us. If he wants the skull so badly, he's going to want to come after us. We're the only other people who might have it, obviously.'

Fuck. I didn't think of that. He could be waiting, watching us from outside the wards right now. If he has Isaac under surveillance, he'll know I escaped the trap. We'll lose one of our strongest elements of surprise. 'How far do your wards extend, Isaac?'

He waves the thought away. 'Don't worry, lad. After all the shenanigans with Franc and your extended absence, I got Nith and Nan on the case. We took your wards and, well...' He looks slightly abashed. 'They aren't really *yours* anymore. We sort of hijacked them in the process of super-charging them — after you gave us permission,' he adds hastily. I roll my eyes and chuckle. Like I care if he holds the wards or I do. If Isaac isn't trustworthy, then life isn't worth living. 'Anyhow, turns out using two angels to reinforce the ward didn't double the effectiveness. More like tenfold, perhaps more. They now cover a lot more distance.'

I'm intrigued. 'How much more distance?'

He points north. 'Montauban.' East. 'Castres.' South. 'Castelnaudary.' West. 'Auch.'

Bloody hell. Colour me impressed. That's roughly twelve thousand square kilometres. 'So no one is sneaking up on us anytime soon.'

He shakes his head. 'Nope, not likely, my lad. He'll have no choice but to go full-frontal assault on the entire region if he wants to go toe-to-toe with us.'

Internally, I heave a sigh of relief that odds are in our favour concerning his ignorance about my escape. I raise a cautionary finger though. 'Don't forget, he was tracking everything Ben was doing without him knowing it. He may have access to his research, the magic against Nith and Nan.'

Isaac nods gravely. 'I expect so. It's something we'll have to watch for, and we're considering it extremely seriously. Nith and Nan are taking it in turns to constantly monitor the wards, looking out for any blind spots or breaks. Nothing so far.'

I cock my head at Aicha. 'And as you slipped off through the back gate into Faerie, he'll not be able to pick up your trail.'

She snorts. 'He wouldn't have been able to pick up my trail anyhow, seeing as how I'm not entirely fucking useless, unlike some.'

Can't really argue with that. 'Okay, so we've seen he likes to play the long game, and he thinks I'm trapped for the next decade and a half plus. He's a schemer, a plotter by nature, so he's unlikely to just come charging in here. He's more likely to try to lure you out somehow and get you to bring the skull with you.'

I recognise the pensive look on Isaac's face as he asks, 'Might he offer you up in exchange?'

It's possible. 'Maybe, but I don't think that'll be his plan A. He worked too hard to put me in that hellhole to let me out if he can help it. No, he wants to move his agenda, whatever it is, forward, but he's not in a desperate hurry. My guess is, he'll head back to his stronghold, wherever that is. He'll take some time to connive his way to getting his hands on the skull without me getting free.'

The other two nod. It makes sense. My relief is palpable. It feels good to have some sort of clarity, to piece together some of his motives, some of his potential actions, even if there are still some genuinely humongous gaps in the complete picture. So I say, 'Next question. Where on earth or anywhere else is his stronghold?'

'That' —Isaac leans back, a wise look on his face— 'is the bloody question, isn't it, lad?'

'I know that's the bloody question, 'Zac; that's why I asked it. What's the answer?'

'Oh.' He goes slightly red-faced and slumps back. 'No idea, lad. Sorry.'

Brilliant. I wonder which is worse for your general health. Grinding your teeth into smooth nubs or screaming in frustration until your vocal cords pop? Maybe a combination of the two together might make me feel better. Honestly? At this point, I'm willing to try anything.

Chapter Thirty-Two

TOULOUSE, 6 JUNE, PRESENT DAY

Less brainstorming, more brain-light-drizzling at the moment.

We take a break from the back-and-forth. Isaac obviously has a few ideas of his own and hurries off to his workshop. Aicha starts sharpening all of her edged weapons, which is as close as she gets to meditating. I take a walk in the forest.

The trees are beautiful at this time of year in Bouconne. The burgeoning buds of new life spring up in evidence everywhere, regrowth pushing through the mulch of broken-down death from the winter. What has been shed is now reused. What has survived has grown hardier, having surpassed hardship. Outside of occasionally having to duck aside to avoid being run down by mountain bikers, it feels peaceful, quiet. Someone wearing rosier-tinted lenses might talk about it taking them back to simpler times. I remember those times well. They were anything but simpler. All there ever was, all there ever is, are moments of calm before troubles sweep them away once more, like the hands of a dandelion clock carried off to root or ruin. Only time can tell. Hindsight is a wonderful thing. Foresight? A myth to justify a set of lucky guesses.

By the time I tramp my way round a small stretch of the vast ancient sprawl and back again, evening is falling. I don't know if it's a side effect of my new fae nature or just having some calm time to reconnect myself to the world around me, but I come back feeling refreshed, recharged. Ready to take on this utterly bizarre set of events, all apparently engineered by one psychotic, reincarnating lunatic. I feel justified in calling him that. Takes one to know one, I guess.

I push my way back into the kitchen to find Isaac chattering away excitedly at Aicha. Her expression, though, tells me he's onto something. It isn't the polite indifference that plasters itself across her face when he gets into the whys and wherefores of academic research. I know the expression she's wearing. It's that of a hound that's caught the scent, straining at the lead, ready to plunge into the undergrowth and find the fox who dared believe itself cunning enough to escape from vicious jaws. Isaac breaks off as I enter, turning towards me, animated, waving me to join them. I do as I'm told, further motivated by the sight of a healthy tumbler-full of whisky awaiting me. My mentor knows exactly how to bribe me into silence.

He beams at me as I sit and take up a suitably attentive position, cradling my drink in both hands. 'Paul, my lad. Perfect timing. Perfect. I've got it. I've got it!'

My excitement builds. 'You know where he is?'

The hesitation brings the optimistic rush back under control. 'Not exactly. But I reckon I've got a pretty good idea. A place to start, anyway.'

I try not to let rising disappointment stamp up and

down on the previous excitement. This is a lot better than the total amount of nothing we had when I went for a walk and pretty incredible work in a couple of hours, actually. 'That's more than when I left. Lay it on me, 'Zac.'

He rubs his hands together. 'Right, so I thought about it. De Montfort's been building his empire since the thirteenth century. You said he took the body of his son, Simon, after his first death, right?'

'Right.' It struck me as odd when he told me that. Simon hadn't been his eldest son. I wonder if it was the shared name that made the magic choose him or if it was because De Montfort favoured him.

'So they had two family strongholds, okay? One west of Paris, not far past Versailles, at Montfort-L'Amaury, as it's still known. The other in Leicester, over in England, where they held a title, although I think the De Montforts had little to do with the lands and titles there prior to the Albigensian Crusades.'

I can follow his line of thinking. 'So you reckon he might still have a stronghold at one or the other of them?'

Isaac nods, only looking slightly disgruntled by me stealing the wind out of his sails a bit. I'll have to work out some way to gruntle him later on. 'Aye, basically. Well, when he took over Simon's body, he handed off the right to the lands in France to Amaury, his oldest lad, in exchange for unchallenged rights to the English territory and proceeded to go and get in the mix with politics and the crown over there for a couple of generations.'

My knowledge of British history is sadly lacking. Here is my great gruntling opportunity, which sounds bizarrely like a Roald Dahl book. 'How much of a mix?' Never let it be said I can't supply an academic with a suitable cue when necessary.

Isaac beams, a look that speaks of the joy of imparting knowledge to the fundamentally unworthy, such as myself. 'Enough of a mix *to rule the country*.'

I look around for a handy shovel to help me pick my jaw up off the floor. 'Wait, what? I'm no scholar of England and English history, but I don't remember a King Simon.'

'He never officially took the crown. He was too smart for that. What he did, instead, was transfer a load of the power to parliament, which he then led, issuing decrees in the king's name, forcing through reform.'

I rub my chin. 'Sounds…pretty bloody reasonable, actually.'

This draws a wry look from Isaac. 'He also went crusading against the Muslims of the Holy Land and drove the Jews out of Leicester, stealing all their money and property. Plus, he led the massacre of Jews across the country under the guise of "cancellation of debts".'

'Okay, that sounds more like De Montfort.'

'Right. Anyhow, he got deposed by some other nobles who supported the king's son and died in battle, along with his eldest.'

I smack my fist so hard on the table, I'm not sure if the resounding crack is the tabletop or bone. 'Then we've lost track of him.'

'Aye, my lad, but that's beside the point. Yes, we lose track of which body he leaped into. The De Montfort family fell from grace, intermarrying with other nobles. A lot of them became mercenaries or sellswords, particularly over in Italy, where they mingled with the Orsini and Di Vico families. From there…'

I narrow my eyes. 'Wait a minute; did you say Di Vico?'

Isaac furrows his brow. 'Aye. Why's that, lad?'

I curse and resist the urge to spit on the floor, which is a very uncivilised thing to do on someone's relatively clean kitchen tiles. 'I met him. You bloody met him! He foiled my attempt to help the Cagots in Rome. The bastard. That's where he found out about me and Susane.'

The cunning shitstain has been weaving his way in and out of my life for centuries, looking for the opportunity to grab some power and to even the scales so he can take me on properly. For a man of action, he certainly learned how to be a proper sneaky wankgoblin after that first death.

We're getting off the point though. 'You said it didn't matter, trying to track his incarnations. Why not?'

Now Isaac's eyes are gleaming. He's already knocked me for six with what he's accrued information wise, having gathered more in two hours than what I'd have done in two weeks, and then some. And he still has a knock-out blow to deliver. 'Okay, so all of this has come to fruition recently, right? In the last few years, the shit wizard got the skull and made his way to Ben, allowing him to put his schemes into place. He already had Susane in his back pocket, but her deal with the Mother came due, and she became another pawn in his game.'

I resist the urge to tell him to skip to the end. Aicha doesn't. 'Skip to the end, 'Zac.'

He harrumphs, but he's too invested in the punchline not to want to deliver it. 'Of course, we're there anyway, lass. We were told it's all about the bones, right? Well, back in 2012, in the parking lot of the Leicester Grammar School, they found the bones of one of England's most infamous kings. Richard III.'

I leap to my feet, hunching over, one shoulder thrust up, the other pulled down. 'A horse! A horse! My kingdom for a horse!'

Both of them roll their eyes. Neither appreciate my

acting chops, apparently. Philistines. 'Yep, that's the one,' Isaac continues as I sink back down to stew over my consoling whisky. 'Well, it wasn't just his body that they found. They buried him with ten others give or take. It used to be the grounds of the Grey Friars Abbey, so that's not so surprising. What is odd is that so many of them were women. Including a surprisingly fancy sarcophagus suggesting whoever the lass inside was, she had been very wealthy or very religious and favoured by the monks. Probably both. Anyway, I got hold of some transcripts, reports from the archaeologists who led the dig. When they lifted the slab off, one of them, a junior student from one of the two local universities, insisted that the pelvis wasn't just astoundingly clean considering the years it was stored but that it was *glowing as well.*'

I shoot to my feet again but this time with excitement. 'Another *talent*-invested bone! The student must have a bit of latent *talent* themselves.'

'Exactly my thought, lad. Considering how bloody powerful the other ones have been, you wouldn't need much more than a smidge to spot it. So I traced where the skeleton ended up. Richard III got a right royal reburial in the local cathedral, and most of the others got distributed to dedicated archaeological teams for further study.'

'But not the girl?' It isn't a hard guess to make that she's the exception that made Isaac say "most" rather than "all".

'Right. Somehow her skeleton got diverted to the historical stores of a nearby castle, Kenilworth, where it should never have ended up going to. Guess whose family home Kenilworth used to be?'

I've got to the punchline now. I'm happy to supply it. 'Demon Fart.'

Isaac nods triumphantly. 'Yes! Demon…' He breaks off,

then bangs his fist down on the table. 'Demon Fart!' He's gone slightly red in the face from the effort but looks immensely satisfied. Good on him. He deserves that for his fantastic research work.

I look over at Aicha, and her grim satisfaction mirrors my own. Finally, *finally*, after keeping us on the back foot for centuries, pulling strings we've never even seen, Simon De Montfort has slipped up. He has no idea I've escaped from Faerie, and he laid a trail to himself he never expected us to pick up. The odds that Simon is over in England as opposed to the Paris outskirts just increased dramatically. If not, we still need to try to get our hands on the glowing set of bones, liberating them from him if he's got them and sticking a thumb in his eye as we do so. Hopefully literally.

If all goes well, it might just mean we'll get our hands on Simon himself. Assuming we do, then we'll have a very long, very bloody chat. It's a conversation I intend to take my time over, and I don't doubt Aicha is looking forward to bringing her own particular brand of pain to proceedings too. We'll make him see the error of his ways. Preferably while he's wearing his own intestines wrapped around his neck like a set of Mardi Gras beads.

Then we'll do everything we can to make sure he becomes history himself. Permanently this time.

I've no idea how we're going to manage it, but one way or another, I am going to end Simon De Montfort. Once and for all.

Afterword

So, we reach the end of another imPerfect adventure, and strangely one of the saddest yet. It's amazing just how hard the death of Lou Carcoilh hit me — and I'm the one who wrote it! Even getting through reading the audiobook version of it took me several attempts as I kept choking up. Pour out a glass for The Snail, the most magnificent gastropod ever.

But we also end on a positive. The team has a lead — and Demon Fart doesn't know they're coming. Maybe things are finally going to come out Team Bonhomme? You'll have to read imPerfect Hunt to find out!

Less historical happenings in the main story this time — what with Paul and Aicha being stuck over in Faerie for the majority of it! — but the setting for their sojourn in the past really did happen as described. Petain's coffin was stolen during the night with the aid of a mortician, and the theft only discovered thanks to an eagle-eyed caretaker noticing the cement joint was too clean. Those named are the fascists arsewipes who were involved in the theft, and all of them were tried and found guilty apart from Tixier-Vignacourt — of course. Although it did tarnish his reputation and ended his attempts to run for President, so small mercies.

One of the most peculiar things about all the reports I read was the two members of the team who weren't named. In all the French articles I could dig out, each time they were simply referred to as 'a Hungarian and a Pole', with their time served in the Foreign Legion mentioned. Nothing further was said about them. I'm sure if I dug into police reports I could have got the details, but I liked this weird mystery about them — it felt very much like a *don't-look-here* thrown on the media. So I picked names for them, and so Gabor and Casimir were born. And then killed with aplomb.

As always I've tried to place things with historical accuracy so the cultural references they make, the dates of the motorways etc, should all correspond correctly. If they don't, it is because I am a Bear Of Little Brain, and you must excuse me my foibles and failures.

In the meantime, turn the page and you can read the first chapter of Book 5 of the imPerfect Cathar series. imPerfect Hunt.

The game is afoot…

imPerfect Hunt: Chapter One

There's cold as ice. Then there's cold as Aicha...normally.
Today? Not so much.

Flying with a control freak is a vision of Hell even Dante couldn't imagine.

I actually enjoy flying on the rare occasions I do it. As long as I go on my own. The whole experience – from the moment you arrive at the airport and huge metal signs guide you towards which grade of car park you're allowed access to up until the moment you get free from the maws of the glass-and-steel giant at the other end – involves following. It's a herding process. That's why I find it relaxing. I don't have to think for a while. Just arrive with time to spare and then go with the flow. Arrow here; queue there. Flash a piece of psychic passport at a perennially bored border guard and then wait in a pen with all the other human sheep till the ground staff shepherd you onboard in groups.

Aicha does not enjoy this. Aicha takes the whole "owner of her own destiny" thing very seriously at all times. People telling Aicha what to do and where to go is like someone following her around, constantly tapping her on the back of the head. With a cattle prod.

So I use my *talent* for the first couple of encounters with airport staff, smoothing away the suspicious glances and ridiculous questions. Problem is, I'm fae now. This is not an environment made for fairy creatures. Except perhaps in the sense of "made to torture them and slowly drive them mad".

You see, they build airports on a gigantic scale to have tens or hundreds of thousands of people tromping through, gawking and chittering and hopefully consuming on a massive scale. That concrete needs reinforcing. Which means rebar concrete – steel bars driven through every column. And I can feel each and every one of them, making my teeth itch, sapping away my fae strength.

So by the time we get to the border guards, I have enough *talent* left to persuade them that the pieces of paper we wave are valid passports even under the intense scrutiny they subject them to, but I've not enough left to stop them from deciding to bombard Aicha with a thousand and one questions.

"Where are you travelling?"

"Why?"

"Where have you travelled recently?"

"Are you carrying anything sharp, anything that can be used as a weapon?"

That she isn't carrying any might well be one reason she's so pissed off. I think it makes her feel the same way most people would strutting through the airport in the nude. She tried to argue for carrying all of her various knives, swords, and other assorted implements of the exceptionally pointy, death-dealing variety onboard with her, using a *don't look here* spell to keep eyes off them. I pointed out that metal detectors go *brrrrrr* even if the security staff don't clock them. Images get flagged automatically by the machines. The poor sucker she convinces magically to look the other way would probably end up answering some very hard questions. They'd lose their job over it. That's not on. In the end, she begrudgingly allowed me to stash them in my etheric storage, where I can have them back in her hands at a moment's notice. She also informed me if I did my usual trick of getting myself killed in some idiotic manner, stranding her without access to them, she'd take great pleasure in demonstrating the usage of each and every one of them on me once she got them back.

By the time we get onboard, Aicha looks like she's been chugging some chemical soup caffeine energy drink for hours while mainlining gorilla testosterone through an IV drip. The cabin crew, masters of human psychology that the job requires them to be, take one look at my companion and offer us two empty rows towards the rear of the aircraft. I think they want the crew at the back to be able to keep a careful eye on us. Keeping us as far as possible from the other passengers doesn't hurt either. I don't care. We've space to relax. That's a win.

The airline's colour scheme, a florid orange against crisp white, carries on throughout the cabin, offset by the muted grey of the seats and the crew uniform. I settle into my row of seats, my bum in one seat and my legs sprawled out over the others, my back half pressed against the window. Then I close my eyes. It'll probably be an hour before we get high enough up that they'll pass round to sell me some much deserved booze. Chaperoning Aicha through the airport is enough to drive anyone to drink.

I'm feeling considerably better being on the aeroplane. The amount of iron composites is pleasingly little. Weight is ever a consideration in aviation, and there are lighter materials to build with. I'm just about dozing off when Aicha drops herself into the seat at the aisle end of my row, booting my feet out of the way in the process.

I sigh. Apparently, now she wants to talk. 'Yes, *laguna*?'

Aicha's scowl could strip the paint off the plane. Seeing as how I'm pretty sure it plays an integral part in the aerodynamics, I prefer she keeps it concentrated on me instead. 'Why can't we just drive?'

Oh, good. We're having this conversation. Again. 'Time, essence, et cetera. C'mon. You know all this.'

'We could do Paris en route then.' My goodness me. There's a truculent tone approaching a whine to Aicha's voice. She really isn't happy.

I shuffle myself further up the window, pulling into a sitting position so as I can look at her properly. 'Aich, we've talked about this. We've got two leads. One is much more clearly linked to De Montfort than the other.'

'But we know there's that rib cage in the capital!'

'Yep. Safely in the care of Leandre – the Lutin Prince and one of the major Powers of France, hell, of the whole of Europe.'

'You think De Montfort cares about that, dickhead?'

I pause for a moment. She has a point. De Montfort isn't going to let anyone or anything get in his way. He wasn't even fazed when he tackled a tower-block-sized snail-dragon. But he'd made sure he knew exactly how to deal with him first. 'I don't think he cares. I *do think* he plans. He's not going to go off half-cocked against Leandre. He'll be plotting and planning, especially now he thinks I'm out of the way.'

'He doesn't care about that. He'll come back if he's killed.'

I frown. That's the sort of ill-thought-out conclusion that Aicha would normally have delighted in tearing strips off me for having. She's taking this whole "trapped in a tiny metal tube and hurtling through the sky at impossible speeds and height with zero control" thing even harder than I expected. 'Aich. Think it through. Quite the opposite. He's spent endless lives plotting how to get this current body so he can have access to *talent*. His reincarnation isn't as simple as mine. It's direct bloodline only. This is the first time in centuries that he's ever had *power*. He'll be protecting that body like a nerdy collector would an ultra-rare Pokemon card. I'm honestly surprised he even leaves the house.' I think this through. 'In fact, I bet he only does when he's supremely confident he's stacked all the odds in his favour that he'll make it home again safely.'

I want to lean over and pat her knee to reassure her. Problem is, I'm attached to my hands. Literally. Something Aicha will modify with extreme prejudice if I patronise her in such a manner.

'I still think we should do Paris first.' Good God, she's sulking. She has her arms crossed, her lower lip jutted out, and she's actually sulking. I've never seen the like.

'We discussed this!' A passing crew member turns a querulous frown in my direction, and I lower my voice, suitably chastened. 'Paris and the surrounding banlieues are packed full of magic creatures and major Talented, several of them fae of origin, Leandre included. All sorts of powerhouses likely to pick up if a potential threat moves into the area. Too risky for a main base of operations. Demon Fart has to have a stronghold somewhere, a safe house or bolt-hole, and family connections are important. Literal life-savers for him. It's got to be Paris or Leicester, and combined with the discovered bones, Leicester makes much more sense.'

Isaac made that connection because research, obviously. If anyone was going to track down De Montfort, aka Demon Fart, as we've childishly rechristened him, through tenuous scraps of information and obscure knowledge, arcane or otherwise, it was always going to be Isaac. Especially now that he's intellectually supercharged by having his brother Jakob along for the ride with him in his head, as well as two brain-meltingly powerful angels.

About a decade ago, archaeologists made one of the strangest and most exciting discoveries in a long time in the UK. Beneath a school car park, they discovered the body of Richard III, the supposedly hunchbacked king of England, eternally reviled as a villain thanks to a certain Billy Shakespeare. That was interesting enough, but what caught Isaac's attention were the other bones discovered on the same site, including a female skeleton bizarrely entombed in a prestigious sarcophagus. Pretty odd for a woman back in those days. Even stranger was that one archaeologist reported seeing the bones glowing before his chief sent him to have a refreshing cup of tea and a nice lie down, the British equivalent of strong anti-psychotic meds. The funding of the archaeological dig remains shrouded in mystery as well, and somehow, the skeleton didn't end up winging its way for further study at one of the universities or laboratories set up for just such a purpose. It got strangely re-routed and ended up at Kenilworth Castle. Guess which family used to own that?

So Leicester it is. Kenilworth looks like the obvious

target, but it isn't the only one. There's an area called Mont-fort-L'Aumery just outside of Paris. It was a De Montfort residence for a long time. But the odds are still on Leicester and Kenilworth as the most likely location. And I want to go straight to the place where I stand the best chance of getting my hands on the bastard.

Thing is, De Montfort has proven to be endlessly resourceful and an intricate planner. We need to find his hideout without alerting him about our investigation. I don't want him to do a runner. What I want is to make sure he does no running ever again by sawing off his kneecaps with a rusty hacksaw. Tetanus and immobilisation for the win.

'I still think we should have driven.'

Oh good. It looks like we've circled right back round to the start of this conversation. Which I suspect is how the rest of the flight is going to go. I check my watch. About twenty minutes till they start the service, by my reckoning. I can survive the hour or so of flight afterwards if I buy —I perform the requisite mental calculations for the ratio of booze to Aicha's whining— the entire bar.

Probably.

imPerfect Hunt: Chapter Two

Shipshape and Bristol fashion. Strange saying. Seems to
imply having a large barnacle-covered bottom.

By the time we exit through the swooshing doors of the
airport, Aicha is back to normal. She makes this clear when
she threatens me with evisceration by nail clipper if I ever
mention the flight again. She wraps a *don't look here* around
us and thrusts a demanding hand in my face a second after
the doors close behind us. A huge part of the stress lining
her face evaporates as I pass them all across. Guess they're
her emotional support bladed weapons of death. I decide to
skip pointing that out to her now that she's armed again.

The weather obviously didn't get the memo about
summer having started. We left a heat just the right side of
baking back in Toulouse, the sweet spot of the year where
you can enjoy being outside from morning until night,
without being a walking buffet for the bastard mosquitoes.
Here? We've arrived just after nine in the morning, and the

297

chill to the air is being carried deeper into my bones by the wind, which blows hard enough to apparently bypass my flesh altogether. There are warmer mornings than this in February in the south of France.

I decide not to mention it to Aicha. I don't really need to get her riled up about something else already. She's back in hyper-vigilant mode, her eyes scanning from near to far, clocking every movement from here to the horizon. At least we don't really stand out. There are people of every nationality and ethnic background milling around outside, and Aicha isn't the only one with a facial tattoo by a long stretch. It's astounding how purposeless the general movements are. People seem lost, disoriented. After anywhere from hours to days of the airports and airlines directing their thoughts and actions, the people seem bewildered to be in control of their own destiny once again.

I scoop up the car keys with a minimum of fuss from the car hire desk. I considered just stealing something from the car park but decided against it. Getting back off holiday is hard enough. I don't want to add to some poor fucker's post-holiday blues, finding themselves stuck without transport at some ungodly hour of the morning. It isn't like we can't afford the hire prices.

The Kia Sportage I've rented is just what we need. Comfortable but concealing. We aren't about to turn heads as we drive down the street, which is good news. The Koreans make sturdy, cheap cars. Functional and discreet is the aim of the game, however much it makes Aicha's lips pucker in distaste.

'We're trying not to draw attention to ourselves,' I remind Aicha as we pull off.

She looks at me similarly to how she looked at the car. 'Have you seen us? Or *seen* us? Subtle isn't really an option.

We both radiate *talent*. Plus, between me being me and you cosplaying as Princess Zelda, people look.'

She has a point. Since we got to the airport, we've spent most of the time being hit on. I tried to make myself look as drab as possible with the glamour I wove, but cities and airports wear me down in this body. The unnatural, other-worldly aura and beauty of it pokes through. It used to belong to Maeve, the Queen of the Winter Court, after all. You don't get much more beautiful. Or deadly. Until Aicha just made her dead -- beautifully.

Aicha herself is stunning too. It's weird thinking about it as I don't see her like that at all, thankfully for both our sanity and my life expectancy. She's like a sister to me. Still, objectively, I can see how beautiful she is. Her dark, almost-black eyes set back into the shadows of her aquiline nose burn with passion and personality. A certain subset of men have a tendency to think that makes her "fiery" and in need of taming, like Shakespeare's Katherina. Said men quickly find themselves choking for air, mainly because of Aicha having kicked their bollocks up into the back of their throat.

Two drop-dead, otherworldly women like us are going to draw attention whether we drive a Prius or a Porsche. I still haven't got used to the lascivious gazes we get from men, often while their wives deal with grizzling infants. The looks we get from their wives are similar, which surprises me. Unless they clock their husbands looking. Then darker, more jealous storm clouds gather in their expressions.

We have to try to be discreet though. I don't want to alert Demon Fart we're coming for him.

I heave a sigh of relief as the satnav directs us away from the airport. Within five minutes, it leads us onto winding back roads that climb and fall away through rolling greenery. The presence of nature recharges me; though the fields lie tended, neat, and precise in their division, the land remains ancient. It reaches out to me through overhanging branches, through the granite, sand, and limestone that form its bones, through restless dreams of days before some jumped-up monkeys smothered it in concrete and tarmac.

By the time we reach Bristol itself, the rush hour has eased, and we skirt the city easily enough. The huge suspension bridge by Clifton provides a magnificent view over the docks and the estuary and the cheerily painted houses on the opposite side set back in rows into the hillside. This is a city built on gradients. You end up with some serious calf muscles living here, I suspect. I wonder what it is about this place down in the south-west, in touching distance of Wales, that makes it such a hotspot of creativity. It birthed trip-hop and drum'n'bass and always seems to be at the centre of cultural originality for the UK. I promise myself a proper visit if time allows. Right now though, we need to get to Leicester.

It's a short enough drive from Bristol that after a fuel up and a coffee grab at a motorway service station, we drive the rest of the way without stopping.

By the time we pull into Leicester, the sun is approaching its zenith, which means it's finally stopped being a lazy git and started providing some actual warmth. The city itself has seen investment in recent times. Modern bulging glass fronts act like makeup that's been slapped onto the long-dead industrial architecture prevalent where money can't reach. I nearly snap a tooth clenching my jaw when we come down the Narborough Road. A bustling melange of bars and fast food, students and immigrants blur by, but it's all the signs labelled De Montfort that throw me. I quickly clock it's the name of a university. Apparently, being a murderous anti-Semite doesn't matter after a few hundred years. Though I suspect it was named for De Montfort's son, the man who was almost king. As it was the same shithead bastard just wearing his offspring's body like a zip-up onesie, I don't really care. They both would've been absolute arseholes even if they hadn't been the same person. Their memory shouldn't be honoured for posterity. Naming a lavatory after them would be more appropriate. I'm aiming to name a shallow grave in their honour...with them inside it.

We park up in a multi-storey car park near the centre of town, then walk down the high street. There was some debate about where to head first. We know the excavated skeleton got sent to Kenilworth Castle, which is outside the city centre, so Aicha was all for heading there and storming it like raiding Visigoths. I felt reconnoitring the dig site and the city itself first to be more sensible — get a lay of the land, see if there are any obvious traces of Demon Fart's involvement. Isaac sided with me before we set off, so here we are.

The city is intriguing. You can see where the money got invested. Swathes of renovated buildings stand proud, if entirely unoriginal – fronts cut out to allow glass panelling; cleaned brick and pedestrianised alleys, all replete with the same mixture of chain restaurants; and quirky pop-ups that masquerade as character but remain money-grabbers. Behind it, though, you can see the real city. Rundown old pubs run down side streets and spill a strange mixture of individuals out onto the pavement. Punks and drunkards, steamed-glass academics and tattooed suits. The mingling is real, and attempts to gentrify the city can't cut the rough diamond weirdness out of its occupants.

The dig site is just a couple of streets over from the high street. They've transformed it into an interactive museum.

Our hope is we'll find some official to pump for information. Otherwise, we'll perform a bit of breaking and entering, see what we can find behind the public façade. Either way, we aren't going to linger right now. I can feel my stomach rumbling, and Aicha's eyes assess every eatery we pass. Hangry Aicha is a horror too hideous to contemplate.

We cut through by the cathedral, the new final resting place of Richard III, unless someone digs him up again in the name of historical science. His statue stands at the end of the open square in front of the church doors, his hand stretched aloft. In it is his crown being waved at the sun. I think it's supposed to be dramatic. It just makes him look like he's auditioning to play tambourine for the Happy Mondays.

I suspect the money spent on the area is directly proportional to the amount of interest generated by the discovery of Richard III's body. Pedestrianised again, the area is all neat green rectangles and pennants on lampposts stamped with the Richard III logo. Prior to this, Leicester was best known for Daniel Lambert, the fattest man in English history. Oh, and Engelbert Humperdinck. Neither brought in the big tourist moolah though. The strangest archaeological story of modern times and a missing king found? That's a draw. Clearly the local council knows it and is ready to do what they need to in order to maximise it.

Various wooden and stone benches squat, artfully scattered among flowerbeds and street lawns. It's surprisingly quiet. I'd have imagined this to be the sort of place people might decamp to from their offices to scoff down their sandwiches during their truncated breaks. But only one bench is occupied. A guy slumps in one corner, dead to the world. He doesn't look homeless, or if he is, it must have happened recently. His clothes aren't super new, but they don't look slept in, however prominently his trainers display their long usage. Outside of that, the only other occupants are a trio of goth kids, black liner face-paint over the kind of white primer that a Parisian mime would be proud of. There are a few ancient gravestones still clustered in the south-eastern corner of the square.

I'm ready to just cut through, to get on our way, but Aicha's hand shoots out, checking me. Were I a normal human, she probably would have caved my chest in. As is, she nearly winds me.

'Something's not right here, *saabi*.' Her eyes rove around, seeking what has set her Spidey sense tingling.

I wave a hand at the group of new New Romantics. 'Was it that the eighties called and wanted their tragic subculture back?'

Aicha's gaze tracks over to the group and stops, fixed on them. Her posture changes to a new state of readiness. In the same moment, their heads snap up, and as one, all their attention turns in our direction. They open their mouths and hiss, and I catch a gleam of fang in each open orifice. Sadly, I don't think they're wearing ornamental teeth caps.

'Vampires,' Aicha hisses.

The three of them glide towards us, taking up position in the most un-hip, undead pincer manoeuvre of all time.

Vampires. At midday. In Leicester. That makes perfect sense.

imPerfect Hunt: Chapter Three

If these guys start sparkling, I'm going to set them on fire.
Turn them into proper sparklers. Guy Fawkes, eat your
heart out. Or drive a stake through them.

I get a better look at them now they've closed the distance.
The one on the right is squat, with arms that speak of
manual labour and a gut that speaks of daytime drinking.
He's wearing a black pork-pie hat, and lightning bolts are
painted out of his eyeliner across his cheeks. His T-shirt is
some sort of shimmery grey wife-beater, perfect for when
you want to look like you live in a trailer park and have a
fetish for mithril silver. The guy on the left is tall and broad.
His hair is pulled back so tight into a ponytail, I'm surprised
he hasn't torn the skin off his face. I wonder if he can still
do anything as advanced as smiling. Or talking. It seems
impossible without him doing himself an injury. He clearly
spends a lot of time in the gym, a fact he takes great pleasure in displaying by walking around topless. He shaved his

chest, if I'm not mistaken, and oiled it too. Although he obviously mixed some of that same white makeup primer into the oil, so at least his chest matches his face colour-wise. His eyes have round black circles with splodges coming off like lava-lamp fluid. It's supposed to make him look mysterious, magical perhaps. Instead, he looks like a panda someone just splashed with hydrochloric acid.

The fellow in the middle is obviously the leader. His hair hangs down around his face. It's supposed to be jet-black, but obviously no one bothered to tell him his roots are showing, meaning his natural ginger is poking through. I guess it becomes more difficult to spot these things when you can't see yourself in a mirror. He's tall and thin, which is only accentuated by the floor-length leather trench coat he wears. It must be the equivalent of taking the guts of the Tauntaun that Luke Skywalker cut open on Hoth and wearing them constantly. Only in the middle of summer. Admittedly, an English summer, which means I only need a jumper and a coat instead of a full set of thermals, but summer nonetheless. He's gone for swirling curves off his eyes that are admittedly pretty, though I doubt that's the effect he really wants to go for. The smear lines where sweat has picked up the eyeliner and carried it in smudges down his cheeks aren't deliberate additions, I suspect. The price we pay for style. Even shit style, apparently.

The overall impact is less than menacing. They somehow aren't aware of that fact. They leer at us like we'll somehow be terrified of them, as if they look like deadly creatures of the night instead of monochrome geishas whose makeup artist got pissed on sake beforehand.

'Jesus Christ, this is beyond painful. Actual vampires dressed up as goth wannabe vampires. Is this like cosplay or something? Please tell me this is some sort of surrealist theatre that English undead are into. Is this the "creatures of the night" equivalent of Morris Dancing? Preserving ancient, forgotten traditions or something?' If ever there is a time in my life when I am delighted to be fluent in English, it's this one. It allows me to categorically rip the piss out of these three and for them to understand every word.

Aicha isn't going to be outdone. 'It's like the Insane Clown Posse. Only without the posse. Or being insane. The Lame Clown Trio?'

'Sounds like an experimental jazz outfit.'

'I think it's great they're so open about being into glam rock. What's your favourite Slade song? "Merry Christmas Everybody"?'

The three of them have gone from looking baffled to faintly insulted to deeply mortified. I suspect at least one of them is blushing, but under the layers of eyeliner, it's impossible to spot. They keep trying to speak, but we're not letting them get a word in edgeways.

I point at the leader. 'Hey, I think that one's got some kind of hair and mouth disease.' His lips clamp shut, and wild panic settles in his eyes. 'Yeah – he's got ginger-vitis.'

Aicha groans. 'That's dreadful.' She turns her full-watt attention on him. 'How does that work, by the way? Ginger vampire? Like, does that mean you've lost your soul twice? Are you negative one for souls?'

The outrage in his expression is comedic. Every time he moves, it sends more black streaks running down his face. It makes him look like he's crying ink. Which would, were it to actually happen, be very fucking metal. As it is, he looks like he just got dumped by his partner and sobbed his little heart out in the grimy toilets of the local goth dive. It makes his attempts to snarl at us just look like desperate pleas for attention. I actually find myself feeling sorry for him, wanting to tell him that whoever it was isn't worth it, that there are plenty more fish in the sea.

We leave enough gap in the conversation for him to put his oar in finally. Unfortunately for him, we've knocked him so far off balance, all he can do initially is splutter and spit, apparently incapable of forming syllables.

'Deep breaths. Think before you speak. Let it all out,' I advise in my most soothing voice. He looks like he's having a rough day. Because of us, admittedly, but a rough day still.

He gets hold of his use of language again. 'Who are you? How dare you come into our territory? Are you the Hob King?'

I think this through. 'I mean, I cook a pretty mean stir fry, if that's what you mean?'

Aicha makes a T symbol with her hands, the universal sign for a time-out. 'A moment to speak to my colleague, please?'

The poor little undead fucker is totally lost by this point. He looks left and right, desperately asking for advice and support. By the time his two goons, who look even more confused than he does, shrug their utter indecision at him, we've already taken several steps backwards, forming a huddle to talk privately.

'What's up?' I keep my voice as low as possible and my eye on the vampires.

'What if they work for De Montfort?'

They are also now huddling, obviously trying to come up with some sort of game plan for dealing with our non sequiturs.

I frown. I did not even think about that. 'They said this is their territory.'

'They'd say that if he gave it to them too. Even if they

worked for him. Vampires. Egos the size of small planets. Plus, have you seen how they're dressed?'

She has a point. It takes a level of utter ballsiness and self-confidence to strut around a grim post-industrial city like Leicester dressed like that in the middle of the day.

I shrug. 'What are you saying?'

'There're no wards here. None I've felt, anyhow. You?' I know what she's getting at. De Montfort wears a fae body too. Maybe I might pick up some sneakily woven faerie magic that she's missed. I shake my head. Nothing rings a bell magically around here.

She nods. 'Think about it. He travels a lot. Nefarious plans clock up the air miles. Can't protect the city or keep it warded. Plus, doesn't want to draw attention. What would you do?'

I can see where she is going. 'Strike a deal with another Talented or group thereof. Let them keep an eye on the place…'

'…and report back if anyone comes sniffing around.'

Damn. It's a valid point. 'So we can't let them report back.' I turn to head towards them, but she grabs my arm and pulls me back. Apparently, she isn't finished.

'Have you seen their earrings?'

I have to be honest; I've not been paying attention. Their botched-job face-painting has drawn most of my attention. I sneak a peek while keeping my head close to Aicha's.

In one of each of the vampires' ears, there's a skull and crossbones with tiny green jewels for the eyes. I swear silently. 'They're the same as what De Montfort has on his ring.'

She nods. 'Something else. I was having a *look* at that jewellery while you were busy with the banter. They're powerful. Best guess? They send an alarm in certain circumstances.'

I can well imagine what sort. 'Like someone getting attacked with *talent*?'

She nods grimly. 'My thought exactly.'

So we're going to have to take these fuckers out in a two-on-three physical brawl, where they can use all of their natural abilities. Or, rather, unnatural abilities. And we have to rely on our sword skills. While also making sure I don't get this body killed, or I go back to being a Talentless schmuck, the magical equivalent of a reality TV star. Surely a fate worse than death.

Guess I better make sure I don't die then.

We wander back over to the significantly baffled group of goth vampires. 'Sorry for the delay.' I smile brightly. 'What can we help you fine gentlemen with?'

The leader opens his mouth, but I hold up my hand to cut him off, pointing at the shirtless muscle head. 'Hold on a second. Didn't you play the rock saxophone in Santa Carla? What were the two Coreys like? Who was nicer, Kiefer Sutherland or Alex Winter?' The blank looks that come back underline a certainty. They've never seen *Lost Boys*. They need to die.

I wave graciously at their head honcho. 'Sorry, continue. You were just about to tell us what you were doing here and who you work for.'

He nods. 'Quite, well this is where we live and... Hey, hold on. That's what you were supposed to be telling us!'

I frown and look at Aicha. 'That doesn't sound right. I wasn't ever going to tell these bozos anything, were you?'

'Only to go fuck themselves.'

A sage expression spreads across my face. 'True. Very

true. So you were going to tell us everything we wanted to know?'

The one in the middle's panic levels are rising exponentially, in direct correlation to his confusion. This conversation isn't going the way he expected it to. 'No. No, I wasn't?' There's a definite question at the end.

'Sure you were! How many of you are in your nest? Who's your master? Who does he work for? All the basics, you know.'

'First line of your address, mother's maiden name, social security number.'

'Sure, Aich. We'll take those too while you're at it.'

I think the fact that we aren't going to suddenly stop being weird and play ball finally sinks in. The Ginger Prince of Darkness hisses, his fangs on display. 'If you want to play rough, that suits us down to the ground. We will feast on your flesh!'

I chuckle. 'Oh, look. He actually believes they can beat us!'

Aicha sighs, throws up a *don't look here* spell, and pulls out her katana/wakizashi combination. 'Just goes to show there ain't no sucker like a bloodsucker.'

I pull my sword from my etheric storage. 'Too damn true, *laguna.* Too damn true.'

The three of them crouch, their fingers elongating out to form claws, their eyes glowing red, ready to pounce. Looks like the fight is on.

Grab your copy...
vinci-books.com/imPerfecthunt